BROKEN
BAYOU

BROKEN BAYOU

JENNIFER MOORHEAD

THOMAS & MERCER

Text copyright © 2024 by Jennifer Moorhead
All rights reserved.

Published by Thomas & Mercer, Seattle

www.apub.com

Amazon, the Amazon logo, and Thomas & Mercer are trademarks of Amazon.com, Inc., or its affiliates.

ISBN-13: 9781662518775 (paperback)
ISBN-13: 9781662518768 (digital)

Cover design by David Drummond
Cover images: © DeawSS / Shutterstock; © Ethan Daniels / Stocktrek Im / Getty; © mel-nik / Getty; © Perspective Jeta / Shutterstock; © SeDmi / Shutterstock; © westtexasfish / Getty

Printed in the United States of America

To Mike, Mackenzie, and Mia. You are my sun, my moon, and my stars.

January 2002

Suzy Weatherton was sick and tired of everyone in this casino yelling "Go Tigers!" LSU won the Sugar Bowl. Big deal. They beat Illinois. Even with her bad knee, she could beat Illinois. If they'd played her alma mater, they'd all be a little quieter. But Suzy knew better than to yell "Roll Tide" in this purple-and-gold crowd.

She reached into the plastic cup of coins in her lap, slid one in the slot, and pulled. She prayed the cherries would line up for her tonight. She'd been here hours already and gotten bupkis. Last week they'd also not been kind. She'd promised herself on the four-hour drive from Houston this would be her last trip. The Louisiana boats might not be as lucky as they advertised. At least the *Cajun Belle* was permanently connected to the shore. Thanks to the Louisiana loopholes, Suzy wouldn't have to worry about getting seasick.

She lit another cigarette and motioned for the young waitress, who'd taken her last two drink orders with a smile. She thumbed in another coin. "Come on, baby." And it hit. Bells started ringing. A light above her slot wailed like a siren. Suzy jumped up, spilling her coins as she clapped.

"Must be your lucky night," someone next to her said.

Maybe this wouldn't be her last trip to the boats after all. This jackpot could keep her and her daughter settled for a while and help with the baby on the way. Her first grandbaby.

Suzy left with her winnings and smiled as she made her way out to the parking lot, fumbling for her car key, then dropping it next to the car door. As she bent over, she heard a voice behind her. "Here, let me help you with that."

Suzy jumped as a flash lit up her face, followed by the sound of an old Polaroid.

Stunned and disoriented, she said, "Did you just take my picture?"

"Say cheese."

The flash popped again, and that was the last thing Suzy remembered.

Chapter One

My hand hovers over the inside car-door handle but refuses to open it. Through my windshield, I study a pale brick building whose dirty front window announces boudin is on sale. Its torn awning flaps in the breeze, and above it, chipped cornflower blue letters read **Sa k and Save Food Store**. You'd think after twenty years they'd have replaced the *c* in the word *sack*, but I guess it sounds the same, so why bother? I wonder if Mr. Bendel is still behind the register inside. If the smell of Virginia Slims still permeates every wall. If the back door still leads to the alley where one could easily escape when shoplifting.

Yesterday, as the incessant notifications started on my phone, this trip seemed like a good idea. Now, though, after sneaking out of my Fort Worth high-rise like a thief, carrying a duffel bag full of pencil skirts and blouses way too formal for this sleepy little bayou town, I seem to have lost my momentum.

Blistering afternoon sun blasts through the windshield. I crank up the AC.

My eyes dart to the large coffee thermos in the seat next to me and, propped beside it, the letter with its creamy paper and crisp typed words from the law office of LaSalle, LaSalle, and Landry. Wings flutter in my chest. I stared at that letter for weeks, ever since my mother handed it to me. Throwing it away and digging it out of the trash several times. A letter notifying us some of my mother's things were found in the attic of my great-aunts' old house, Shadow Bluff. Things we may want to come get. Things left behind years ago. Forgotten. On purpose.

Then that television interview happened, and responding to the letter seemed like a better option than staying in Fort Worth. I don't want to take a chance that a certain object in that attic falls into the wrong hands.

I kill the engine. I'm going in. I'll get what I need for the few days I'm here: some snacks, a wheelbarrow full of Community Coffee, maybe some wine. That's it. Except that won't be it. Not here. Someone will remember me. Once I walk in there, the whole town will know Krystal Lynn Watters's eldest daughter is back, and she may have fancy clothes and be a big deal back in Texas, but in Louisiana, she's still the sad, messy-haired little girl who always tried to return everything her mama stole, clutching her little sister's hand like she might float away. People in small towns don't forget. They also ask questions. Questions like, Why'd you stop visiting Broken Bayou? Why didn't you come to your great-aunts' funerals? Why'd y'all skip town so fast that last summer you were here?

I take a deep breath and open the car door. The heat of a thousand suns smacks into me. Hotter than Texas. Despite the ground looking painfully dry, the air is wet with humidity. I wouldn't be surprised if the people who live down here have adapted by growing gills. The air smells of the salty gulf, of my past. Even though I've only crossed one state line, I feel like I need a passport to be here.

My skin tingles under my long sleeves. Sweat rolls down my back. A tailored suit with a jacket may not have been the best clothing choice for this . . . errand. But this is the wardrobe I've grown accustomed to. The complete opposite of Krystal Lynn's tube tops, bell-bottomed jeans, and bright plastic bangles. I saw what that wardrobe would get you and hauled ass in the opposite direction.

My cell dings as I slam the car door shut. Somewhere on the long bridge over the Atchafalaya Basin, I thought it'd be a good idea to turn my ringer back on. Part punishment for my stupidity, part motivation to keep driving.

It dings again. And again. Finally, I look. New notifications. Trending now: #1 Entertainment, Dr. Willa Watters, *Fort Worth Live*, hashtag honestly hot. A reality TV star from Dallas had retweeted *the* clip and tagged me, hashtag put me on your couch. A sour taste fills my mouth. But comments like that will wither on the vine soon enough. It's the comments about my emotional stability that have the acid in my stomach building.

Dropping my cell in my tote, I teeter across the crumbling parking lot on my heels. I earned a full ride at Baylor, trudged through five years of grad school, and defended a dissertation on spectrum children being integrated into a traditional school setting. I wrote a damn book. I helm a successful podcast, for God's sake. And now I'm being reduced to entertainment and hashtags on social media while working up the courage to shop in a Sack and Save.

I stop just as I'm about to open the store's glass door. Something catches my eye, parked on the far end of the lot. My hand slips off the door handle. My pulse quickens. A white news van, off by itself. It's not for you, I tell myself as I rub my sweaty palm on my jacket. Stay focused. In and out. No big deal.

As Krystal Lynn would say, time to cowgirl up.

Inside the store, I keep my head down, grab a cart, and start heading for the closest aisle.

"Well, forevermore, look what the cat dragged in."

Four seconds through the front door, and a woman in a denim tent of a dress and a gray permed head works her way from behind the checkout counter. That must be a record.

Maybe I should have skipped this stop and driven straight to Shadow Bluff.

"Willamena Pearl," the woman says.

Hearing my full name always makes me cringe. I better live to ninety so I can grow into it.

She wraps her meaty arms around me, then pulls back as if she's been waiting on me and I've finally shown up. I don't move.

"I mean Dr. Willa, now." She beams; then her smile falters. "Sugar, it's Johnette. Johnette Bendel. Mr. Bendel's my daddy. I used to know the Aunts too."

I search my memory for this woman but can't place her. "Of course," I lie. I smile. "Good to see you."

"You haven't changed a bit. Well, 'cept for the highfalutin clothes." She sizes me up. "You must be scorching in that suit." I nod, smiling again. I'm needing the wine more than the coffee now. A few patrons mill around us, pretending to look at canned peas and studying a Stove Top stuffing display, but I know they're listening. They're always listening.

"You don't remember me, do you?" she adds, her smile faltering.

I swallow. I'm distracted and jittery from the long drive and can't think of an appropriate response. I settle on "It's been a long time."

"Right," she says. Her smile is gone now, replaced by an irksome smirk. This highfalutin city girl has offended her. I've unintentionally told her she's not important enough to remember.

"How's your mama?" she says. The glint in her blue eyes tells me this is a prod. Kudos to her. Mama is indeed the best way to taunt me.

"Fine," I say because answering with *She's had four falls in three months, two broken hips, a broken collarbone, and COPD and somehow still managed to steal cigarettes from nurses at the Texas Rose Rehabilitation Center* seems a little TMI. Mama's laundry list of ailments reads like one for an eighty-year-old woman. Not a woman in her late sixties. But Krystal Lynn burned her candle at both ends with such intensity I'm amazed she made it this far. Seventy seems like a lofty goal for her.

"Good. Good," Johnette says to my one-word answer. "So," she adds, "what in the world are you doing down here?" Her right eyebrow lifts slightly.

What's your game, Johnette?

"I'm just in Broken Bayou for a few days to unwind and relax." It sounds ridiculous even as I say it, but ridiculous has become my new area of expertise.

Johnette tilts her head to one side. "Unwind? Really?"

My shoulders stiffen.

Johnette shrugs. "Odd time to be here, but I guess you might need a place to unwind after that live television interview yesterday. That was something."

And there it is.

Shit. How has this woman, in this town, seen that? How viral was I? And if Johnette Bendel has seen it, who else has? It doesn't bode well for my thinking this place would be a social media graveyard.

"Well . . . ," I start, then finish with "I better get to my shopping."

"Okay, sugar, let me know if you can't find something. I'll check the back."

Nothing in her voice tells me she'll do any such thing.

I push my small cart with a wobbly wheel toward the nearest aisle. Between the squeaky wheel and my absurd heels on the linoleum floor, I'm making quite a ruckus. I pause and look back at the end of the aisle. Johnette is gone, but her words linger in my head. What did she mean it's an odd time to be here?

"Oh my God!" A woman's voice booms through the store.

I jump and snap my head in the other direction. The aisle is empty. No one is standing there pointing a finger at me and laughing. I exhale. I'm too jumpy. I need to take my own advice and find a healthy way to navigate my anxiety. The seven-dollar bottle of chardonnay I'm putting in my cart is probably not the best start.

"We're going to put that back," a woman shouts in the next aisle over, and a loud, high-pitched scream follows. Definitely a child's.

Two women round the endcap onto my aisle shaking their heads.
"Spoiled brat," one whispers.

"He needs a good old-fashioned spanking," the other replies.

I redirect my cart toward the sound and when I turn the corner and see the child, I know those women have it wrong. He looks to be about two or three. He's sitting on the floor, flapping his hands, and screaming. A sound so specific that if your ears aren't trained to listen for it, you'll miss the root cause.

Two stock boys have gathered at the end of the aisle now, and it looks like one is videoing. Idiots.

"Honey, please stop," the woman says, her voice cracking, her face red with embarrassment as her son starts biting his own arm.

I saw this behavior more times than I can count when I was in private practice. So much so that I kept a sensory kit on hand to help de-escalate the situations: soft things, shiny trinkets, snow globes.

His mom is combing through her tote and doesn't notice me as I scan the shelves. He needs a distraction.

I abandon my cart and race back to the aisle with the salad dressing. I spot a clear bottle of Italian. Bingo. Next best thing to a snow globe. I slip it off the shelf, remove the label, and head back to the screaming child. I push my cart past them, shaking the bottle so the herbs, oil, and vinegar start to mix and change colors. The boy tilts his head, stops screaming. I shake again and he reaches for it.

"That should buy you some time," I say to his mom with a smile as I continue past them, leaving her in stunned silence and me thinking how I'd put Occam's razor up against a degree any day.

There is no bank of checkout lanes or self-checkout at the Sack and Save. Just good old Johnette behind the counter, currently occupied by a group of men and women huddled around her and looking down at something. I stop behind them.

"Oh, bless her heart," a woman says.

The hairs on the back of my neck tingle.

"I couldn't believe it when I saw this," Johnette says, leaning over the counter, pointing at what I now see is her phone screen. "'Member her? Used to visit here in the summers."

Shit. I wonder again if that back door still exists and, if so, if it's still unlocked.

"I do remember her," one woman says. "Had that poor darling little sister."

"Well, I can tell you this," Johnette says. "She don't remember any of us."

The YouTube video has started. I hear my voice coming from the phone. I hear the perky voice of host Harper Beaumont say, "Good morning, Fort Worth, and welcome to *Fort Worth Live*. We have a special guest with us today." Harper continues, "She's here to talk about her new bestseller, *Honest Healing: Parenting a Child on the Spectrum*. A book that shot up the *New York Times* bestseller list after celebrity influencer Charlotte Dalton posted about how it's helped her family on Instagram. Since then, the phrase *honest healing* seems to have caught fire, not only locally but nationally as well. Welcome, Dr. Willa Watters."

Shit. Shit. I could run. Go to Shadow Bluff and hide. But it's been a long two days, and I'm just too damn tired to run.

I stay where I stand and, in the words of another Krystal Lynn saying, take my licks. Which unfold in blinding HD at the checkout counter of the Sack and Save Food Store.

I watched old *Fort Worth Live* clips with Amy, my best friend and show producer, to prepare for my interview. The set was more cow town than glossy pretense, just like the city I chose to live in compared to its sister city, Dallas. It's the reason Amy picked that show. "It's a perfect fit," she said, even though I wondered if that was true. The outfit I chose for that day screamed glossy pretense: pencil skirt, kitten heels, silk shirt.

Amy was hovering too close yesterday at the KTFW television studio. She sensed my nerves. But it wasn't exactly nerves. It was something else. I was off kilter. A combination of the feelings that letter drudged up and the hangover from too many Texas Twisters, as the bartender called them, the night before. I clipped out of my thirty-fifth-floor apartment that morning with my . . . overnight guest, giving him a thumbs-up when we parted ways in the lobby of my building, his flip-flops slapping across the marble foyer. Flip-flops.

Getting hammered the night before my first live television interview and bringing home a stranger was classic self-sabotage. Willamena Pearl in her youth may not have known better, but Dr. Willa in her midthirties certainly did . . . and yet . . .

The makeup artist did her best with the beard burn I showed up with, and Amy did her best to assure me everything would go smoothly, and it did. At first. The mic techs wove a microphone through my blouse buttons and secured it to my bra and then to a Velcroed pack on my back. Harper stuck to the script, asking beautifully mundane questions.

"So after practicing child psychology for a few years, you switched to writing a column for the newspaper, then radio." She added with a silly laugh, "Some of our viewers probably don't even know what a newspaper and radio are."

I gave her a courtesy laugh even though I couldn't imagine she had even one viewer who didn't grow up on radio and newspapers. That's why I was there. Those were the people who would buy my book. Avoiding too much of a soapbox, I explained how dealing with insurance made it too difficult to maintain a private practice and how I felt I could reach more people if I expanded my scope. So I started a column for the *Fort Worth Tribune*, then was approached by execs at KWKP radio station about hosting a show. And it took off from there. The *Honest Healing* podcast was a natural pivot. A way to stay current.

Harper nodded and smiled and led me down a lovely risk-free path. We briefly discussed my lack of children, but it was nothing I hadn't said before. My explanation simple and true. I raised my sister, and it was grueling and challenging. So instead of having children, I chose a career where I could focus solely on helping them.

"Awww," the woman in the cutoffs says. The group nods. None of them look at me, though. Not the real me. They're engrossed in the screen me.

I haven't watched this clip yet. Too soon. I was waiting for the right time. So much for that theory.

Harper's voice rings out: "I hear you're headed to *Good Morning America* next. Glad we could catch you before you get too big for our little old show." I laughed, politely.

Oh, the smugness in that laugh.

"Okay, how about we open up the phone to callers." That was something I didn't expect. That wasn't on the script.

The calls were typical at first. A distraught woman with an estranged son, followed by a resentful woman whose husband refused to have their child tested. I referred to certain chapters in my book and told them what I tell so many: You can do this. Your child needs an advocate. Always.

I hear a voice on Johnette's phone, and I'm back in that studio, under those lights, Harper staring at me. The caller on the phone is a girl.

Maybe I've seen enough. I start to slowly back up, but the cart's bad wheel gives me away.

"Ho-ly mother-of-pearl," the woman in cutoff shorts says when she spots me. Her gaze isn't judgmental, it's worse. It's sympathetic. "What are the damn odds?"

Math didn't have to be my best subject for me to understand the odds are staggering, for them, not me. For them, looking up to see me in the flesh as they watch Johnette's screen is insanely shocking. For me, wandering into a group of random people watching me make a complete ass of myself on live television is now, unfortunately, highly probable. Johnette could have at least waited for me to leave the store. But what fun would that have been?

11

I smile at the group. I fucking smile at them. What is wrong with me?

"I need your help," the girl on Johnette's screen says.

Her voice sounds so young, so helpless. Something in it so familiar.

I see the group weighing their options now they know I'm here.

"Dr. Willa?" Harper Beaumont says on the screen.

The group turns back. Decision made.

"Can you repeat that?" I said to the caller.

"Can you help me find it?" the girl said.

I watch my face on the screen. I look frozen in a state of shock. I heard "Can you help me hide it?"

"Excuse me?" I said.

"I need help finding it."

Again, in that moment, I heard the word *hiding*, not *finding*.

"I'm sorry," I said to the caller. "Are you asking me to hide something?"

Harper tilted her head and blinked her spider-leg lashes. She smiled a painful smile. "She's asking about your book."

"My book?"

The caller drew out one word, one syllable. "Uh . . ."

My train of thought was so gone by that point that when the caller spoke again, I heard a word from my past. A word one child gave to another child. A safe word. One that should've made me laugh as an adult, but it didn't make me laugh. It set my chest ablaze as if a hot brand was pressed onto it.

"Did she say *okra*?" I said to Harper.

Harper laughed an uncomfortable laugh and tried to keep her composure, but her voice cracked. "What?"

"Okra. Did she say the word *okra*?"

Harper looked at me like I was a complete lunatic.

"How do you know that word?" I said to the caller.

"Um." Harper's eyes darted around the room. For the first time, she looked her age. She fumbled over her words. "Maybe, um, we are all out of time."

I sprang up, tugged at the microphone threaded through my shirt. "I'm sorry. I can't do this anymore. I need to go." I detached the mic pack from around my waist as Harper gaped at me, but I still couldn't unhook the mic and wire from my blouse. So I ripped it off. The mic, the wire, the pack. And my blouse.

I stood there on live television in my bra, claw marks from my manicured nails on my chest.

I looked down. "Fuck."

And I ran away.

The clip ends. The gaggle of strangers in front of me, now silent, look up. My face flushes with heat. I choke down my bitter pill. "Can I check out now?"

Chapter Two

It takes every ounce of self-control I possess not to unscrew the chardonnay I just purchased and drink it straight from the bottle. Mama would have. But I'm not my mother, I remind myself. If I wasn't so tired, I might laugh at that thought, as the image of me clawing my shirt off on live television flashes in my head.

A familiar heaviness settles on my chest. A heaviness I welcome. All the good I've experienced lately, my podcast, the book, it all makes me nervous. It always has. Accepting good fortune was the hardest thing for me to learn, and I still slip. Still look over my shoulder, looking for the bad, waiting for it, and in a completely unhealthy way, hoping for it. When the bad shows up, I can exhale. Then I know what I'm up against.

Guess I can exhale.

I cruise south on Main Street, passing the ditch where Mama wrecked the old station wagon, then bragged to the tow truck driver she hadn't even spilled her beer when we crashed.

Memories, like poisonous vines, curl around my throat. Memories of Mama and me and my little sister, Mabry, and our trips to this town every summer to visit my great-aunts on Mama's side. Down here, it never failed that some kid would ask where I was from because of my accent. As if I was from some faraway land, which in a way, I guess I was. In Greenhill, our northwest corner of the state, we had clipped words and no Mardi Gras until the riverboat casinos showed up. The local news included Texas and Arkansas. *Dressed* referred to clothing, not what you wanted on your po'boy. But this place, this town, was what Mama referred to as our escape. And what we were escaping from fluctuated every summer. Her job slinging soggy Tater Tots and Salisbury steak onto plastic trays for the ungrateful students at Greenhill High. Her latest boyfriend. Her bench warrants. So when summer came, we'd load up the station wagon and head south. My great-aunts' home, our refuge.

The adrenaline from the moment at the Sack and Save has receded and left in its place an edgy jitteriness I can't seem to shake. The guy tailgating me on this tiny two-lane road isn't helping. I lower my window and motion for him to go around but he doesn't.

Something on the far side of the street catches my eye. A white news van like the one at the Sack and Save. I slow down, study it.

My phone rings next to me and I jump. Then I see who it is.

"Hello, Mama." Of course it's Mama, tethered to me despite the miles between us, calling at the exact moment I think of her.

"You sound so far away," she says.

Her voice sounds small and fragile and lonely. I fight off the guilt it triggers and remind myself for the hundredth time she's where she needs to be.

"I am far away, Mama. I'm in Broken Bayou."

I refocus on Main Street. There's no traffic. It feels like a ghost town. And in a way, it is. Full of my ghosts. Everything looks how I remember. Narrow and potholed and quiet. The street names come back to me: Vine, Hill, Church.

"What! Why the hell are you down there?"

I glance at the letter again. A letter that states my great-aunts passed away. Within minutes of each other. Just like how they were born. My throat constricts at the thought. I hadn't been in touch with them in years. Neither had Mabry or Mama. The Aunts, as everyone called them, hugged Mabry and me, fed us pancakes and coffee, and showed us how to gather eggs from the henhouse without even ruffling a feather. We helped fertilize plants in their greenhouse while Dolly Parton crooned

"Here You Come Again" from a small cassette radio. And sometimes, we slept on the floor outside their bedroom door, our little-girl bodies curled like cats around each other. But after our last summer here, and with each passing year, those memories had grown smaller and smaller until they finally dissolved into nothing but dust. I wonder if a VHS tape left in an old attic could turn to dust as well.

"I'm getting your things, remember? The boxes left in the attic?"

There's a long pause. "Mama?"

"I remember now. That's right. You said you were gonna go down there."

She's lying, but I'm not sure I'm up for exploring her memory loss at the moment. That can wait. Besides, maybe I'm just tired and only hearing lies from the past, not the present.

"The letter," she says as if she knows she needs to prove something.

"Right."

Mama says, "You're getting my things."

I pull at the collar on my blouse, adjust the air so it blows directly on my face. Mama doesn't know all the things I'm here to get. I protected her from that.

"Have you seen the news?" Mama's voice cracks, and she starts to cough.

"Take a breath. Are you wearing your oxygen?"

Her voice rakes over her smoke-ravaged vocal cords. "Listen to me, sweet girl. That bayou is all over the news."

I straighten, thinking of the news van I just passed, the one I saw earlier. "What do you mean?"

"There's a drought."

I shake my head. "Well, that's . . . terrible."

"And there's a schoolteacher missing. Her parents think she drove her car into that bayou."

"What? That's horrible."

I approach the corner of Main and Bridge Streets. A flashing stoplight sits at the corner. That's new. I roll to a stop even though it only flashes yellow. The guy behind me revs his engine. Late-model truck, no muffler. Then he lays on the horn.

"What in the world is that?" Mama says.

"Some asshole behind me." I yell out the open window, "Go around!" There are still no cars in sight. He'd have no problem passing. I motion again.

The old truck revs a second time, then starts to ease past my window. His windows are down, and his eyes stay on me as he rolls by. He looks rough. Thin, unshaven face marked with scars. I make sure my doors are locked, but he doesn't stop. He turns left on Bridge Street and disappears. Once he's gone, I release my breath. I'm not in danger, I tell myself. The fear I'm feeling is from an internal source, not external. I don't need to shift blame to a random guy driving an old pickup.

"That place is gonna come back to haunt us," Mama says.

I scan the intersection. Ned's Pharmacy sits on the corner to my right, next to Ace's Hardware and Farm Supplies. Not Ace Hardware. Ace's. You'd be hard pressed to find a business in this town without the owner's name in front of it. The two stores are part of the same white clapboard structure with a deep overhanging eave and small wooden steps leading up to the doors. Steps, no ramps, which is surprising, considering the median age in this town has to be north of seventy. Young people don't stay in small towns anymore. Then I notice another storefront next to Ace's. An antique store. I squint through the setting sun at it. It seems familiar, even though I don't remember an antique store ever being there.

"Nothing's coming back to haunt us," I say. I ease north of Bridge Street, past an overgrown parking lot with an abandoned, rotten shell I remember as a Dairy King. "Screw Dairy Queen. We got the Dairy *King* here," Mama always said.

"I'm tired, Mama. I gotta go."

She coughs and clears her throat again. "Love you, sweet girl."

That's when I hit the brakes. Krystal Lynn is not a *love you* kind of lady. "Mama, what's wrong?"

There's no answer. I check my phone. She's hung up, but my screen is full of missed emails, messages, and voicemails. A text from Amy asking if I'm okay; a voicemail from a reporter wanting a comment. The buzzards are circling indeed. Even Harper Beaumont has chimed in. She messaged me that she hopes I get the mental care I so obviously need. As if. That's *my* lane, dammit. My fingers itch to reply to Harper. Something smart and snarky. But I understand once you are in the hole, quit digging. I'm just the new bull's-eye for them to shoot at. To be fair, though, I did hand them the gun.

I start moving again, and the last building on the corner catches my eye. A small redbrick box with a sign reading NAN's CAFÉ over the door. But it's not the sign or the building that has my full attention. It's the parking lot. Specifically, the two news vans sitting off by themselves in it. I may not be from this town, but I know enough to understand four news vans is not the norm here. Would four news vans be here for one missing person?

The sun is lower through the front windshield but still as hot. Just because it sets doesn't mean relief is coming. I remember that. Just like I remember the building I glimpse as I start driving again. Taylor's Marketplace and Bait Shop. There was a little silver bell above the door. The smell of stale tobacco and burgers frying coated the interior. I had a part-time job there every summer thanks to a sweet woman named Ermine Taylor. She taught me about making money and saving money. And she paid me in cash, always slipping a few extra bills in for "fun money," she'd say with a wink.

The white paint around the large transom windows and on the clapboard exterior looks fresh. The covered porch looks new, too, and the double-hung doors are painted pale pink, not green like when I was here last. Its two-story facade looks like a square wedding cake with the adornments on the front instead of the top.

I see Mama inside in her red cowboy hat and red cowboy boots. Her cowgirl phase. Her throaty laugh as she poured peanuts into my sister's Coca-Cola bottle while purring to Ermine Taylor about how there were no good-looking men in this town. Mabry clutching my hand, laughing as I pretended to smoke my candy cigarette. That memory is quickly replaced by another that recalls a name I've so far kept out of my head. But seeing this old place brings it charging back.

Ms. Ermine and her husband, Mr. Billy, taught me to use the register the summer I turned fourteen. I was ringing up a customer when a long-legged creature with tanned arms and a lean body sauntered in and promptly ignored me, making me wish for the first time that I liked makeup as much as my mother.

"Travis Arceneaux," I whisper.

His name on my lips conjures up images of late nights on the levee and long hot days on Shadow Bluff's front porch. But teenage infatuation isn't all it conjures up. I shut out the next thought as if I've slammed a door. The ability to compartmentalize is a gift every therapist should embrace. A way to keep the negative aspects of the job from seeping into everyday life—the patients you can't help, the frustrations, the trauma of children. It may also be the only thing that can get me through being back in this town.

I refocus on the road and slow down even more. If I don't, I'll miss the narrow unpaved path I'm looking for. When I spoke to the lawyer Mr. LaSalle yesterday, he sounded a bit perplexed that I'd be traveling to Broken Bayou for some very old boxes. He offered to ship them, but I declined, explaining I had a few days off work and really wanted to revisit the town where I'd spent my summers. That's when he told me the Aunts donated their home and land to the local preservation society, and that group was in the process of taking ownership, but he was sure they wouldn't mind if I stayed there while in town. I agreed before I realized what I was agreeing to, and now that I'm this close, and after the events at the Sack and Save, I wonder if I should've chosen a hotel in Baton Rouge instead.

A telephone pole with a Missing poster stapled onto it marks my turn. The eyes of a young woman watch me from the torn paper. Is this the missing schoolteacher Mama spoke of? I try to place her, maybe someone from this town, from my past, but I can't. Like with Johnette, I don't recognize her. So much of this town stayed sharp and in focus, while other parts dulled and faded like that picture. There's a number to call with information, and I hope for her sake, and her family's, she's not in that bayou. But the news vans I saw earlier might indicate otherwise.

I turn and crawl down the narrow dead-end lane, through a tunnel of live oaks. Twenty years have passed, yet it still looks the same, over-grown and remote. The closer I get to the end of the road, the more shallow my breathing becomes, like I'm somehow going up in elevation instead of driving below sea level.

I stop at an open gate at the dead end. The same gate Mama charged in her cutoffs and boots, flying over it *the cowgirl way*, as she called it. Hands high on the top rung and flipping her body over like the Kilgore Rangerette she never was. Always reminding Mabry and me she would have been if her mama hadn't been so drunk that she'd been unable to drive Krystal Lynn to the tryouts.

I glance at my phone, swipe it open. I want to call Mabry, tell her where I am, but she won't answer. She was so angry the last time we spoke that she promised we'd never talk again. I figured it was an empty threat. A way to scare me. But she kept her promise.

I decide to text instead.

Guess who? You'll never believe where I am.

I inhale a slow breath and release it even slower; then I pull through the gate.

Dusk has settled in among the thick, twisted live oaks flanking the narrow driveway. Veiny roots sprout from the ground and spread in all directions. No manicured lawn or landscaping here. The Aunts always complained about how the trees' shadows prevented any grass from growing, but from the looks of things now, weeds grow plenty. They choke every square inch of the yard.

Something moves deep in one of the shadows. Probably a raccoon or possum looking for food. Or maybe it's just the ghosts of two little girls running around in oversize Hanes T-shirts, catching lightning bugs in mason jars. I picture Mama running around with us, her T-shirt always shorter and tighter. The Aunts yelling at her from the porch to "Put some britches on, Krystal Lynn!" Mama, of course, ignored them. We brought the full jars inside, up to the front bedroom. Mabry and Mama jumped into bed, and I turned out the lights and opened the jars. Tiny dots of light filled the room, and Mabry whispered, "Magic." And we all fell asleep, watching the light show, Mama humming "Delta Dawn." But the magic ended the next morning when Mama and I awoke to Mabry's wails and small dead carcasses covering the beds.

I teared up as well. "I didn't know it would kill them."

Mama smoothed Mabry's hair, pulled me in close, and in a rare moment of clarity, said, "Shhh, sweet girls. Of course you didn't. Sometimes we do things for fun and don't realize the consequences. That's just how life is."

Every inch of this property holds a story from my childhood. I wonder how long I'll be able to live among them.

The old house looms in front of me in a hulking mass. Greek Revival columns that have seen better days hold up a sagging porch that looks like it's given up. Weeds have made their way here as well, twisting through the wooden slats as if nature decided to take over since the Aunts were no longer around.

White peeling paint covers most of the exterior of the house, interrupted by bare patches of wood and windows with a thick layer of grime. Shadow Bluff is not like its closest neighbors to the west: the stately Rosedown with its extravagant gardens and smooth columns, or the haunted Myrtles Plantation with its 125-foot veranda and Baccarat crystal chandeliers. No, Shadow Bluff is different. Smaller, not on hundreds of acres, and certainly not fifty-three thousand square feet like Nottoway, a few towns over. Shadow Bluff lives in the shadows of the moss-hung oaks in a town nobody wants to visit. The local Historic Preservation Society may have more on their hands than they bargained for.

The summer air feels like a heavy blanket when I fling open the car door. Frogs croak in the shadows of the large oaks that give this property its name. Bugs flit around my face. I grab my things and crunch across the oystershell drive toward the ramshackle porch. My handgun slides into view through my open duffel. I added it last minute, along with a box of bullets. "A girl's day out," Amy said about our conceal-carry class. Laughing, she added, "It's practically mandatory in Texas." I shot ten different guns in our class that day, but this handgun fit me best. Even my ex-husband argued it might not be a horrible idea to have protection. A single woman living alone in a big city and gaining notoriety. Notoriety. Jesus.

I drop my bag on the old porch and stare at the heavy front door. I pinch the bridge of my nose and squeeze my eyes shut. I could turn around, get back in my car, and go back to the mess in Fort Worth. It's not too late. I could tell the lawyer to throw Mama's boxes in the trash. But as I open my eyes, I know I'll do neither. This is not just about old boxes. It's not just about running away from public humiliation. It's about protecting what means the most to me: my career.

I lift up the front mat and find the key the lawyer told me about and slide it into the lock. Mama's young voice fills my head. The one from that night down here so long ago. Soaked in vodka, warm, and slurred in my seventeen-year-old ear as I leaned over her bed.

Get rid of it, sweet girl.

I turn the key.

Chapter Three

A whoosh of dusty air escapes when I open the door, like I've broken the seal of an ancient tomb. My hand finds the light switch out of habit. Bright LED lights illuminate the foyer's splintered and warped wood floors. The lights are new, but judging from what's around me, they're the only new things.

The two rooms sitting off the foyer are filled with sparse cloth-covered furniture. On my left is the formal dining room, connected to the kitchen by swinging doors, and on the right, a parlor where Mabry spent most of her time drawing in her sketchbook. The rooms are nothing like the blond hardwood floors and tall windows of my high-rise. They are dollhouse rooms, separate and boxed in and much smaller than I remember.

The floorboards creak as I walk farther in, and along with that sound, I hear our voices ricochet off the walls as we hauled our gear in that last summer here.

"Hey, y'all, we're here!" Mama yelled, a cigarette balanced between her lips.

Mabry clung to my side. She was always shy when we first arrived.

The Aunts shuffled down the hall in unison. They reminded me of fairy-tale creatures . . . Grimms'-fairy-tale creatures. Made of sharp bones and loose skin and topped off with salt-and-pepper frizzy hair and thick eyeglasses. In sync, right down to their missing molars. Their matching muumuus hung on them like bright tents, baggy and wrinkled like their skin but with lots more color.

"Lookee here, Pearl," Petunia said, wrapping her arms around me. "We got us some scalawags come to visit."

Petunia grabbed Mabry, and we all hugged in an awkward circle full of pats and coos and smelling like mothballs and Rose Milk body lotion.

"I need a wine cooler after that drive. Where y'all keep the hooch?" Mama ran a hand through her hair and exhaled a perfect ring of smoke.

"Sweet sugar, you know good and well we don't keep *hooch* in this house. And we don't smoke in it neither." Pearl pursed her lips. "Maybe one of these summers your memory will kick in."

Mama rolled her eyes.

"What are we gonna do for fun this summer?" I asked Pearl, or maybe it was Petunia. They looked more alike than usual.

"Ever milk a goat?" they said in unison.

I laugh at the memory, but the laugh fades as my eyes fall on the straight staircase in front of me. The last time I saw it, I was hauling bags down, not up. Oblivious in some ways, complicit in others. Not understanding it'd be almost twenty years before I stepped foot in this house again. I missed this place so much that first summer we didn't return. I'd packed my bags and Mabry's, and we raced home after our last day of school to load them in the station wagon. That's when Mama told us we wouldn't be going back, ever. Mabry cried for days. The Aunts called and wrote letters, and Mama told them we'd try next summer. Mama and I fought, and I told her I'd take Mabry without her, and Mama slapped me so hard my teeth rattled.

"We'll never step foot in that town again," she said. "If you try to go, I'll take Mabry and disappear."

That was all the threat I needed. Mama knew my weakness.

I shift the paper sacks from the Sack and Save as my duffel strap digs into my arm. I glance down the hall toward the kitchen, then back to the staircase.

My phone trills in my purse. I shift the sacks, fumble for it, look at who the caller is. I've sent her to voicemail too many times already. If I don't answer, she may call the National Guard next. Besides, now would be a good time to hear a friendly voice.

"Hi."

"Willa! Finally. I've been worried sick," Amy Owens says over speakerphone. Friends for longer than I can remember, Amy and I bonded because of our mothers. Hers an alcoholic, mine bipolar. Two incoming high school freshmen living with dysfunctional mothers have a way of finding each other. Gravitational attraction. Amy had just moved to Greenhill, Louisiana, and was looking for a friend. I'd lived in Greenhill my whole life, and I was still looking for a friend. She didn't care that I charted my mother's moods on a calendar with red and black markers, and I didn't care that sometimes she ran away from their apartment and slept under my bed. Now, our after-work, happy hour childhood-one-up matches keep our other friends laughing. They sip their special old-fashioneds and swear we are lying. Amy and I laugh with them. Only not as loud.

"Sorry. I've been avoiding my phone." For obvious reasons, I want to add.

"I got the text you sent early this morning. What the hell are you doing in south Louisiana?"

I glance at the stairs again. "Quick errand," I say.

"Well, convenient timing on this errand," she says.

I make my way down the narrow hall toward the kitchen. "I made it convenient timing."

Like the rest of the house, the kitchen is smaller than I remember, but unlike what I've seen so far, it's been updated. Stained wood floors, faux-distressed cabinets the color of a robin's egg, a white farm sink under a window. A small square table with four mismatched chairs sits in the middle of the room like an afterthought. The appliances all look new and unused. I wonder if my great-aunts were still here when they died or if they were in a nursing home. They must have been in their nineties. I hope they were here. As soon as those words enter my head, my heart clenches. An image comes to mind of my mother at Texas Rose, tangled hair and an oversize robe, falling asleep sitting up.

I set the groceries next to the sink.

"Wanna talk about the interview on *Fort Worth Live?*" Amy says.

"Nope," I answer before she finishes her question.

I snag the bottle of wine from one of the bags and find a glass in the cabinet.

"Well," Amy says, "wanna talk about our podcast and when we're getting back to work?"

That one is trickier to answer. I have a podcast thanks to Amy. She's the one who told me years ago to switch from radio. My radio program was losing steam, and so was I. She helped me reinvent it into a show averaging over five thousand listeners per episode and growing.

I unscrew the top, pour a small glass, and sip. I don't even care it's warm.

"Soon," I say.

"Talk about it soon? Or we're getting back to work soon?"

"Both."

"I guess the good news is your social media followers have quadrupled," Amy says with a short laugh.

"Yay, me." I drain what's left of my wine and set my glass down. That's when I see the note propped up by the coffee maker.

"Willa," Amy starts.

"Hang on."

I pick up the note. *Make yourself at home. Your mother's things are in the attic. Be by soon to check in.* It's signed in small neat cursive by my aunts' lawyer, Charles LaSalle II.

"This isn't the end of the world," Amy says in my ear. She starts talking about a few show ideas and ways to navigate this minor incident, but I'm not listening anymore. I'm back at the front staircase.

I pick up my duffel and head up. When I reach the top, I pause, my heart pounding faster than it should be for my slow ascent. Like downstairs, the second floor is compartmentalized. One bedroom at the top of the stairs. One across the small landing. And two down a short hallway to the front of the house, overlooking the driveway. The door to the bedroom Mama claimed every summer is cracked open.

A chill passes over me.

"Are you listening to me?" Amy says.

"Yeah," I lie.

She continues talking as I ease toward the bedroom and peek inside. The antique four-poster bed is stripped as bare as a skeleton. No tangled sheets. No empty vodka bottles. No smoke curling around its carved posts. I swallow the lump in my throat and close the door. That's not the room I'm here for.

Goose bumps cover my arms despite the warmth of the house. I drop my duffel and flip the light switch by the stairs. A single lamp illuminates in the corner, but the ambient light does little good. Shadows still linger in the back corner, near the other set of stairs. The ones that are cramped and narrow and lead to an attic.

"But we're not going to worry about that," Amy says and keeps talking.

I place my foot on the first step, and it creaks so loudly I pause, like I'll wake someone up. But there's no one here to disturb. It's just me, alone, in this house. I chew the side of my thumbnail, then continue up. The higher I climb, the lower the ceiling becomes thanks to the slanted roof. Hunched and struggling to maintain my balance, I pause at the top of the stairs. The air feels cooler up here. The Aunts must have added air-conditioning at some point.

When Mabry and I played here as kids, it wasn't. The summer heat culminated up here like molten lava. Once we played hide-and-seek, and Mabry hid in the attic for so long Aunt Pearl made her drink pickle juice when she finally came down, sweaty and shaking. I'd been terrified and lectured Mabry until she cried. Then I apologized and let her crawl into bed with me that night so I could tickle her back until she fell asleep.

"I mean, how do you want to handle it?" Amy asks.

I close my hand around the knob and turn it. Nothing happens. I twist it again. Still nothing. I pull and push and rattle the door. It's locked. I smack my hand against the wood, shut my eyes, count to three because it's as far as I get before I start looking around the small landing for a key. Only dust hides in the corners.

"Willa?"

Of course it's fucking locked. I rub the back of my neck. "Sorry, Amy, what did you say?"

"How do you want to handle it."

I head back down to the landing. "Handle what exactly?"

"Willa. The press. They know about Christopher."

I trip on the last step. "What?" I recover, move from the attic stairs to the stairs leading to the first floor. "Wait. Give me a second."

I scamper down the steps, back to the kitchen. I refill the wineglass and sit at the table. "Okay, I'm ready."

"An old classmate of yours posted something on her feed. A picture of him and you. Said she always thought y'all had dated during clinicals. Hashtag honest healing. Hashtag what honesty. Local reporter from the *Tribune* saw it, remembered you."

I choke on the sip I've started to take but manage to say, "Shit. Shit, shit, shit."

My ex. Dr. Christopher Fulton. A licensed psychologist twenty years my senior. But it wasn't his age that was the problem. It was his position. I worked for him the year I did my clinicals. I was twenty-seven and ready to start my career. He was close to fifty and nursing wounds from an ugly divorce. It started innocently enough but quickly turned into something not so innocent. Our relationship was secretive and highly unethical. Although students dating professors isn't unheard of, in our field, it's a deal-breaker. He and I could have both lost everything we'd worked toward.

We married in a private ceremony at a town hall a year later, after I passed my boards. I kept my maiden name and went into practice with two others. We divorced four years later as quietly as we wed, leaving each other with the understanding no one would ever know about our yearlong tryst before we married.

Even after my podcast took off and the book started gaining momentum, I didn't worry. My former husband had nothing to do with either. I kept him out of it, and no one had gone digging. Until now.

Amy says, "You still there?"

"Yeah."

"You gave the buzzards a little taste of scandal yesterday, and they liked it. They want more, and they'll dig until they find it." She pauses, then adds, "Willa, what do you think the fallout will be with the Christopher thing? Could you lose your license?"

"No," I answer too quickly, and I can picture Amy rolling her eyes. "Look, what we did was unethical but not illegal. Our relationship had no bearing whatsoever on my clinical internship or my ability to pass my boards. Period. Besides, it's so far in the past; no licensing board would touch it."

There's a pause, and I hear her sip something. No doubt she has her own wine in hand.

I take another sip. "It's going to be okay," I say, but I don't sound convincing, even to myself. Because what I don't say is, even though my license is safe, I still need to be very careful when it comes to the court of public opinion. My field is held to a higher standard of ethics than most. Sleeping with my adviser is not going to do me any favors in the credibility department. If this snowballs, it will not be good. For me or for Christopher.

"When are you coming home?" she asks.

"Couple of days." Now, it's my turn to sigh. "In time to turn around and get to the *Good Morning America* spot."

Amy sighs.

"What?"

"They canceled."

In my head, I see the first domino in a long line tip over. My silence says it all.

"Willa." Amy clears her throat. "They said they had a scheduling conflict. That's it. We'll reschedule."

I exhale, finish my second glass of warm wine. "I'm sorry for all of this. I feel like an idiot."

"You're human, Willa. That's all. And don't apologize."

I nod. Even though she can't see me, Amy understands. "It's gonna be okay," she says, echoing my own words.

All the energy drains from my body. I tell her good night. That I love her. And hang up.

Back on the upstairs landing, I grab my duffel and peek into the remaining three rooms. They are empty except for the last one. The one Mabry and I once shared. The twin beds are bare except for a set of folded sheets on one. Did the lawyer know this was the room I once stayed in? How could he? More than likely, this room was chosen based on the size of the sheets they had.

Just like in the foyer, this room holds Mama's voice as well. Our last summer here, she waltzed in with her cheeks glowing. "Isn't it just great here? We're all going to have the best summer ever. Who knows what will happen?" She twirled around the room with her arms out wide and danced over to Mabry and scooped her up. Mama dipped her and blew raspberries on her neck, and Mabry squealed with laughter. Then Mama started into a raucous rendition of "All My Ex's Live in Texas," stomping her feet and shaking her hips and sashaying Mabry with her. I watched and hoped Mama's mood would make it to the end of summer, but hope was dangerous in the Watters' house. And Mama never made it on a high three solid months in a row before. Still, though, what if? I was almost seventeen and knew better. Mabry was twelve and did not. But Mama's laughter and bright eyes and wild hoots of joy were contagious, and soon I was tapping my foot and jumping into the fray right along with them, swinging around the room and laughing as if everything would be okay.

Exhaustion floods over me. I slip off my heels, study my duffel. I could unpack, but how long do I plan on being here? Unpacking may be too much of a commitment. What I do is make the bed, change, and crawl under the sheets.

My mind runs through my conversation with Amy. Christopher. If I could take back that relationship, I would. The problem with it, with me, was a basic one and somewhat insulting in its simplicity. Daddy issues. Christopher, the men I dated after Christopher, the guy I brought home the night before my interview all fit that mold. Emotionally unavailable. It happens when the only thing you remember about your father is he smelled like spearmint gum and chewing tobacco the day he left. I was five. Mabry a newborn. Mama yelled after him from the front yard, holding Mabry, who was wailing. "You're gonna be sorry you left me!" I wondered for years if he was sorry. In my twenties, I tracked him down. He lived in a nearby town. I drove to his house, ready to confront him. His new wife opened the door. Two young boys stood behind her. I told her who I was, and she asked me to come in. She made me tea I didn't drink and told me my father died of a heart attack six months earlier. I'd just missed him.

I force myself to clear my mind, breathe away my thoughts.

This house, the boxes, that letter have been applying their weight for too long. Maybe it's a good thing I can't get into the attic tonight. Maybe it's a sign I'm moving too fast for what's in there. I'll figure it out tomorrow. Tonight I'll let sleeping dogs lie.

June 2015

Destiny Smith didn't like the music at this festival anymore. It was fun at first, but now the acid rock music in Louis Armstrong Park was grating on her last nerve. Her fix was gone. Her buzz wearing thin. And it was so crowded she could barely move. People moshed around her in a wild, rhythmic dance. An elbow landed in her cheek, and Destiny screamed and shoved back. She enjoyed New Orleans when she first arrived. The people were nice, and the drugs were even nicer. Everyone seemed to want to share. This park was good too. Safe. Safer than her house in Birmingham. And she found a job. A shit job dancing on Bourbon, thanks to her fake ID, but the tips were good. Soon, she'd have enough saved to get to California. She'd clean up there. Live next to the ocean. Meet a sweet boy who wouldn't hurt her. Maybe she'd let her mom visit her one day. Maybe. If she cleaned up too.

Destiny pushed her way through the drunken crowd, with no idea of where she was going.

"Excuse me," a voice in the crowd said. "Hey, you."

Destiny turned. A flash went off in her face. She held her hands up. "What the fuck!"

"Say cheese."

"Cheese, motherfucker." And Destiny punched him.

He stumbled, but he didn't fall. He smiled. Every warning bell in Destiny's tiny body sounded. She knew this type of man. She saw it in his eyes. He was trouble. She turned to run, but he was quick and grabbed her ponytail. Destiny yelled, but her voice was lost in the loud music of the festival. Then something stung her neck, and she couldn't scream anymore. All she could do was fall into his shoulder and whimper for her mom to please come get her.

Chapter Four

Someone is touching my arm as I sleep. My skin registers it, but my brain is still tangled in dreams and memories. For a moment I think Mabry is next to me in the twin bed, tickling my arm.

My eyes fly open. I leap from the bed, swatting at my arm and scanning for my handgun, only to find the intruder is a daddy longlegs, now scampering across the wood floor. Shit.

My breath is shallow as I rub my arms and settle my heart rate. It's a strange feeling waking up in this house again. In one way, it's too familiar. In another, too foreign. A purgatory of sorts.

In the bathroom, I find fresh towels and a bar of soap to wash my face. I catch my reflection in the mirror. I look tired but not as bad as I expected, considering I tossed and turned all night. I smooth my hair back into a neat bun. One strand breaks loose, but I tuck it behind my ear. I'm wearing the XXXL black T-shirt that reads *Fort Worth Live* across the front. Seems appropriate. It's what my handlers at the show gave me to leave the studio in. I have no idea what happened to the silk blouse. Maybe some intern has fished it out of the trash by now and sold it on eBay. Hashtag honestly stupid. I shouldn't have brought this T-shirt. A reminder of what I've put at risk. But that's what I do, keep things I shouldn't.

I dig through my hanging cosmetic bag for my moisturizer. Something shiny glints through one of the clear plastic pockets, but I ignore it. I shouldn't have brought it either.

I rub moisturizer on my face, then dig a short silk robe from my duffel. The robe's inappropriateness is on trend with everything else in my bag. Too formal. Completely unnecessary here. I tie it tight around my waist, glance at the bedroom door. Time to wake up sleeping dogs.

I climb the attic steps again and fold my hand around the knob and pull. Come on, I silently encourage. It still only rattles in place. I study the landing in the dusty light coming from the window at the bottom of the stairs. I didn't miss anything last night. No key. I try the knob again, pulling harder. The door gives slightly. And with that small give, my sense of urgency to get inside grows. I pull and pull and pull, then yank the door as hard as I can. Something cracks on the doorframe, but instead of the door opening, my hand slips off the knob. I sway backward, balancing on the top step and somehow catching myself before I fall and become a heap of broken bones at the base of the stairs. I exhale, slow my breathing, regroup. I need a different plan.

The kitchen is warm and humid and filled with the sounds of birds, almost as if they're in the room with me. I search the drawers but don't find any options to accommodate a breaking and entering. Only a few paper plates and plasticware. I do, however, spy the coffee maker and a bag of chicory coffee.

I pour water into the coffee maker, as well as a generous amount of grounds. I find a coffee cup and set it on the butcher-block countertop my decorator would approve of. Unlike the marble ones I chose for my kitchen at home. "Scars too easily," she said. "That's okay," I told her. "I like scars."

A throbbing starts in a vein on the inside of my arm, high up next to the crease in my elbow. Next to the small tattoo I thought was a great idea five years ago. Amy got one too. A spur-of-the-moment decision as we walked past a tattoo parlor in Deep Ellum after a concert. We chose hearts. A symbol of the love we felt for our family members who are sometimes hard to love. I rub the spot. Amy didn't know what was under that tattoo. The scars from when I didn't love myself.

I don't wait for the coffee to finish dripping before I pour some into a cup, then sit at the table with my phone. I'd silenced my notifications before bed, and I see a text from Amy sent an hour ago. I check the time. What the hell was so important that she sent a text at six in the morning? I open it.

Stay off Twitter until I can call you.

Seriously? I thought she knew me better than that. I open Twitter. I scan for any mention of me and find it immediately. Christopher's first wife retweeted my old classmate's tweet from yesterday as well as the clip from *Fort Worth Live*. Under it she wrote, This is what a homewrecker looks like. There are hundreds of comments.

HOT!

I'd let her heal me anytime!

What a fucking idiot

She needs a boob job

NUTCASE!

Sad emoji, laughing emoji, flame emoji. The things people have the courage to say when they're hiding behind a screen.

I developed a thick skin growing up with Krystal Lynn as my mother and after grinding my way through nine years of higher education without any support at home, but these comments find a way to pierce my armor. And in a way it feels good. Pain, I understand. The word *homewrecker*, however, I do not understand.

I keep scrolling, and that's when I see her second tweet, stating Christopher and I engaged in an illicit affair while he was still married to her.

"Bullshit!" I yell to the empty kitchen. And that's when I see her final tweet. It gets my hands shaking so much I almost drop my phone. This is not the role model we want for our children. She's only an expert in cheating. How did you do so well on those clinicals? Time to be honest Dr. Willa!

Acid churns in my stomach. My breathing shallows. I scroll to Amy's number and press it. It goes straight to voicemail. I send her a text instead: Call me!

I finish my coffee, talk myself out of responding to that insane tweet, tell myself that platform will only bring attention to something I want to disappear. Still, though, I'll need to address it at some point. I can't preach to people about how to handle bullies and not handle my own.

And there's something else I have to handle. Of all the things I don't have control over, finding that tape is something I still do. I need it in my possession. After that, I'll hang tight for a couple of days, make sure the social media fallout dies down. Make sure the vultures don't get anything else to feed on. Then I can go home, confront the allegations from Christopher's ex, coddle whomever necessary at *GMA* to get my spot back, and reboot my career.

The shrill cry of a crow startles me and I jump. It sounds as if the bird has gotten inside, but the kitchen is empty. I'm too keyed up. Maybe I don't need coffee after all. Then I notice something's off. Something creaks near the door that leads outside, and I raise my coffee cup, ready to hurl it if anything tries to come through the door. Nothing comes in but a breeze. I lower the mug and study the door. It's cracked open. I ease up to it and try to push it closed, but a hot wind pops it back open. I push it again. And again. Each time it opens on its own; the wind enough to jostle it free. The wood near the latch is warped and rotten. And it takes several more tries before I finally get it to stick. Even shut, the wind whistles through it. If only the attic door was this rotten. Then my gaze stops on something on the other side of the door's window. My pulse kicks back up.

Clusters of rusted wire-fence pens fill the backyard. Once they were filled with goats and a henhouse and even peacocks. I loved yelling "Pretty, pretty" at them and watching them fan open their bright feathers. There are no bright colors back there now. Just browns and dull greens. And a rusted, leaning shed sitting off to one side. The Aunts kept their gardening tools in there. Like the attic, Mabry and I were forbidden from playing in it. Too many sharp objects. I wonder if those sharp objects still exist, especially one that might open a locked door.

I stand in front of the attic door with a hammer in one hand and a screwdriver in the other. My trip to the old shed proved quite fruitful. I tap gently at first. I don't want to damage the lock too much. But the longer I stand there, tapping and getting nowhere, the antsier I get. Maybe I could hit it a little harder. I wedge the screwdriver into a crack by the knob and bring the hammer down hard on top of it. A ripping sound erupts from the wood frame. A piece splinters away, and the doorknob jostles. The damage sounded worse than it looks, but I'll still need to leave some cash behind to fix it.

The smells of mothballs and mildew smack my face when I open the door. Sunshine floods in through two dormer windows facing the front of the house. The room isn't an attic anymore. It's a bedroom. An odd, sloped-roof bedroom, but a bedroom nonetheless. The Aunts once had a plan to make this place a bed-and-breakfast. Maybe they succeeded. My heart aches with the knowledge strangers could have enjoyed this space, made memories here while I was forbidden from doing the same. Another thing to add to the long list of things to forgive. But forgiveness is like a house of mirrors in the Watters family. Just when I think I've found a way to it, a memory will surface or, in this case, a room, and I'll discover I'm even more lost than when I started.

My eyes stop on a stack of moving boxes against one wall. My fingers tingle. My mouth goes dry. Three boxes are separated from the others, in the back corner. I move toward them on shaky legs. On the side of each, in Petunia's or Pearl's loopy cursive, is a name: *Krystal Lynn*. My stomach drops as I drag one of the boxes to the middle of the room and stare at it. I test its weight. Then I test the others. I can get them all down the stairs and into my car without a problem. But do I really want to haul them back with me? Then what? Now that I'm looking at them, I'm not sure that's the best idea. Dragging my past around doesn't need to become a habit. What I need to do is throw them out. Be done with them for good. I could take them and toss them in a small-town dumpster on my way home. But first, I want to make sure what I'm looking for is here.

The packing tape has come loose on the box in front of me, peeling up on both sides, and that's all the invitation I need. In a matter of a second, I'm kneeling beside the box and ripping the tape off. I pull back the top flaps and sit back on my knees. Inside are old clothes and books and odd pieces of jewelry. I exhale. My shoulders relax. This isn't the box. I extract an old children's book and my heart flutters. P. D. Eastman's *Are You My Mother?* Mabry's favorite. I fish out a dry-rotted and faded yellow dress from the box, which pulls me back to when Mama got it in her head that Mabry could win *Star Search*, and the first step would be entering Mabry in kiddie beauty pageants so she could get used to being on stage. Mabry was terrified. I was appalled. But Mama went down to the Goodwill and bought what could have been the ugliest, yellowest thing I ever saw, then went to town on her sewing machine. She said by the time she was done, every little girl in northwest Louisiana would be jealous. Mama was on a peak. There was no touching her.

Mabry, looking like Big Bird from *Sesame Street*, entered the Little Miss Cornbread beauty contest and came in dead last. Every girl, even the one with the lazy eye, won something. Not Mabry. She stood on the stage in that hideous dress, her giant ears, her little freckles standing out against her pink cheeks, and her brown doe eyes watering. Mama came unglued. How dare those judges judge her daughter. Who did they think they were? She proceeded to cause such a scene that she was escorted from the convention center and told no child of hers would be entered into another pageant in the state of Louisiana, ever. At home, Mama grabbed the sewing machine and, with incredible strength, hurled it through the front window, where it crashed onto a row of shrubs. She then snatched a bottle of vodka from the freezer, climbed into bed, and stayed there for days. On the fourth day, she called Mabry to her side and hauled her into the bed next to her, clutching my little sister even harder than the bottle of vodka. On the fifth day, I decided Mabry needed a safe word.

I dig past the dress until I see something that really gets my heart pumping. Mabry's sketchbook. I wedge it from the box and open its worn cover. Mabry's sketches look even more spectacular than I remember. She may have been grades behind in school and misspelled everything she wrote and wrote everything she misspelled backward, but the girl could draw. Her attention to detail was eerie. The first few portraits are of me. One of Travis and me, sitting by the bayou. One of the bridge. Then one of Mama and a man I don't recognize, in what looks like a restaurant booth. I wonder if this is a real moment or one Mabry made up. Then I see one of old Mr. Billy Taylor and his wife, Ermine. Again, it looks like a moment Mabry watched. They are sitting, staring at one another at a table. Maybe Mabry watched them too. Although she was rarely anywhere without me. And I don't remember seeing her at Taylor's with her sketchbook when I worked there. But Mabry had a sneaky side. A few times, I remember the Aunts calling Taylor's to tell me Mabry had snuck away, and could I go find her. Usually she was hiding on their property under a bed, behind the oaks, hiding from Mama. But maybe sometimes she snuck away, and we didn't know, taking her sketchbook and capturing moments. From the looks of it, moments with a woman and a man. My heart clenches. Mabry knew even less of our father than I did. At least I can remember what he looked like.

I flip to the next page and see a sketch of another couple. A little girl I don't recognize, holding the hand of a boy I don't recognize. The girl has a single finger over her lips. Something about the girl looks familiar, a tickle of a memory I can't quite place. The next drawing is a parakeet. Ralph, one of Mabry's pretend pets. Some kids had pretend friends. Mabry had pretend pets. I liked Ralph. Mabry always had her finger out, cooing at him.

I wrestle the next box to the middle of the room and open it, bracing for what could be inside and, again, releasing a long breath when its contents are still a mix of clothes and jewelry. Nothing looks special to me. I dig through the pile of outdated clothes: crop tops, cutoffs, plastic bangles. Krystal Lynn's summer uniform. A black cowboy hat is crammed in with the other items and stands out against the faded neon colors. I put it on my head, and it falls almost to my eyes. Mama did have a cowgirl phase, but I always remember her hat being red. I drop the hat back into the clothes and focus on the third box. That's the one. I feel lightheaded and touch my fingers to the carpet to ground myself.

Open it.

I yank the tape from the box and peel back the cardboard flaps. My breath catches in my throat. This is what I came for. A messy pile of black VHS tapes sits inside. Old dinosaurs. Most recordings of Mama's soap operas. Bile rises in my throat. Most.

I hear Mama's voice from when I visited her two evenings ago to tell her I'd changed my mind; I would be going to Broken Bayou after all. She looked at me suspiciously from the firm sofa in the overly warm TV room of the Texas Rose Rehabilitation Center, a place filled with functional handrails, lovely gold-framed landscapes, and plenty of guilt.

"I want you to have your things," I said.

"Sure you do." Her wrinkled lips formed a smile around the clear tubes leading from her nostrils to a small oxygen tank resting on the sofa in a cloth bag. An empty wheelchair sitting on her opposite side. An oversize white robe meant for someone twice my mother's size covered her frail body, and a bird's nest of gray hair covered her head. Krystal Lynn Watters was always reckless and unpredictable and constantly in need of a hairbrush. That certainly hadn't changed in that place. If anything, it was amplified . . . even with all the meds. She looked as fragile and empty as the cicada shells my sister and I collected off pine trees when we were kids. She shifted and tapped a rhythm on the side of her leg. Mama's press-on nails provided the soundtrack for my youth. She was always tapping them on something: the steering wheel, her teeth, a can of Fresca. I learned the timing in those clicks like a master thief learns how to tumble a lock. Her long acrylics were replaced by paper-thin ghosts of what they used to be, but their telling rhythm remained. And two days ago, it told me to be on guard.

I'm reaching for the first tape when I hear the doorbell downstairs ring. I freeze. Wait. It rings again, this time like someone has their finger pressed on it and won't let go.

I race to the bottom of the stairs and fully expect to see the lawyer, LaSalle, on the other side of the door. Instead, I see a police officer wearing a navy polo shirt with a badge sewn on, khaki cargo pants, and mirrored sunglasses. Tall, with cropped hair, and built like a baseball player. His weapon is fastened onto a nylon rig belt around his waist.

He looks me up and down, and then I remember what I'm wearing. I tug at the hem of my short silky robe and straighten my shoulders.

"Can I help you?"

The officer studies me with a serious expression. "Yes, ma'am. Are you Dr. Willa Watters?"

"Yes."

He pauses. "You're under arrest."

I stare at him, barefoot and gawking. "Excuse me?" I think of my car, sitting in front of what should be an empty house. Somebody must have called the police. But under arrest?

"I'm not trespassing. I swear. I have a letter—"

The officer laughs. "Willa, I'm just kidding." He removes his sunglasses. "It's me. Travis Arceneaux." The dimple pops out next to his crooked smile.

A blush rises to my cheeks, and I clear my throat before I speak, which still takes several seconds. "Oh my God. Travis." His blue eyes shine. Most of him is just as I remember. Tall, with broad shoulders, dimpled smile. But fine lines form beside his eyes when he smiles now, and a deep crease sits between his brows. I wonder what he thinks, looking at me. Is he noticing my creases as well? I'm not sure I've held up as well as he has, even with the dermatologist I can now afford. I wish I'd brushed my teeth before I came down. Hell, put clothes on. I try to remember if I'd put deodorant on this morning.

"You should've seen your face," Travis says, still laughing. "You looked guilty."

A small knot tightens in my stomach, but I ignore it. "I look tired is what I look."

"Nah. You look great."

His smile matches mine. It's been almost twenty years since I've seen that smile. Since we rolled on a levee together, his hands making familiar territory of my body. Since I showed up at his house in the middle of the night, panicked and scared, asking for his help. Since he helped me. The knot in my stomach turns into a hard stone. And now he's a cop.

"How'd you know I was here?" I say, working to keep the nerves out of my voice.

He lowers his chin. "Really? You think you could have kept the fact you were back in town secret? News travels fast in small towns. Not to mention my brother said he saw a fancy woman driving around yesterday. And Charlie LaSalle likes to talk loud at Nan's too."

The truck that roared past me yesterday on Main Street. His brother. If I remember correctly, Travis had six brothers, most of whom had moved away by the time I met him. I figured Travis would have moved, too, considering what his homelife had been like. He called it shitty back then. I've learned enough to call it what it actually was, toxic at best, abusive at worst. It's one of the things we had in common.

Travis nods and looks around. An awkward silence settles around us. I shuffle on my feet, toying with the idea of lying and saying I have to be somewhere so he'll leave. This reunion doesn't need to happen. Definitely not part of the get-in-and-get-out-quickly plan.

"Well, thanks for coming by."

"Sure. I'm glad I—" Travis starts, and I interrupt.

"Want a cup of coffee?" So much for my plan.

"You bet." He whistles as he crosses into the foyer. "Been a few years since I've been in here. Sorry to show up unannounced. And I was sorry to hear about your great-aunts."

"It's fine. Thanks. Been a few years since I've been here too." Our eyes linger on each other a fraction too long. I glance down at my small robe. "You can head on into the kitchen. I need to change."

He peeks at my legs. "If you insist, but don't change on my account."

The heat in my cheeks deepens. What is wrong with me? I feel like I'm fourteen again. I hurry up the steps and return to the kitchen a few minutes later. Travis looks out the window over the sink. "Didn't this place seem bigger when we were kids?"

"It did."

He turns around and chokes on his sip of coffee. "What are you wearing?"

I look down at my pressed suit pants. "What?"

He laughs. "You going to court or a funeral?"

I fill my coffee cup. "Ha. Ha."

He pulls a kitchen chair out for me, and we both sit. He holds his cup up. "Hope you don't mind, I helped myself."

"Of course not." This little reunion seems to be much more comfortable for him than for me. I'm having a hard time keeping my foot from tapping under the table. He looks completely relaxed, like no time has passed.

"Confession," he says. "I've followed your career a little." He looks down into his coffee. "I even bought your book." He glances back up. "You really got it together, Willa."

I cock my head to one side and eye him. "Guess you don't watch YouTube."

He grins. "Except for that."

"Yeah. Except for *that.*"

Another awkward silence creeps in. Travis's eyes land on the large silver thermos tucked beside the sink. "Damn, Willa. How much coffee do you drink on a daily basis?"

"Whatever it takes to get the job done."

"Willa, Willa, Willa," he says.

He's staring at me with a faraway look. Travis and his brothers who'd stuck around were like a pack of wolf pups every summer, all paws and tripping over each other to get to me, the only viable out-of-town teenage girl in the entire parish. And I encouraged it. Hell, I'd learned at the knee of the master. I'd been raised in a testosterone vacuum: Krystal Lynn, Mabry, the Aunts. As soon as those Arceneaux boys made an appearance at Shadow Bluff, with their dirty fingernails and tanned chests, I was done for. I smelled their pheromones and damn near got drunk on them. Travis was a couple of years older than me, and even though some of the others tried for my attention, my attention stayed on Travis. Mostly because he ignored me. But he didn't ignore me long.

Soon, he was sneaking me out of Shadow Bluff in the middle of the night with a six-pack of beer and a blanket. Then one night his rough hands found their way under my shirt, and I didn't stop him. Travis was my first. I was fourteen. The first time was awful, but we got better at it. We couldn't keep our hands off each other. And every summer was the same after that. I'd come to town, and we'd start back up like no time had passed. It was so easy, so comfortable. Until that last summer.

I clear my throat, and the sound breaks the silence. I try to think of something other than his skin against mine. That was a long time ago.

But being in such close proximity brings it back like it was yesterday. I have an urge to reach over and hold his hand. But I don't know that hand anymore. And he doesn't know mine.

"You know," I motion around the room, "this house is going to the Historic Preservation Society."

"Is it?" He's still staring at me with that crystallized stare.

"Yep. It is." I sip, shift in my chair. Silence falls again, and I work to come up with something to say, usually not a problem for me. I built a career on talking. But this setting and this man have me flustered. "My mom got a letter asking her to clean out anything that belonged to her. So here I am." Shit. Why did I tell him that? He doesn't need to know that. He doesn't need to know anything about that box of tapes in the attic, especially given his profession.

"So how long you going to be here?" Travis asks, bringing me back to the kitchen.

"Not long."

"Too bad." He checks his watch and grabs his sunglasses, then pushes back from the table. "I guess I better be going."

I walk him to the front door, where he pauses. "Um." He slips on his sunglasses, clears his throat. "Maybe we could grab dinner before you leave. Catch up."

I smile. "Sure."

"Tonight?"

No, absolutely not. "Oh. I . . . sure. Why not?"

He smiles back at me. "Great."

"Great."

We look at each other, and the moment drags a little too long. "Okay then," I say.

"Guess I should get your number."

I give it to him, and he punches it into his phone. He starts for the porch steps, then stops and looks back at me. "Actually, are you hungry now? I haven't had breakfast, and you could join me in town if you want. I know a great breakfast spot." He exhales a laugh. "It's pretty much the only breakfast spot."

Tell him no thank you, Willa. Tell him you have things to do. The box in the attic is waiting. My foot starts tapping again. I shove my hand in my pocket to keep from chewing on the side of my thumbnail. No plans, no dinner, no breakfast with a cop, even if it is Travis. Especially because it's Travis.

"Well?" he says, smiling.

The answer is no, the voice in my head says.

But I am hungry, and I need to eat somewhere, and those boxes are fine for now. I found what I needed. Taking an hour to regroup and eat something isn't going to make a damn bit of difference. Those tapes are worthless until I can figure out a way to watch them.

Besides, avoidance as a coping mechanism doesn't sound so awful at the moment.

"Breakfast sounds good," I say.

Chapter Five

Travis navigates his truck down the narrow lane, away from Shadow Bluff. The truck is spotless. A Ford F-250 with a leather interior and a dashboard that looks like the inside of a cockpit. A siren rests on the top of the dash.

"Nice truck," I say.

"Thanks. Took me forever to save up for it."

"No patrol car?"

He laughs, and there goes the dimple again. "Hell, no. Even the chief doesn't have a patrol car. No damn money. We're lucky we even have a police department. Lots of small towns have lost theirs. It's just me, the chief, and two other officers in a run-down rented building north of Bridge Street. Oh, and we do have Margie, who works the front, but she volunteers because she's married to the chief." He side-eyes me and winks. "A real coup." He glances at me again. "You know, Nan's is pretty casual."

I look down at the suit pants and navy-and-white-striped blouse. Silk, like the one I ruined on *Fort Worth Live*. "Unfortunately, this is my casual."

"Suit yourself." He slides his gaze at me with a smile. "No pun intended."

I roll my eyes. It's strange, being in a car with him again. One of the last times I was in a car with him, Travis snuck me to a spot outside the town. His uncle's place, where Travis worked during the summer.

Then he took me for a joyride. In a crop duster. I remember the sinking drops in my stomach as he dipped over the fields. I was laughing and crying at the same time. No roller coaster came close. I'd never been that out of control. And by the time we finally landed, I'd discovered a piece of me actually liked it.

I gaze out the window. The town looks tired. The ditches are overgrown with weeds, and the small houses are sagging, some even boarded up. The complete opposite of the town down the road. St. Francisville capitalized on its antebellum homes and gardens, and created a quaint place for tourists to ooh and aah over a past we have no business oohing and aahing over. Maybe that was Broken Bayou's hope for Shadow Bluff. Even though Shadow Bluff isn't technically antebellum. It's old, yes. But not a plantation. The Aunts liked to brag it was, but it's just an imitation. I looked it up, researched it when I was in middle school and looking for a history project. Shadow Bluff was built in the nineteenth century but well after the Civil War ended. Beautiful, but never even had a crop. And as I look around, I don't think the restoration of that place will bring this town back to life. Broken Bayou looks . . . broken.

Travis pulls into the parking lot of Nan's Café, a small box building with windows on two sides. We hop out, and Travis opens the glass front door for me. A lively hive of clinking silverware and slow southern drawls greets us. Inside, it looks like most small diners. Booths against one wall, tables in the middle, and in the back, a long counter with stools facing the open kitchen. A menagerie of jelly packets, salt and pepper shakers, and Louisiana-brand hot sauce jars adorn every table. Beige walls and linoleum floors finish out the look. No cutesy decor like I expect in a southern establishment, only kids' drawings taped on the walls. Which is odd considering there don't seem to be many kids here.

We head for an empty booth. It's overly warm and smells like sweet perfume and bacon. Topics of conversation float around us as we weave through the tables, most people commenting on the worst drought in this region's history. As we pass, one man takes off his cap, rubs his thinning hair, and says to the waitress taking his order, "Some people talk about hundred-year floods. Well, this here's the hundred-year drought."

We slide into the booth, and a waitress with a messy ponytail and a sour look on her face approaches, turns over our ceramic coffee mugs, and pours coffee before we ask. Then she abruptly leaves.

"So much for southern hospitality," I say.

"The locals can be a little cranky." Travis nods to a table in the back. "You look like one of *them*."

I look around more closely and notice a table where the customers are dressed like me, suits and slick city hair. "What's going on?"

"Media."

The waitress reappears, tops off my mug to overflowing, and onto the table, drops two plastic menus that announce Nan's proudly serves breakfast all day. Before she can walk off, Travis stops her and orders spicy sausage and biscuits with white gravy, a side of fried green tomatoes, and a crabmeat omelet with grits.

I stare at him with my mouth open. "Really?"

"You have to try all the house favorites. Besides, I remember you liking a big breakfast."

My cheeks flush, and I study the menu until it subsides. When I look up, he's watching me.

"What else do you remember?" I say.

His smile mirrors mine. "I remember it all."

What does *that* mean? His tone is flirty, playful, but so is mine. Maybe he's following my lead. Or maybe he's testing me. Or maybe I'm overthinking it all, and it means absolutely nothing.

I need to think of something to say. Anything that keeps the conversation from drifting to the past.

"How's your mom? Your dad?" I say and immediately regret it. That might be the worst topic I could've picked.

Travis rolls his eyes. "My dad died a few years ago."

"Oh, I'm sorry."

"I'm not. He got drunk and fell off the dock, drowned."

"That's horrible." I remember his father. A burly man who watched Travis like a hawk.

"My mom is still out at the house."

An image of Liv Arceneaux comes to mind, and it's not a pretty one: of her holed up in their run-down house, staring out the window when Travis would run out to meet me. Although I didn't go over there much. The Aunts forbade it. I don't remember much about that house except that it sat tucked into the woods at the north end of town and that I could always see Liv peeking outside. She would have made a good research study in grad school.

"My brothers Doyle and Eddie live with her," Travis continues. "The rest of my brothers escaped this place. And Emily," he pauses, swallows. "Emily passed away a long time ago."

I set my coffee down. Emily. The sister. I'd forgotten all about her. I only met her a couple of times, even with all our trips down. I want to ask him more about his dad and sister, but I can see the sadness in his eyes, so I settle on, "I'm so sorry."

He nods, sips his coffee.

I point at his outfit. "And how did you end up in law enforcement?"

He laughs. A deep, hefty laugh that brings with it the memory of a boy and a girl and fireworks. "Thought I'd try out life on the other side for a while."

"A while?"

"Yeah. Till I get bored, and the juvenile delinquent side comes back out."

I hold my coffee mug up, and he clinks it, grinning. The scar under his eye crinkles. The one I know he got from falling through a glass-top coffee table while wrestling with one of his brothers. But there's something unspoken in his eyes. It's in mine too. I hope to God he doesn't bring it up. I'm not ready for that topic yet.

I glance at the media table again. The Missing poster and the news vans come to mind along with the conversation with my mother the day before. "I saw several news vans yesterday, then the Missing poster at the turn to Shadow Bluff."

He shakes his head. "The media's not here for that missing schoolteacher. They're here for the barrels."

I sit up straighter. "What barrels?"

His mouth falls open. "Are you serious?"

That bayou is all over the news. I nod.

"Christ." He rubs his face. "It's unbelievable." He pulls his cell phone out.

"Travis?" I say. "What barrels?"

He holds his finger up. "Hang on." He taps on his phone, then turns it around so I can see the screen. "Watch." He hits play on the video.

Two newscasters, a bright-eyed woman and a coifed, lean man, from a Baton Rouge affiliate fill the screen. They look very serious as they discuss the drought plaguing the area. Water levels are dangerously low. Crops are dying. People are worried. Down here, the concern is always too much water, not the lack of. For the first time ever, people are praying for a tropical storm. The two anchors look desperately at the meteorologist, who shakes his head and informs them there's nothing spinning in the gulf, no rain in sight.

I reach for one of the individual liquid creamers on the table and pour it into my cup. When I look back at the screen, the newscasters have switched gears, and the woman says, "Now, Grace Morgan will follow up on that bizarre story out of Broken Bayou. Good morning, Grace."

I turn up the volume on the side of Travis's phone.

"Good morning, Sherri. As you can see, I'm here on the banks of Broken Bayou this morning, following up on a story that has some of the folks here quite concerned."

I lean in.

Grace says, "In a moment, I'm going to talk with Alice and Calvin Boudreaux, the parents of Katharine Boudreaux, the young teacher who went missing after a night out with friends in New Orleans." A picture flashes on the screen. The same face I saw on the Missing poster. "The Boudreauxes believe Katharine took a route home that night three weeks ago that would have led her through Broken Bayou. Specifically, over the bridge behind us." She points to the bridge in the background. A bridge I fished and swam under every summer. And every summer, there was always some story about kids swimming in the bayou and becoming violently ill from swallowing the water. But not Mabry and me. We never got sick. The Aunts said our stomachs must be made of stone. But it wasn't stone that hardened our insides. We had Krystal Lynn to thank for that.

The reporter continues, "They believe Katharine never made it over that bridge and are pleading with local law enforcement to help in their search. So far, they say, the local police have been less than helpful, undoubtedly due to the other major story in this small town." Grace straightens. I do as well. "We have new information on the grim story surrounding the barrel, containing human remains, found a few days ago in Broken Bayou."

"Oh my God." I hit pause on the screen and look up at Travis. "What the hell?"

He nods. "Yeah, like I said, unbelievable." He presses play. "Keep watching."

I struggle to swallow my next sip of coffee.

"Thanks to items found inside that barrel," the reporter is saying, "the remains were identified as those of Destiny Smith, a fifteen-year-old runaway from Birmingham, Alabama. Her last known location was New Orleans, where she went missing in 2015." After an appropriate pause, she adds, "Back to you."

The camera switches back to the studio, with both anchors shaking their heads.

"Tragic," the man says to his coanchor and to the camera. "We will keep you updated on this story as we receive more information. We'll be back in just a minute with Grace, live on the bayou."

I lean back against the booth, speechless. The poor parents of that fifteen-year-old girl. Runaways think any place is better than home, and sometimes, that's true, but an overwhelming percentage find a place that's much worse. My heart breaks for that young girl. She needed help, and instead, a monster found her. I wonder what her story was. Where her issues lived. Was it abuse, addiction, both?

Travis pockets his phone. "That's the second barrel that's been found."

I stop my coffee cup midsip. "What?"

"The first one was actually found over a decade ago. It's been unsolved forever. Then some kids stumble upon this latest one. It's insane. Chief Wilson called the sheriff. This shit is way out of our league. Then the sheriff called the state police, and now with the second victim being from out of state, the state police are talking about calling the feds. But I don't know if that's a great idea. Everyone will be stepping on everyone else's toes. We're still waiting for the crime lab to send us the DNA analysis from the first victim. My guess is it will be another runaway."

"Travis." A disturbing thought pops into my head. "Could this be a serial killer?"

He shrugs, nonplussed, as if I've asked if he wants more coffee. "Maybe. We've had our fair share down here. Hell, we've had our fair share in this parish. You remember Derrick Todd Lee?"

I shake my head no.

"He was the Baton Rouge Serial Killer. Stalked girls at LSU. Killed seven. And he was from our parish. Died in prison. Hell, the police chief in Derrick's town knew it was him. He told the state police, the sheriff, the lead investigator. Nobody listened. And he was right. You just know when it's one of your own."

My coffee has lost its flavor. I set it down. "And do you think this is one of your own?"

"I sure as shit hope not. Anything's possible, I guess, but we're not saying the words *serial killer* yet. We don't want to create any hysteria."

The waitress clanks our breakfast order onto the table, and I jump. "Here you go."

"Perfect," Travis says to her with a smile.

My fingers unroll the paper napkin from the silverware and place it in my lap even though I have no appetite.

"This is crazy, Travis."

"I know. And they're not helping." He nods toward the table beside us. "Only one reporter was here a few days ago. But the AP picked up on it, and you know, once they get a whiff of death, they come running." He scoops a bite of grits into his mouth. "Waiting to see if there's more."

I stare at him as he chews.

"What?" He says around the bite in his mouth.

"How can you eat?"

"I'm hungry, that's how." He swallows the bite. "And I'd better eat now. It's going to be a long day."

"What's going on?"

"You'll see."

Before I can question him, Travis turns to the older ladies sitting next to us and says, "Ladies." He looks back to me. "Think you might have been spotted."

"Wh-what?"

He points to the ladies. They wave, then lean in and begin to whisper. I look back at Travis. "Great."

"Well, I'll be," a voice from the table says. "Willamena Pearl Watters."

Travis and I both look up as an elderly lady approaches our table. Her white cotton candy hair perches on top of her small head. I picture her wrapping that hair in toilet paper at night like Pearl and Petunia used to do so it'd *keep* until the next beauty parlor appointment.

I nod at her.

"I'm Ermine Taylor, darlin'."

"Ermine!" I jump up from the table.

She wraps her little bird arms around me and whispers in my ear. "You sweet angel. Bless your heart."

I hear pity in her voice. Ermine's been watching more than just the local news. She's been watching YouTube, and from the looks we're getting around the room, she's not the only one.

Ermine took her daddy's bait shop and turned it into a business that actually thrived in this town. She offered hot food, cold beer, and easy conversation. And she bucked every stereotype about a Black woman owning a business in the South. Ermine Taylor had been a force to be reckoned with, and from the steely gaze in her dark eyes, she still is.

I smile at the woman who became like a second mother to me over the years. Her store and her hugs something I looked forward to every summer. Then, like so many other things in this town, I'd let her fade away too.

"I . . . I . . ." I stumble over my words. "I should have kept in touch."

She waves a hand in front of her. "Water under the bridge, honey. Tell me, how's your mama?"

Again, that question. And again, I answer, "She's fine."

Ermine looks at me like I'm a lost puppy. She pats my arm and tells me to come by Taylor's Marketplace if I'm in town for a while. I promise I will.

A few of the other ladies are up now that Ermine led the charge. They surround me in a huddle of hugs and sugary perfume, going on about how good it is to see me and how much they miss the Aunts. I don't recognize most of them as they say their names in one continuous stream. June, Lydia, Barb, Sally. They ask questions all at once about living in a big city and how Mama's getting along and why I haven't been back sooner, all in slow rolling accents that sound more Brooklyn than southern gulf. The Yat dialect, as it's called in New Orleans.

I answer the gaggle in front of me in order: wonderful, just fine, working too hard. None broach the topic of *Fort Worth Live*, but I see their sparkling curiosity behind their smiles. What they wouldn't give to have me sit at their table and replay that tale. Then Travis saves me.

"Ladies," he interrupts. "I hate to steal the main attraction, but we have to go."

"Thank you," I mouth to him, then turn, and say my goodbyes, leaving with promises to keep in touch, although I have no way to back that up.

◆ ◆ ◆

Travis pulls out of the parking lot, crosses Main, and parks his truck sideways in front of Ace's hardware store. The whole process takes less than a minute. I don't even think he checked for traffic when he crossed the street. Not that he needed to. There's not a car in sight. It unnerves me a bit. I've grown used to city noise, cars, people yelling, airplanes overhead. This town is way too quiet.

"So Ace's is where we're going?" I say.

He opens his door. "No. We need to do something about those shoes before our next stop."

I look down at my kitten heels, but before I can respond, he's out of the truck and disappearing into Ace's.

Ned's Pharmacy is next door, like I remember when I first drove through town. Then my eyes land on the business next to it. The antique store. The fine hairs on the back of my neck stand on end. Something about it still seems familiar.

A woman is out front, sweeping the stoop. Ancient high chairs, crates of old colored bottles, and rusted **DIXIE BEER** signs overflow onto the front porch. The woman waves. I wave back. Then a thought hits me. I open my door, glance at Ace's. Travis is still inside. But for how long?

"Excuse me," I say to the woman.

She stops sweeping.

"Would you happen to have a VHS player in there?"

The woman shakes her head. "I don't think so, but you're welcome to come inside and look."

I study the glass door behind her. "I'll stop in later," I say as I climb back into Travis's truck.

What is it about that door?

My mouth goes dry. It's not the door that's the problem, it's what used to be on the other side.

A vision of Mama racing into Shadow Bluff, out of breath, one hot, muggy evening flashes in front of me. We'd been in Broken Bayou about a week that last summer, and the Aunts had made it clear we would all sit down for supper at six sharp.

"Let's eat. I'm starving," Mama said, sliding into her seat at the table. She wore her tightest pair of jeans and a top that would have fit better on Mabry.

The Aunts scowled and simultaneously asked the Lord to bless our food and forgive us our sins. The last part directed at Mama.

"Guess who got a job today?" Mama said in a singsong voice as she slung mashed potatoes onto her plate.

I studied her. Mama getting a job during summer was not normal. She liked her months off. Said it gave her time to think, whatever that meant. Something was up.

"Why'd you get a job?" I said.

She smirked at me. "You're welcome."

"Where you gonna be working at?" Pearl said.

"Oh, just a temp job at a little office up the road. Guy who runs it is a real hotshot. Drives a Cadillac. Probably a bookie, but whatever; he's paying me cash." She winked at me. "He's a pill, but I can handle his type." She hoisted up her already-hoisted breasts. "He would not stop staring at the ladies the whole time he interviewed me. Perv." She found my gaze and winked. "But the pervs are the easiest to control."

My eyes stay fixed on the glass door. A door that once led to a dark narrow office. My seventeen-year-old self never stopping to think *why* that door was unlocked at two o'clock in the morning. Papers were scattered all over the floor, the phone off the hook and hanging over the side of the desk. A chair overturned. A safe in the corner, open and empty. But I found what I needed. I punched the eject button on the antiquated video recorder, snatched the black tape that shot out, then ran as fast as I could into the night.

Travis opens the car door, and I snap back to reality. He studies my face. "You okay?"

I blink several times. Away goes the memory. Professional Willa is back. "I'm good. But I think I better get back." I leave off the last of my sentence: *to a box of forgotten tapes.*

"Sure, but we need to make a stop first. That's why I got you these." He smiles and presents a pair of bright orange rubber boots. "I guessed your size."

I stare at his hands. "What are those?"

"Bayou boots."

Oh no. Absolutely not. My next stop needs to be Shadow Bluff. "Travis, I don't—"

The radio on Travis's dash crackles. "Hey, Travis. You out there?" The woman's voice on the other end contains the distinct gravel of a lifetime smoker. She sounds tired and bored.

He unhooks the radio from the dash. "I'm here, Margie. What's up?"

"Is your phone off or something? Chief needs you. Now. Crowd's getting out of control. It's a circus down there. Check your gosh-darn phone." The radio goes silent.

He looks at me and shrugs. "Sorry. You can wait in the car if you want."

He shifts the truck into drive and pulls away from the antique store. Away from the woman sweeping. Away from the glass door. Toward a place that has me regretting I ever said yes to breakfast in the first place.

Chapter Six

Travis takes a hard turn, and I grab the side handle of the door as the truck bounces through the ruts on the dirt road.

"Sorry," Travis says and slows down.

On my right is a long narrow hill I haven't seen in decades. The levee. Echoes from the past fill my head. Of me showing up at Travis's house in the middle of the night. *I need your help.* I exhale in an attempt to slow my heart rate, but it doesn't work. I don't like the momentum right now. I can feel it shifting. Like one of Mama's moods. The memories. The tape. The bayou. Every turn in this town leads to something I want to forget.

Travis eases his truck off the road and pulls behind another large truck, which is parked behind a line of cars. I want to insist Travis take me back to Shadow Bluff, but he's already slammed the car into park and opened his door.

"Travis?" I say as he starts to step out. "What is going on?"

He faces me, takes a breath. "Divers are going into the bayou."

My pulse switches from too fast to completely stopped. "What?"

"Willa, it's gonna be fine."

At breakfast, I asked him what he remembers, and he said he remembers it all. Of course he does. "This doesn't feel fine, Travis."

He clears his throat. "It might be nothing, but I wanted you to see it firsthand, just in case."

"See what firsthand? Just in case what?"

He steps out of the truck, leans back in. "The divers think they found a car."

My mouth falls open, but no words come out. "Willa, it's probably the schoolteacher's," he says, studying my face. "But I thought you should be here, you know, in case it's not."

"Oh my God." I drop my head in my hands, press my fingers into my forehead. "Why would you think me being here is a good idea?"

"Because it's better to know now. Might help with damage control." His radio barks again. "Listen, it's going to be the teacher's car. Okay? Don't worry. But . . ." He shakes his head. "Just don't worry either way."

He shuts the door. I tell myself I will not scream. I will not lose it. I will stay in control. This is not about me. This is about a missing person. I'll sit here and wait for Travis to come back; then he'll take me home, and that will be that. But the heat in the truck is suffocating me. My silk blouse sticks to my back. And the thought of divers in that bayou, finding what I dumped there decades ago, has me feeling like I'm breathing through a straw. I stare at the hill, then slip on the orange boots and fling open the door. I'll walk back to my great-aunts' house. It can't be more than a mile.

I'm tucking my pants into the boots when I hear the low rumble of a truck and men shouting for people to get back. I look at the dirt road leading to Bridge Street; then I look up the levee. *Because it's better to know now.*

I scramble to the top of the levee and freeze. It takes a minute to grasp what is happening below me. Margie was right. It's a circus.

The scene beside the bayou is surreal. The crowd looks like they are lined up for a parade. People cover both banks and the bridge connecting them, most with cell phones out and pointed at the bayou. Two officers dressed like Travis are attempting to make a wide path through the crowd so a tow truck can back its way to the water. The air crackles with electricity as if a storm is coming, but the bright, hot sky shows no signs of trouble. The levee, on the other hand, does.

A gaggle of elderly ladies who look identical to the ones in the diner watch me from afar. I see their stares, their huddled whispers, no doubt about Krystal Lynn's oldest daughter. The apple doesn't fall far from the tree and all that. And I understand for a brief moment what it would've been like to be Krystal Lynn in this town. Long legs and outsider ways, always drawing the attention. I look down. The bright orange boots certainly don't help.

Broken Bayou weaves below me like a muddy S. Eighteen miles of river water, four of which amble north to south through town. The side I'm standing on has a few large oaks scattered along the levee, but most of the trees and scrub brush are on the opposite bank. Broken Bayou diverts from a river east of here, whose name I can't remember, and meets back up with that same river somewhere downstream. It's narrow but deep, like a lot of waterways in this area. Well, it used to be deep. The drought I've been hearing about is taking its toll. The original waterline is now several inches above the actual water.

I once loved trying to swim bank to bank in one breath, but I never succeeded. It always took three breaths. Along with the smell of fish and hot mud, I can almost smell the pineapple-scented suntan oil Krystal Lynn used to slather on me, telling me I needed a good base tan for boys to like me.

Mama. *Get rid of it, sweet girl.*

Sweat rolls down my back. I unbutton my sleeves and roll them up, but the heat isn't just external; it's coming from my veins as well. I need to turn around and leave, but I catch a glimpse of Travis halfway down the levee and do the exact opposite. I walk toward him.

"Travis." As I say his name, a large man with a belly that looks like a lumpy pillow shoved in a shrunken pillowcase turns from the water and faces us.

"Hey, Chief," Travis says.

The man waddles up to us. "This is turning into a three-ring, dog-and-pony shit show. Hell, even the DAR ladies broke up their morning bridge game to come have a look-see." He sucks on the dip in his front lip and spits a brown stream onto the muddy bank.

"Chief." Travis points to me. "This is Dr. Willa Watters. Her great-aunts owned Shadow Bluff. Willa, this is Chief Jute Wilson."

I nod and hold out my hand. "Nice to meet you."

He cocks his head to one side. "I'll be damned. You're Krystal Lynn's daughter." He rocks back on his cowboy boots and disappears into another time for a moment. He draws another long pull on the dip, spits, and trains his bright eyes on me, rubbing his chin with sausage-like fingers. "Damn shame about Pearl and Petunia. Good people. I heard after Pearl passed, Petunia just laid down and never woke up again."

I nod. That was the rumor. I have no idea if it's true or small-town lore.

"When was it, last time you were down here?" he says.

My eyes dart to Travis. I swallow. It's a simple question, but it feels loaded, like he's fishing for something.

"Been a while," I say.

Chief Wilson pats my shoulder. "Tell your mama, Jute says hi." He scratches his stubble. "That one was a real firecracker."

Another man approaches. He looks to be around my age, and he, unlike Travis, has a real uniform. It's brown with ironed creases and topped off with a brown hat and a real badge. As I look around, I notice other officers, too, dressed in blue uniforms.

"What's with all the different uniforms?" I ask Travis.

"Blue is state police. Brown is sheriff. And polos are Broken Bayou's finest." He grins, but I hear an edge in his voice. Bitterness. Something tells me Travis had bigger dreams than being a local cop. Or maybe, because of his father, he has a problem with anyone who's got more authority than him. That would fit. Of course, there was his mother too. I tell myself to stop diagnosing Travis. He's not a child. And I'm certainly not his doctor.

The officer in the brown uniform whispers something in Chief Wilson's ear. Chief Wilson tugs the dip from his lip and smacks it to the ground. "Goddammit." He looks at Travis, then at me. "Excuse me for a minute, sweetheart."

I step back, tucking the *sweetheart* comment away along with my terse retort.

The officer studies me. Like he knows me. I smile but can't place him. Like so many other faces I've seen since my arrival, his hovers just beyond recognizable. I wonder if he remembers me from the past or if he's been trolling social media sites. Then his eyes shift to my chest, and I get my answer. To his credit, at least he blushes when I catch him looking. I don't say a word, just stare at him. He clears his throat, tips his hat, and walks away.

Travis cuts his eyes to me. "You okay?"

"Not really." My eyes dart to the muddy water, then down to the orange boots. I look up at Travis. "This is why you asked me to breakfast, isn't it? To bring me here."

He shifts on his feet, sighs. "I wanted to catch up but . . . yeah. I figured it'd be better if we were here together. You were in town. This drought's got everything coming up. Then I learned about the car. Seemed like I should include you. But now that we're here, maybe that was a mistake. This is even crazier than I expected." His face hardens as he looks past me, over my shoulder. "Shit."

"What up, bro?" a man says behind me. I know his voice immediately, even though it's been years since I last heard it.

Doyle, one of Travis's older brothers, grins at me when I turn around. He's built like a praying mantis. His jeans and stained T-shirt both look two sizes too big for him. His face is covered in acne scars. This face I recognize. Not just from the past but also from the corner of Main and Bridge Streets. He's the one who honked at me when I was on the phone with Mama. The one who told Travis a fancy lady was driving around town. I shift away from him.

At Doyle's side is another of Travis's brothers, Eddie. A grizzly bear wearing cargo shorts and a purple-and-gold LSU T-shirt. He was another reason Travis and I connected with each other. We both had siblings who needed us to parent them.

The years had not been kind to these two men, and I wonder what stories their deep creases and tough hides could tell. I also wonder about the other brothers. The ones Travis said left town or maybe he had used the word *escaped*.

Eddie shuffles his dirty boots rather than picking up his feet, and when he stops, he rocks back and forth like he's on rough seas. I remember Eddie the most. He followed Travis around like Mabry followed me. Limited speech development, no eye contact. Again, like Mabry.

During my third year in grad school as a research assistant studying children bullied on playgrounds, I made a special trip home to my mother's latest apartment, where Mabry still lived, and hugged Mabry so tightly she coughed. Most of the children I was studying needed genetic testing, something Mabry was never offered. She fell through the cracks, somehow managing to get her GED despite not being able to even get a driver's license. Then I learned about FAS and knew Mabry didn't need genetic testing after all. Fetal alcohol syndrome strikes randomly in families, and it struck Mabry. Hard. Cognitive defects, abnormal facial features like large low-set ears and the smooth philtrum above her lip. And yet, I'm sure Mama didn't abstain when she was pregnant with me, and I turned out fine enough to graduate summa cum laude from Baylor without even having to try that hard. It took years for me to harness my anger at the unfairness in that, at Mama for denying Mabry her full potential.

"Not sure why these Texas folks had to come in," Doyle says in his thick south-Louisiana drawl, breaking off my thoughts. "Look, see, we coulda done this for free."

I remember Doyle as a lanky kid with severe acne who scurried around during those lazy summer days, shy and sneaky and always watching.

Travis motions toward the water. "These Texas folks *are* free. They're volunteers."

"Huh. Well, you should of kept it local, bro. These boys might go diggin' where they shouldn't."

"She don't wanna be alone!" Eddie's agonized cry cracks through the heat, startling me and several people near us. He rocks and hugs himself.

Doyle slides a look at me. "Don't mind my brother, ma'am. He's an idiot." He tilts his head. "Hang on a minute. You that girl that used to run around with those crazy old twin ladies in that big ole house?"

"Hi, Doyle," I say, keeping my shoulders back, spine straight. Ready for whatever he says next.

He lets out a long whistle. "You look different with your shirt on." That one I'm not ready for, and as I stutter and try to craft a smart retort, he adds, pointing to my chest and laughing, "Guess TV does add ten pounds."

Travis pops his brother in the chest with the back of his hand. "What the fuck is wrong with you?" He lowers his voice; his jaw is tight. "Get the hell out of here."

"Yeah, yeah. Was just leaving."

As Doyle walks off, my eyes burn a hole in his back, pissed I hadn't pointed to his crotch and said that even a camera wouldn't help his cause.

Eddie pauses a moment. I turn my attention to him, but he won't look me in the eyes. Instead, he reaches into his cavernous front pocket and extracts a metal object, holds it out to me in his massive palm. I glance at Travis, then take the small object from Eddie. It's a metal doll, little arms and legs soldered to a round body, like a small misshapen baby Frankenstein.

"Thank you," I say, even though it gives me the creeps.

Eddie smiles at the ground, then lopes off to catch up with Doyle.

Travis says, "Sorry about that. Doyle's the one who's an idiot." He points to the metal object. "Eddie still doesn't talk much. I think those dolls are his way of communicating. He doesn't normally give them away, though. He must like you."

I think of Mabry's sketchbook and wonder if, even though she spoke more than Eddie, that was her way of communicating; I'm surprised I haven't thought of that before now. It's common in children exposed to trauma. I start to quiz Travis more on Eddie, but as I go to speak, a woman's sharp high-pitched scream cuts through the low rumble of the crowd.

People gasp and lean in to look toward the bayou. The tow truck is backing up. A diver is standing on the bank, taking the chain from the truck, and heading back into the water.

"They found it!" A man in the crowd yells, and I feel Travis's hand find mine and give it a quick, almost imperceptible squeeze.

I'm starting to feel dizzy, maybe from the heat. Maybe not. "Travis."

He follows my gaze to the area downstream where the divers' boat launched. A man and woman stand at the water's edge. The woman is crying. Another woman moves to where the couple stands. It's a woman I saw in Nan's Café this morning, sitting at the media table. She's wearing an expensive navy pantsuit. Her slick hair swept from her face in a tight black ponytail, a microphone clutched in her hand, and a cameraman following closely behind. In her element, I recognize her. Rita Meade, an investigative reporter for a national news program. She's got quite a following, both on and off air. And earlier, at Nan's, I'd caught her staring at me.

"Oh, hell," Travis says, looking her way. "Stay here."

Travis tries to block Rita from getting to the couple as a young deputy steps in and escorts them away from the water and toward me, Rita fast on their heels. The deputy tells Rita to leave these poor people alone, but he obviously doesn't know who he's dealing with. Rita Meade's reporting style is notorious, ruthless. She's famous for helping solve the Kansas City murders back in 2016. An entire family was slain as they slept, and Rita pounded on doors and interviewed neighbors, coworkers, lovers for almost a year. She'd even interviewed the family's minister, who, it turned out, was in a long-term affair with the wife and distraught over her calling it off. Rita had used that footage to help the police get enough evidence to arrest him. Covering that case put Rita on the map and thrust her into a new echelon of investigative reporters.

And now she's here, feet from me, homing in on this sad-looking couple.

A light on the camera behind Rita flares. She glances in my direction, pauses on my face, then refocuses on the man and woman. She pulls them off to the side, ignoring the deputy who is trying, and failing, to stop her.

"What are you hoping will happen here today, Mrs. Boudreaux?" Rita says.

Boudreaux. The last name from the newsclip I watched on Travis's phone. These are the missing teacher's parents, Alice and Calvin Boudreaux.

Alice looks directly into the camera. Her husband keeps his head down. "I'm hoping we'll learn something, one way or the other."

"Are you prepared for what the divers might find today?"

My stomach clenches. I know I'm not.

Alice shakes her head. "We just need closure."

Indeed you do. Alice holds her tears in check now. Much stronger than I would be in that situation. She's got a good wall up, but I have bad news for her. They haven't invented a wall strong enough to keep grief out. Eventually, it will find her. And when it does, I hope she has someone besides the man next to her to help her get through it. The husband, Calvin, has my attention. He hasn't spoken a word, but his body language is interesting: arms crossed over his chest, eyes constantly shifting to the muddy water, jaw working side to side. Like he's nervous. Like he's hiding something.

Rita turns her attention to him.

"Mr. Boudreaux," Rita says, "do you think your daughter could be a victim of foul play?"

He snaps his head up, eyes wide. He flexes his hands, then balls them into fists as he glares at Rita. Probably not an uncommon reaction to her, but the way he watches her makes the hair on my arms rise. He looks like he wants to punch her.

Mrs. Boudreaux answers, "No! We know our child. She's not a drug addict or a runaway like the one they found in that barrel. She's a schoolteacher. And she had an accident. I just know it."

I'm tempted to go to her, put my arm around her shoulder, and get her the hell away from Rita's hyperfocused gaze. I want to comfort her and tell her she will survive this. But really what will happen is she'll feel like it should kill her, she'll pray for it to kill her, but it won't. Then the slow realization will hit that she will have to live with it. And there's no comfort in that. I stay rooted to my spot, watching.

Calvin Boudreaux is still now, very still. Almost like a child who thinks if he closes his eyes and doesn't move, he can't be seen. But Rita sees everything, and she turns her focus on him again.

"What about you, Mr. Boudreaux? Do you have anything you want to say?"

His eyes narrow. "What's it matter. She's gone."

Rita lowers her chin. "Maybe you'd like to comment on some information I've recently become aware of, regarding your domestic-abuse charges?"

Mrs. Boudreaux gasps. "Those charges were dropped."

Mr. Boudreaux balls his hand into a tighter fist. But before anything else can be said, a sharp whistle cuts through the thick air.

Rita, the Boudreauxes, and I all swing our heads toward the tow truck. Chief Wilson is motioning for it to back up even more. A winch begins to unspool. I barely turn back to the scene in front of me before Rita snaps at her cameraman and rushes back toward the water's edge. Mrs. Boudreaux is fast behind her, yelling "My baby" over and over.

Pulsing energy ripples through the crowd around me. Locals yell about something coming out of the water. Travis yells "Get back!" to everyone. Then police and divers swarm to the tow truck's back end. A large heavy chain lowers from the tow truck into the bayou. One diver on shore walks into the depths with a hand on the chain, and both disappear under a layer of algae.

I crane my neck to get a better look. The young deputy tries to move me back, but I refuse to move. My orange boots stick to the dry grass.

Chief Wilson shoves his radio to his ear, then places two fingers in his mouth and whistles to the tow truck driver again. The chain stops.

The silence that follows is deafening. Even Rita falls quiet. A bull-frog croaks from its hidden spot, and a woman in the mass of people screams. Nervous laughter follows.

It's the teacher's car, I tell myself over and over. But something in my gut twists to the point that I want to double over.

Then the thick chain reverses direction. The back tires of the tow truck start to sink into the bayou mud, and men begin to shout again. The driver grinds the gears, and the smell of smoke fills the air. One of the divers yells, "It's a car, all right."

I cross my arms over my stomach and dig my fingers into my ribs.

Mrs. Boudreaux releases a howl and claws her way toward the tow truck. "My baby. I told you! I told you she was here!"

I watch Travis grab her, and she pounds at his chest. The crowd moves back except for Rita, whose cameraman stays with Mrs. Boudreaux. Mr. Boudreaux is nowhere to be seen.

The edge of a bumper starts to emerge from the water.

Breathe, I tell myself.

"Easy, Scooter," Chief Wilson hollers at the tow truck driver, and the driver backs off the winch. With a sucking, gurgling sound, the back end of a car rises from the muck and is pulled onto dry ground. Water and algae drip from it. Several officers inch up to the car like it's a ticking bomb. It was once a convertible, but its ragtop has long since disintegrated.

My knees buckle.

Chief Wilson runs two fingers through the thick grime on its exterior, winces, and turns to another deputy. "Donald, what color's the teacher's car?"

"White!" Mrs. Boudreaux screams. She crumbles from Travis's grasp and falls to the ground.

Chief Wilson wipes his hand on his pant leg and kicks the ground. Travis's gaze finds mine for a split second, but I keep my eyes on the red swath left behind by the chief's fingers.

Chief Wilson yells to no one in particular, "This ain't the teacher's car!"

I suck in a breath that chokes me. He's right. It ain't the teacher's car. It's my mother's.

May 2006

Teri Thompson hated leaving her boys when she traveled, especially when she traveled for fun, like this weekend. But her girlfriends told her Jazz Fest would be worth it. Jimmy Buffett, Paul Simon, Lionel Richie. Hard to say no to that. Besides, Dan promised he had it under control. She'd left him a three-page, single-spaced letter, just in case, about the boys' homework schedules, sports practices, and eating habits, then realized an hour outside of Biloxi, she'd forgotten to put the pediatrician's number on it. Her friends told her to relax, but Teri rarely relaxed.

Except for now, oddly enough, as she strolled Bourbon Street with a large hourglass-shaped plastic cup in her hand full of something that tasted like grain alcohol and Kool-Aid. The Big Easy is right. This felt easy.

Teri gawked at the flesh on display in the doorways as she strolled. She checked her watch. Two in the morning. She hadn't been out past midnight since college.

She watched her girlfriends up ahead of her disappear through the throngs of people into a karaoke bar. Teri quickened her pace to catch up. Then she felt a tap on her shoulder.

When she turned, a man smiled at her. "You shouldn't be alone in a crowd like this. It can be dangerous."

"I'm not alone." When Teri tried to move away from him, a camera flash lit up her face.

"What the hell?"

"Say cheese," the man said.

The flash sparked again, followed by the sound of a Polaroid. "Get away from me!"

Something stung her neck, and Teri's vision started to swim in front of her. Her head became heavy and lolled to the side. She felt a hand on her waist, guiding her in the opposite direction from her friends. She wanted to look back and yell for them, but her head refused to move, her mouth too dry to open. Instead, she allowed the stranger to walk her through the crowd until they disappeared. Her last thought was of Dan and if he'd gotten the boys to sleep on time.

Chapter Seven

The crowd disperses, and I follow Travis back over the levee. Show's over. The tow truck dragging a huge rotting chunk of my past pulls onto the levee road, then heads for town.

Travis and I climb into his truck. My entire body is numb. He blasts the AC and glances over at me, his eyes wide and knowing. A nervous energy radiates off him. His eyes study me, a crease forming between his brows. I see the worry in his expression, worry for me. But he quickly reaches for my hand and squeezes it in a way that tells me he's confident this will still be okay. I need that right now. My confidence got towed away with that car.

Both of us are silent as he pulls away from the levee. My throat constricts around the questions in my head: How much trouble am I in? How worried should I be? But I remain quiet, my mouth unable to form the words.

Sweat rolls between my shoulders and down my back. But I know the heat isn't the real problem. The real problem started years ago, that last summer in Broken Bayou. When the hot, lazy days had lulled me into a state of laissez-faire, as the locals called it. That is, until the day Mama whipped into the driveway of Shadow Bluff, yelling "Girls!" at the top of her lungs. Mabry and I ran to the porch and found her draped across the hood of a bright-red convertible, waving her arms like a *Price Is Right* model and laughing her throaty laugh. "Look what I got!"

"What the hell is that?" I said.

"It's a car, Willa."

"Where's the old station wagon?"

"I traded that piece of shit in. It was on its last leg anyway."

"Does this car even have a back seat?"

"Of course it does." Mama scanned the inside. "Kind of."

"You can't afford to buy Mabry colored pencils, but you can afford that?"

"Well, sugar girl, colored pencils can't drive us to the grocery store, can they?"

Mama sauntered onto the porch, fanning her face, speaking with a soupy accent she didn't normally have. "I'mma need some lemonade, y'all."

As she passed us, I noticed a smudge of purple high on her cheek. At first, I thought it was makeup, but one thing Krystal Lynn never messed up was her makeup, not ever.

"What's that?" Mabry asked, pointing.

Mama's long fingernails hovered over her cheek. "Nothing, baby girl. Mama just ran into a door at work is all." And she flitted into Shadow Bluff without a care in the world.

My heart thumps in irregular beats. Travis pulls off Main onto the lane leading to Shadow Bluff.

"Travis," I say. "I think we need to talk."

He turns into the driveway and stops in front of the porch. It feels like we've been gone for days.

He finally looks at me. "Don't worry about the car."

I can't see his eyes through his sunglasses, but his voice sounds earnest, not angry. "I'm a little worried." I inhale a long breath and let it out.

My hands start to shake. Travis lowers his sunglasses. His expression matches mine. On edge. "I'll take care of it."

"No. This is my mess." One of many, I think. "I'll take care of it. I'll talk to Chief Wilson. I'm the one who dumped the damn thing in the bayou all those years ago."

He lowers his chin like he's dealing with a petulant child.

"No one will know you were with me," I add quickly. There, it's said. There's no dancing around it anymore.

"I wasn't with you," he says.

"True, but you were close by. And you knew what I was up to."

"Because you came to my house and asked me for help." His tone has changed. The frustration in it is palpable. I wonder if it's geared toward me or himself. Probably both. And I don't blame him. I was young. And, despite thinking otherwise at the time, so naive.

"I'm sorry, Travis."

His dash radio squawks, and he slides his sunglasses back on. "I have to go. Look, Willa, I'll help you figure out a way to handle this." I open the car door. He adds, "Just don't say anything yet. My job is all I have. I don't want anything or anyone to jeopardize that."

"I understand." And I do understand. Vulnerability starts when you have something to lose. And I have something to lose as well. But I have no idea what taking care of it will look like. Do I tell the police the same story Mama told me all those years ago? That she wanted me to dump that car for insurance money.

I may have been able to convince myself money was the reason then—a crime, yes, but one I could eventually make right, justifiable because of my age—but now that I'm back here, now that I've seen the car, I'm starting to understand insurance fraud could have been just another one of Mama's many lies. I certainly don't remember us ever receiving a check. I do, however, remember a large stack of cash in the glove box of our old car the day we left town. Insurance companies don't operate that fast, and they don't pay cash.

I stop my thoughts from going any further. I need to stay present, in control.

I look at Travis and say again, "I'm sorry." Knowing that my career hangs in the balance based on my stupid actions makes me sick to my stomach. If Travis had done something years ago that could jeopardize it, I'd be furious. But these days, I'm the only one jeopardizing what I've accomplished.

He nods but keeps his gaze forward. "I'll try to come by at some point. And, Willa," he adds. "Don't go anywhere."

I climb down from the truck and watch as Travis leaves in a cloud of dust.

As I walk past my car, I notice a note slipped under the wiper. It's from the lawyer, apologizing for missing me this morning and saying he'd like to come back by and introduce himself. I sigh. Great.

Now what? I look at my car. I could load those boxes and drive out of here, that's what. But Travis just asked me not to go anywhere. And I probably need to straighten out this problem rather than run from it. Dumping my mother's car in a bayou may turn out to be only a stupid stunt that hurts no one. At least, that's what I need to tell myself right now in order to placate that part of my brain that has my nerves sizzling like downed power lines.

Birds whistle in the oaks around me as I trudge up the steps and open the front door. The house greets me with a cough of dust. I pause in the foyer. Sunlight scatters through the front windows onto the white-sheeted furniture. I'm halfway up the front stairs when a sound comes from somewhere down the hall, a thumping noise. Close to the kitchen. It's probably nothing, but with everything that's happening in this town, I'm not taking any chances.

I bound up the rest of the stairs and find my handgun sitting on the bedside table in the front bedroom. I start to pull up Travis's number, then realize I never asked for it; he asked for mine. I type in 9-1-1 but feel too foolish to hit call. I settle my breath. It's daytime. There's nothing to steal in this house. No one would break in and be that loud. I ease back to the staircase and listen. It's quiet. But just as I start down the stairs, a loud thud comes from the dining room, and I scream. A bird flies from around the corner, past the stairs to the parlor. Shit. I lower my hand, grab the railing, exhale. At the bottom of the stairs, I find the bird flapping wildly against the parlor window.

I open the front door, take one of the sheets off the chairs in the parlor, and shoo the bird back to freedom. The house is quiet again. No intruder. Thank God. All I've ever shot is paper. If a person had come running at me, I'm not sure I could have pulled the trigger. The exact opposite of what my conceal-carry instructor said. "Don't buy a gun unless you are mentally capable of shooting a person. And," she'd added, "if you do shoot an intruder, you'd better kill them. Otherwise, they'll sue you."

I move to the kitchen and check the warped door. Sure enough, it's open. I push it closed and pop it with my hip until it stays shut. In an instant, I see Mama dancing into this very kitchen the night of my seventeenth birthday in a swirl of smoke and Cinnabar perfume. She wore a skintight stretch-denim jumpsuit with a thick gold zipper running from her crotch to, in theory, her neck. The zipper was nowhere near her neck, though.

Mabry looked up from her sketchbook. Her little mouth fell open. "Boobs."

Mama flipped her curled hair and smiled. "Darn tootin', boobs." She pointed at the both of us. "And if you girls don't grow a pair soon, I highly recommend figuring out a way to buy them. These suckers will open doors you didn't even know existed."

The Aunts gawked at Mama over their Coke-bottle glasses.

Mama grinned a smeared red grin. "Mabry, sugar, you can come with me after all. Let's let your sister have *her* night." Mama's voice slurred a little as she zeroed in on me. "You made it clear you don't want either of us around. We wouldn't want to mess up your birthday plans, now would we?" She stumbled a step.

Mabry chewed on her fingernails and stared at me. I wanted to tell Mama no, Mabry was coming with me. But the thought of my date with Travis and having a night to myself shut that voice down before

I even had a chance to form the first word. Mabry would be fine. She would be with her mother, for God's sake. But that argument felt as flimsy as Krystal Lynn's bra.

"Don't wait up!" she yelled, pulling Mabry toward the shiny red convertible, then whipping out of the driveway, the Judds belting into the hot August night.

Thoughts of that car and Travis and Mama swirl in my head. What had Mama asked of me?

In my late twenties when I thought my years of education made me wise, I told Mama I forgave her. She'd said, "For what? I did my best." Couldn't argue with her there. She had done her best. Unfortunately, her best was mediocre, hovering around abusive.

Once when I visited her at Texas Rose after my book deal, she said, "You're so lucky you had a crazy mother and a retarded sister to help you get all this fame." It took every ounce of self-control I possessed not to slap her across the face. I'd slapped her before. She'd slapped me, and Mabry. It was our toxic way of communicating when I was young. Another bad habit I had to fix.

I spent years circling Mama and her responses and trying to understand her, telling myself forgiveness is the only path out. I also spent money. On Mama. Doctors, specialists, medication. All trying to find the right balance for her. But balance isn't Mama's strong point. She's rejected more medications than I can count. So I convinced myself I didn't need her acknowledgment to forgive her. But being this close to my past is showing me just how foolish I've been. How can I forgive Mama for that night when I've never even forgiven myself?

I find a granola bar I bought at the Sack and Save and make my way back up to the attic. Every creak of the stairs has me jumpy. I tell myself I'm going to come up with a plan with Travis. Talk to the chief, and things will sort out. But the tape in the attic has my skin tingling, and with each step up the cramped staircase, memories tingle as well: Travis sitting on the front porch with Mabry and me, playing cards and laughing. His right eye swollen shut after a fight with someone in his house, probably his dad or one of his brothers. Travis and me walking to get ice cream cones at Dairy King, fishing on the banks of the bayou, running through the woods at night with beer and a blanket. Then I see his worried face in the dark as he grabbed my arms and tried to calm me down. *It's okay, Willa. I'm here.*

The boxes filled with Mama's things are where I left them in the attic. Little boxes of chaos. Krystal Lynn had certainly been a chaos seeker. A term I'd learned in undergrad. Yet even though I understood that term and saw it in action, I still managed to make my own chaos as well. When you grow up in a home where crazy is familiar, it's hard to designate a new familiar as an adult. You keep making decisions that turn your world into a disaster zone. Like dating and marrying the man in charge of my clinicals. Making a fool of myself on live television. Saving a videotape I should have destroyed.

One at a time, I take the boxes down to the front bedroom and place them on the floor. A sour taste fills my mouth as I turn my attention to the box of old VHS tapes. *Guiding Light* and *As the World Turns* were as vital to Mama as air and water. She recorded them every day and watched them at night with a vodka and a cigarette. But those tapes aren't important. Only the one I hid among them years ago is important. Now, more than ever, I need to understand what happened that night.

I swallow, pull a black, rectangular tape out, examine it, and toss it back in.

Did I really think that security tape would be found by someone and used against me? That I *had* to come back to this godforsaken town to retrieve it? In my mind, when I read that letter from the lawyers, yes. It stood out in my memory as something that would be recognized as wrong because it was wrong to me. It would physically stand out, announce itself as trouble, because it was trouble to me. In reality, it just looks like junk.

I pick up another tape. I need to be careful. These tapes could turn into quicksand and suck me into a past I may not want to remember. And even though I want to believe what I did all those summers ago was mostly harmless, something still gnaws at me. I stare at the stack of tapes. The one I'm looking for could have degraded over the years. It could be in such poor shape I'll never know what was on it. But what if it is watchable? My instincts that night told me to take it, told me to hide it. Now, I need to find out why. I need to understand why Mama asked me to dump that car. I need answers, and the women in my life who were involved in that night are either unwilling or unable to talk to me about it. Mama and Mabry never said a word to me. Maybe Mabry would have at some point but not now. Poor Mabry. It's no wonder she pushed against me the older we got. After grad school, I'd pulled away from my role as her caretaker. I'd studied in great detail about toxic codependent relationships and thought the distance between us would fix ours. I was young and foolish. The distance only made it worse. Then I'd married Christopher, and Mama moved them back to Louisiana. Mabry never forgave me.

The rotted yellow dress from Mabry's failed pageant catches my eye. I look down at my phone. Back at the dress. Screw it. I scroll to my favorites and punch her number. It goes straight to voicemail. Her laugh, like the tine of a fork on crystal. "Leave a message." I hang up. I'll have to get my answers another way.

I open my Amazon app and start searching for VCRs. The irony not lost on me that I'm depending on the most advanced technologies to purchase one of the least advanced. There are several options, but most take a week to arrive. Finally, I find one I can have overnighted. The shipping costs as much as the VCR but too bad. No way I'm waiting a week. And it says there's only one left in stock. I read about the hook-up process and hurry down to the kitchen to check the television I'd seen on the counter. It's as wide as it is deep. Not a new flat-screen, but I hit the power button, and it sparks to life. Only white static fills the screen, but it works. I unplug it and test its weight. I can get it upstairs where the tapes are scattered, where it and the VCR I plan to hook up to it won't be seen by a cop who tends to drop by unannounced.

I add the VCR and corresponding cables to my cart and start to click "Buy Now" when I realize I don't know the address here. I fish the letter from my tote, scanning until I find where the address is printed. I type it into the shipping details and hit purchase. I refresh the screen. It tells me that my order is processing and I'll be notified when it's shipped.

My phone vibrates on the floor next to me. I pick it up. It's Amy. "Hey," I say.

She sounds out of breath. "Sorry it's taken so long to get back to you. It's been crazy here, Willa. I'm out for a walk. Needed to move."

"Yeah, it's been a little crazy here too." I exhale. Christopher's ex will have to move down on the list of things I'm worried about. "Look, I did not cheat my way through grad school, and I certainly didn't sleep with Christopher while he was married," I say.

"I told you to stay off Twitter," she pants into the phone.

"I would have if you hadn't said not to."

"Good point."

"It's all completely untrue." When Amy doesn't respond, I say, "What?"

"Are you sure Christopher wasn't married?"

"Of course, I'm sure." A sickening taste fills my mouth. Was I sure? We spent every minute together. I slept at his apartment. He couldn't have still been married. He talked a lot about his ex. Their divorce. But it's not like I'd ever demanded to see the divorce papers. I just believed him. "Oh Jesus," I whispered into the phone.

"Look, I'm pretty sure the ex is just stirring up shit. She's got some new skin-care line and is looking to get some followers. We're not going to give that rumor any legs, okay? And the one about you cheating on your exams is complete bullshit, and everyone knows it. It's going to die down. We'll mitigate damage. I've been working on a show idea." She pauses.

"Amy, what?"

"There are a few busybodies out there questioning your boards and if you passed because of Christopher."

The temperature in the bedroom rises several degrees. Heat radiates under my skin. "I worked my ass off to pass that exam. I've renewed my licensure every year since. Not to mention continuing education every two years. My job is based on my credibility."

"Easy, Willa. I know. This is what we don't need. We don't need you getting defensive."

"I'm not defensive." My answer is too quick, and I know it. "Okay, maybe a little bit."

"You don't need to be, especially with me. Look, everyone is enjoying your story right now, but it's not going to last forever."

I think of the car coming out of the bayou only hours ago. Of the way Rita Meade looked at me. *Shit.* "When do you want to shoot the show you're working on?"

"The sooner the better."

I want to say *Will do; I'm on my way*, but I don't. I don't say anything.

"Look, Willa, I've given you some grace because you sounded exhausted. But you've got to come back. You can't hide from this. It won't look good."

A heavy silence hangs between us.

"Willa?"

"Give me a couple of days. I need to figure a few things out."

"Uh, no can do. This shit is going to fester if you don't deal with it. Load up whatever it is you went down there for, get in your car, and start driving. And after we clean all this up, we'll book a trip to Cabo and drink mango margaritas all day. Okay?"

"Yeah," I say absently and hang up.

I shut my eyes a moment, open them. Glance at the box of tapes. What I really came here for is control. And now I have anything but.

Amy is only trying to help. And I know she needs me to cooperate, but I don't need her hurry-up mentality right now. Things have changed. I need to take a minute and assess before I go running off again. I thought being out of Fort Worth would help this die down, or maybe, a part of me knew it was time to deal with something other than my career for once. Get my karma in order. Repair the past in order to move into the future.

Whatever I want to call it, I'm here now, and I may have more to repair than I thought.

Chapter Eight

I'm parked in front of the antique store again, this time in my car, not Travis's. The sign in the front window says OPEN but I'm dragging my feet. Not sure if going inside is the best idea. I saw what the Sack and Save had to offer, and I'm not ready for another dose of public humiliation. But this place looks relatively empty of people. It is, however, full of memories.

I searched for electronic stores nearby on my phone and called around in New Orleans and Baton Rouge. A guy at Best Buy suggested I take the tapes somewhere and have them digitized to a thumb drive. That's a hard hell no. I open my phone and check my order. It still says delayed. I click the tracking number, and I'm routed to the shipping site. It says *In Transit*, scanned in Memphis, but now it's expected to arrive tomorrow. I glance up at the store.

Dolly's Antiques is my next option.

Part of me wants to hurry in and look for what I need. Another part wants to run like hell. I open the door before the second option wins.

I step inside and exhale a long, slow breath. No disheveled office. No upturned desk. No papers scattered on the floor. Just a treasure trove of junk that contemporary designers would call *brown furniture*. Large wooden armoires, heavy dark nightstands, bowfront chests of drawers sitting alongside end tables, lamps, and twin iron bed frames. All waiting to be wanted again. Several used televisions and miscellaneous electronics line a wall in the back. Bingo.

I weave my way toward the electronics, past two ladies who stare at me as if I'm an alien. The navy wrap dress with large bright geometrical shapes and the tall heels don't really say local. I smile. They smile. They look suspicious. So much for this store being empty.

The one with wild, frizzy hair says, "You a reporter?"

I shake my head. "No."

"Your people here?"

"No. I'm visiting Broken Bayou."

She scrunches her face into an exasperated look. "Why?"

"Long story." I'm trying to keep my answers short and my gaze down. All the cues she should need to see I'm not up for a chat. But this woman *is* up for a chat.

"You know what's going on here, right?"

"I do."

"It's just awful. But I'm not surprised. There are some real lowlifes 'round these parts."

I nod, start for the electronics section.

"Y'all know they found another barrel," the frizzy-haired lady says to her companion and me, assuming I'm the other half of the *y'all*.

Her friend pops her arm, mouth agape. "Get out."

I stop walking.

"Yep. That makes three." The woman ticks off her fingers. "The old one from 2002 that's been unsolved. The runaway druggie they ID'd, and then this latest one. Saw it on the television."

"It's a serial killer," the other woman says. "I knew it. God only knows how many they'll find."

Another barrel. Cold air prickles the back of my neck. "Did the news say anything else about what was found over there?" So much for not chatting.

The other woman leans in, her eyebrows raised. "I heard that old car they pulled out has been put in impound over at the sheriff's station and that the investigator over there had 'em all diggin' around in it for something."

I stumble back on my heels, work to keep my composure. "What?"

"Well, my cousin—" the woman starts.

"She's the local beautician," the frizzy-haired lady clarifies to me.

"Anyway," the other woman says, giving her friend a quick glare. "My cousin heard it's good and tore up." She pauses, glances at us to make sure we're listening. She lowers her chin and her voice. "I may go by and take a look."

"Why in the world would you do that?" her friend says.

"Why not? It'd probably be easy. *Raymond's* watching the impound."

"Oh Lord." The frizzy-haired woman rolls her eyes. "No wonder. My two-year-old grandson could watch it better."

A woman wearing a flowing dress that looks like a thousand scarves sewn together and sporting long gray hair that hangs loose to her waist appears next to me like a vapor. "Can I help you?" The smell of patchouli surrounds her.

I stutter over my words. "Um . . . I was . . ."

"Wait, you were outside the other day," she says. "Looking for the VCR."

The two ladies next to me pretend to shop, but I see them exchange a look. I nod.

"I'm Dolly," she says.

I shake her hand. "Nice to meet you." I don't offer my name.

"I checked for one that day," she says, following me as I head for the back of the store. "Sorry. No luck."

I stop at the back shelves.

Dolly watches me. "You might find something else you need, though. I've got just about anything and everything. You'd be surprised what grown men with decent jobs think are collector's items." She rolls her eyes. "Then they gotta bring 'em here for me to sell."

Televisions are stacked in rows, a clunky original iPod sits on one shelf, a Polaroid camera next to it, even an old black rotary phone.

"Thanks anyway," I say, heading for the door.

"Found some old tapes, huh?"

I pause and look back at her. "Excuse me?"

Her thick eyebrows furrow. "VCR."

"Oh, right. Yeah."

"You know," she says. "VHS tapes deteriorate over time. Not sure how old yours are or how they were stored, but chances are, they're useless. Just a warning."

My fingers are trembling by the time I climb back into my car. Time to meet Raymond.

The police station sits one street off Main. I park along the shoulder and hustle to the front door. The only thing I can say about the inside is it's brown. Brown chairs, brown floor, brown desk. Behind the desk is a woman with a big brown bouffant. Streaks of gray run through it, and the wrinkled eyes beneath all that hair turn to sharp slits when they see me.

She doesn't look surprised. She, like the ladies in the antique store, looks suspicious.

"No comment," she says and goes back to reading her crossword puzzle.

I look down at my dress. "I'm not with the press. I'm here to see Raymond."

When she looks back up, her gaze is even more suspicious. "He's out back."

I smile. "Thank you. Oh, and would it be possible to get Travis Arceneaux's cell number?"

She sets her pencil down, lowers her readers. "No." She picks her pencil back up and turns her attention to the crossword again.

"Can I leave him a note?"

Without looking up, she says, "Whatever."

I scribble a note asking Travis to call me or come by, thank the woman I'm assuming is Margie, based on her voice, then hurry back into the broiling heat. I spot a tall chain-link fence topped with razor wire behind the station. I look around, then redirect to the rolling gate in front of it. It's padlocked and covered with two signs. One reads **KEEP GATE CLOSED!** The other states **DO NOT ENTER. MUST BE ACCOMPANIED WITH IMPOUND PERSONNEL.** Several cars sit on the other side. A few are wrecked, but one in particular has my attention. It looks like it was dragged from a bayou.

My palms start to sweat. I rub them together as I move closer to the fence and stare at the old convertible. It's in bad shape. Rusted and molded, with the passenger door missing. My throat constricts. I work to swallow as I move down the fence to get a better look at the back end. I press my face against the cool metal, crane my neck.

"Can I help you?"

I jump back from the fence as if it shocked me. A baby-faced officer in a brown uniform stares at me from the other side. It's the same guy I saw on the levee yesterday. The one I couldn't place.

"Willa Watters, right?"

Shit. I nod.

"Yeah," he says, snapping his fingers. "Saw you at the bayou yesterday. With Travis." He studies my face a second. "It's me, Raymond St. Clair. Remember, we all used to run around in the summers down here. Get into trouble every now and then." His cheeks go pink.

So this is Raymond. Raymond St. Clair. I do remember him. He was a shy kid who ran with a group of highbrow boys his older brother hung with. They were always acting cool, usually at the expense of someone else. That group taunted Travis, called him bayou trash. Said his family was trouble. Not necessarily wrong, but cruel nonetheless. Sometimes they made fun of Mabry and Eddie, who were usually tagging along beside us. Raymond was always hovering in the background, kicking the dirt. I'd always felt sorry for him.

"Of course, Raymond. It's good to see you," I say, even though I wish I hadn't seen him. Now, I may get asked questions I'm not ready to answer.

"Did you get your car towed?" he says. "Margie, inside, can help you with that."

That's not the question I was expecting. "No. I . . ." I'm about to say I was just leaving when Raymond nods, says, "It's okay. I know why you're here."

My stomach drops. Has he talked to Travis? If so, what has Travis told him?

"Everyone in town is curious about that car."

I breathe out a raspy laugh. "Yeah. I just had to see it." I lean closer. "But it's hard to get a good look from here."

He scans the area behind me, shuffles on his feet. I don't say a word. I let him sit with his thoughts about me and about how his friends acted in our past.

Raymond's eyes finally come back to mine. "I mean, I guess if you want to come in and have a look-see real quick, it'd be okay. As long as you don't touch anything," he adds firmly.

Maybe being recognized by someone harboring old guilt isn't so bad after all. "I don't know, Raymond. I don't want to get you in trouble."

He swats his hand. "Ah, no. Everybody's down at the bayou anyway. It's fine."

"Well." I pause. "If you're sure? I would like to take a look."

He grabs a key ring from his pocket and opens the lock. The gate swings open. "No touching, though, remember?"

"Got it." I give him a thumbs-up in a lame attempt to be casual. My pulse is anything but. It's pounding in my neck like a jackhammer.

I ease into the yard, past the other cars. Raymond walks with me. As I approach the convertible, I cover my mouth and nose with my elbow. It smells like death.

"Should have warned you about the smell," Raymond says. "Clams. And God knows what else."

The car's frame is dented and rusted. The red paint shows in some places but just barely. It's completely rotted. Back to front. I head for the driver's side and study the base of the windshield. No VIN number.

As I stare at it, my mind rewinds the clock to Mama and Mabry stumbling into Shadow Bluff well after midnight. Even though Mama told me not to bother, I'd been up waiting for them. Mama had snapped a heel off and was holding the shoe in her hand as she limped upstairs. Mabry followed, feet bare and covered in mud. She shuffled past me to our room. I followed Mama into her bedroom. She climbed into bed in her clothes, lit a cigarette. Smoke swirled around the bedside lamp. In the light, I saw one eye was swollen shut.

"What happened to your face?"

She exhaled a plume of smoke. "Nothing."

"What happened to Mabry's shoes? Why are her feet covered in mud?"

"We walked home."

"Walked home? Where's the car?"

She took a long drag.

"Where's that fancy new car, Mama?" I repeated, completely out of patience.

She snubbed her cigarette out and motioned for me to come closer. "I'm gonna need you to do your mama a favor."

The decayed car in front of me transforms into its shiny new version, sitting alone in the parking lot where Krystal Lynn told me I'd find it. Key in the ignition. The faint smell of Cinnabar in the leather seats. I'd wrapped my fingers around the steering wheel and thought about Mabry and the money we'd get. And I told myself whatever I did, it'd be worth it. Mabry would finally get the help she needed. That's when I noticed the security camera, high on the wall in front of the car, pointing directly at me.

"That's too close," Raymond says, and I jerk back, gasping. I've moved around the side of the car, and now I'm staring at the open trunk. My heart rate racing.

Raymond cranes his neck. "Not sure what's going on, but they had a whole crew working this car when it came in. Even the state boys. My guess is, they found something good."

"Good?" I say as something cold dances over my skin.

"Well, bad," Raymond corrects, looking embarrassed again. "You know, I was an EMT in Baton Rouge before I became a cop. I thought I'd seen it all, doing that." He grimaces at the trunk. "Not even close to what I'm seeing now."

I follow his gaze to the trunk, my heart clamoring in my chest, unsure if he's referring to it or the barrels. I back away, slowly at first, then pick up speed as I turn and head for the gate. With my back to him, I say, "Thanks for letting me have a look, Raymond."

As I hurry across the street to my car, he yells after me. "Wait. Wanna grab a cup of coffee while you're here?"

The sun is low in the sky when I turn back onto Main. I'd stopped at the Sack and Save for more wine and gotten hung up by Johnette again as she talked to the man in front of me about barrels and missing teachers and shoddy police work. Now, the other shops are closed, the street empty. I don't like it. I don't want to be out here at night alone.

I turn off Main onto the dead-end road, then through the gate at Shadow Bluff. Through the dusky shadows, I spot an old truck sitting in the driveway. One I recognize. I frown and my guard goes up. Being alone here would be preferable to this. Eddie is standing by the porch steps, rocking, while Doyle sits on the steps with something in his hands.

A small surge of adrenaline warms my veins. Fight-or-flight mode. Some of the men from the sex offenders' groups I used to monitor in grad school gave me this same feeling. I learned from them to trust my gut. Them and some of Mama's boyfriends. Not having a steady, reliable male figure in my life did me no favors when it came to trusting men. It's a miracle I ever married Christopher and no surprise we divorced.

I stare at Doyle a moment through the windshield, then grab my tote and the wine and get out. I keep my shoulders back, walk with a purpose, and I keep my eyes on his. I stop at the porch steps.

"Hi, Eddie," I say. He doesn't meet my gaze but he smiles.

Then I look to Doyle and wish I'd put my gun in my tote. He's carving a large stick with an even larger knife. He pushes off the old step. I keep my eyes on the knife until he shoves it and the stick in his back pocket. He holds his hands out in front of him, his nails long and dirty. "I don't want no trouble."

I stay where I stand. He's blocking the way to the door. "Then what *do* you want?"

"I'm a handyman. Thought I'd see if you got anything needs fixin'."

"What?"

"I used to fix things here. I know the house pretty good."

It feels as if ants are crawling on my skin. What the hell does that mean? "Nothing needs fixing." I think of the kitchen door, but I'm not about to mention that to him. "I've got some things I need to do so . . ." I start to step around him when Eddie's hand locks on my arm.

"She don't want to be alone," he yells, his grip tightening.

I force myself not to react too quickly. I don't want to upset him any more than he already is. I slowly twist my arm, but I'm unable to free it. "Eddie."

"Edward," Doyle snaps, and Eddie releases my arm. It's clear who's in control here.

Doyle moves a step closer to me, and I take a step back, scanning the yard for the best exit in case I need to run. I hear the sound of an engine on the road leading in. Doyle's eyes flick in that direction, then back to me. His jaw works side to side, like a nervous tic. He's muttering something, but I can't understand what it is. All I can think about is the knife in his back pocket and the way he was handling it.

Tires crunch on the driveway near the front gate. "Let's go," he says to Eddie as he heads for his old truck.

Eddie stands where he is, then shoves his hand in his pocket and produces another metal figure like the one he gave me on the levee. He holds it out to me, his eyes staying on the ground. This figure is welded together with misshapen metal bits. I close my fingers over it. It's not quite as scary looking as the first one, but it still gives me pause. The fact Eddie's not only letting me touch this doll but is giving it to me tells me to pay attention. Giving me a second one feels important. He trusts me.

"I said let's go!" Doyle yells, and Eddie runs to the truck.

They pull away just as a shiny pickup truck pulls into the drive and stops behind my car. Travis jumps down from the driver's side and watches his brother drive off as he walks toward me.

"What the hell did he want?"

"He asked if anything here needed fixing," I say. "Said he was a handyman here once."

Travis shakes his head. "Hope he didn't scare you."

"It's fine." I watch Doyle's truck disappear, Eddie's doll cold in my hand.

"I got your note," Travis says.

I look at him, confused, then remember. Right. That feels like days ago, not an hour ago.

He holds a finger up. "And I didn't come empty handed." He runs to his truck and comes back holding a bottle of wine and a pizza box. "Thought we could talk over dinner." He lifts the pizza box and wine. "Best I could do."

Not that I'm hungry, but I'm glad he's here.

We need to talk.

Chapter Nine

Travis follows me to the kitchen and watches me prop Eddie's metal doll next to my thermos where the other one sits. I feel like Eddie's trying to communicate something to me, like his little dolls should tell me something. But what? And who doesn't want to be alone? His mother? Or is it he doesn't want his mother to be alone? And what is Doyle trying to tell me? Showing up here with a knife, waiting on me. If I could get one hour with Eddie, I might be able to find out both. But then what would I do with the information? I need to stay focused on my own issues. Now is not the time to analyze someone else's. I'll save that for when I get back to Fort Worth.

Travis pops the cork from the wine he brought, and I place the bottle from the Sack and Save in the fridge. It's obvious he spends most of his downtime in a gym, and something about the way his hands handle the wine and the way his jeans fit tells me I could be in trouble tonight. Stop, I tell myself. I don't need another mess. And that's what my love life has been since my marriage ended, a mess. Short flings that required little to no attention. I convinced myself it was a way to keep things simple, keep my focus on my career. And it worked . . . for my career. But my heart still aches for something more.

And Travis won't provide that, the voice in my head reminds me. Besides, I'm pretty sure any feelings I have for Travis are left over from another decade, lingering because he and I never got closure. I don't need an NFCS—need for closure scale—to know I'd score high. Down here, closure seems to elude me in so many ways.

I find plates and napkins and paper cups and lead Travis to the parlor. We sit on the sofa. Travis sets the pizza box down and pours the wine. I take a sip. Where the hell do I start?

"Travis."

"Look," he says at the same time. He smiles. "You first."

"First." I take a sip. "The car."

I set my wineglass on the table next to Travis's, rub my face. The light in the front windows has faded to night. I stare at Travis. He stares back at me.

"You showed up at my house that night," he says. "In that car. Told me you needed help. Begged me not to ask why. And I didn't ask." He shuts his eyes a moment, reopens them. "I was so stupid."

"I'm sorry I got you involved. I was the stupid one. I justified something I knew was wrong. And I included you in it." My mouth goes dry. I take another sip. "My mother called it a favor. She came up with this ridiculous idea about hiding that convertible for insurance money. She told me Mabry wouldn't get back in the car that night for some odd reason, so on the walk home, Mama decided to just get rid of it and get some cash. I know it sounds ridiculous, but you have to understand; ridiculous for her was normal. I told her to sell the car, but she said that'd take too long, and we wouldn't get enough. She told me it was up to me. I was a minor, so if I got caught, no big deal. If she got caught, Mabry would go to foster care." I inhale, exhale. "She said we could use the money to help Mabry get the therapy she needed. Not that that ever happened. Said she hoped I wouldn't let my sister down." I swig the rest of my wine. "She knew right where to aim her barbs."

"Insurance money?" Travis says. "That's what this is about?"

I nod even though the pit in my stomach from seeing the car in the impound earlier tells me that may not be all that it's about. I touch my fingers to the sofa to steady my lightheadedness. Why wouldn't Mabry get back in the car?

I'd used Travis's truck to push the convertible into the bayou; then I'd driven it back to his house and left the key inside. I'd walked back to Shadow Bluff with the security tape in one hand and a trash bag full of crap from the convertible in the other. I should have slipped that tape into the convertible and dumped it, too, but I hadn't. Something told me to keep it, just in case.

"All right," Travis says, jerking me back. "At least I know what we're working with."

"I knew it was wrong," I say. "I even thought about calling the police, but Krystal Lynn would've killed me if I did that. And then what about Mabry? I decided maybe hiding a car wasn't so bad after all. It's not like I was hurting anyone. I told myself I was just getting rid of something we didn't need in the first place. To help Mabry." I meet Travis's gaze. "The problem was . . . I didn't know where to put it."

"So you came and got me," he says with a sigh.

"So I came and got you."

I don't tell him the other parts of the story. About hiding that security tape in a box of Mama's recorded soaps. About Mabry shaking in her little bed. About Mama's bruised and swollen face.

"I'm going to talk to the chief," he says. "Tell him the truth. With all the other stuff happening right now, I doubt this is going to get his dander up. I'll find out what needs to be done and let you know."

He's downplaying it, trying to make it sound less than it is. Or maybe it really is less than it is. Maybe you're the one trying to downplay it, the voice in my head says.

I reach for the bottle of wine and refill my glass. Travis chews his bite of pizza and swallows it. Insects tap against the front windows.

"So Doyle and Eddie came over here to give you one of Eddie's figurine things?" he says, breaking the silence. "That seems weird."

"It was weird. Doyle had a knife."

Travis sits up. "Did he threaten you?"

"No. It just . . . felt threatening."

"Something's up with him."

"Didn't seem like you two were getting along too well on the levee the other day."

He gives me a look that says he doesn't want to go down that path. And I don't blame him. But it's like the part of me that digs for answers won't shut off, and my next statement comes out before I can stop it.

"Do you want to talk about it?"

"It's just brother stuff." He grabs another slice of pizza and takes a bite. "Actually, Doyle seems to be doing better these days. He's managed to keep a job for once, which is a miracle. Builds playground equipment. Simple and steady, which is exactly what he needs since he's the one supporting Eddie and our mother."

The thought of Doyle handling equipment for children leaves a nasty taste in my mouth. "Well, that's good."

"And Eddie," he says. "He's doing okay, too, I guess. Who can tell?"

I can, I think. "How long has Eddie been nonverbal?"

Travis shakes his head. "Since he was a kid really. Then it got worse later, and he started making those dolls." He takes another sip. "I don't really want to talk about that."

"I understand." I shift to face him more and venture a little deeper. "What about your mother? How's she?" I just can't stop myself.

His eyebrows twitch but that's the only movement on his face. "Same."

"What does *same* mean?"

"Jesus, Willa. You on the clock or something?"

I shake my head and give him a small laugh. "Sorry. Hazard of the trade."

"Look, she's troubled, okay? She could probably do with a little of whatever it is you dish out. But I don't really want to get into all that. I got enough on my plate right now."

"Of course." I clear my throat. "Sorry."

I grasp at something to fill the silence and settle on the topic that's got this town talking. "I heard a third barrel was found."

Travis nods. "We've already confirmed the ID." He leans back against the sofa. "Her name was Teri something. Mother of two. Last seen at Jazz Fest in 2006."

"Not a runaway," I say.

"Nope. Good thing she had an engraved watch. The state boys said getting a good DNA sample would have been tricky. Her barrel was pretty rusted out. Lots of holes. Big enough for aquatic life to get inside and go to town."

"Travis!"

He looks over, unfazed. "Sorry. Hazard of *my* trade." He takes another bite of his pizza.

I set my slice down. "Do you think there will be more?"

He nods as he chews. "Probably. Hard not to call it what it is now. Three barrels. Three women. It's serial for sure." He wipes his mouth with his napkin. "Timing's all over the place, though. After we found the second one, the crime lab had to scrounge up that old DNA from the first one back in '02. That woman had a daughter who loved her. Left a DNA sample back then that helped us match it up. Crazy."

"So that victim wasn't a runaway either."

He shakes his head. "She'd been at a casino. There seems to be no pattern to this one. One old lady gambler, one runaway addict, one mother of two. Makes no sense."

"Even if there was a pattern, it wouldn't make sense." My stomach sours at the thought of these women having families who loved them, worrying over them all these years. The thought there could possibly be more.

Travis studies me, raises his eyebrows.

"What?" I say.

"Raymond St. Clair said he recognized you by the bayou."

What else did Raymond say? I suddenly don't want Travis to know I was at that impound, digging around. It feels like a betrayal, like I'm hiding something. Which I am.

"Remember him?" Travis says. "Ran with those jackasses that used to hang out at the Dairy King."

"I remember Raymond." I shake my head. "So did all the juvenile delinquents in these parts become cops?"

"Well, yeah. That's all there is to pick from." His grin widens. "You either go to jail or put people in it."

"So you and Raymond, cleaning up this town."

He rolls his eyes. "Technically, Raymond's with the sheriff's office. Brown uniform. But, yeah."

"What was the deal with you and Raymond back then? Seemed like there was something. Other than the idiots he hung out with."

"Ancient history."

"Tell me."

"It's nothing, Willa."

Travis's voice sounds playful, but his eyes look serious. A look that says if I keep going, he'll leave. And I'm not ready for him to leave.

You're getting out over your skis with this one, I tell myself. Stop. Put the wine down.

Travis breaks the tension. "I know something we can talk about."

"What?"

"Oh, never mind. Maybe I shouldn't say."

I swat his arm. "You can't do that. Tell me."

"We may have our sights on someone."

"Sights on someone?"

"A suspect," he says.

"What!" The wine has me overanimated. I tell myself, again, tone it down.

He nods. "Person of interest, for sure."

"Who?"

"You'll know soon enough." He sets his cup down. "Sooner if that fancy reporter gets her teeth into it. I swear that woman has a source in law enforcement. She gets information before the chief does."

"Let me guess. Rita Meade."

He smiles a crooked smile. "Bingo."

I lean in, the wine tightening the hold on my curiosity. "Who's the person of interest?"

"Stop." He points a finger at me, trying to be serious but he's smiling. "I can't."

"Who am *I* going to tell? Besides, if Rita knows, the whole world is going to know pretty soon."

"Then you'll see it on the nightly news." He raises his glass.

I stare at it. "You seem more of a beer guy than a wine guy."

"I'm an anything guy tonight."

More silence; then he catches my gaze. "We used to have fun, didn't we?"

I rub my fingers across my lips. "Yes, we did."

What the hell is wrong with me? Don't talk in that cooing, flirty voice. Don't go to the past. But the warm buzz is nice, and he smells damn good.

"Remember the crop duster?" he says.

"Aerial applicator," I correct, remembering what he told me all those years ago as he buckled me in. "You knew me in my wild days." I tell myself it's time to march into the kitchen and get a large glass of water. But I lean into the sofa instead and stare at him.

"My dad almost killed me that day." Travis's smile fades. Something in his voice changes. I hear a hitch in it, almost like I can hear his heart beating. He's not joking.

"Travis," I start.

"I bet you still are," he says quickly, his voice returning to its normal banter.

I let the moment slide away. Now's not the time. "Still are what?" I say.

"Wild." He scans my outfit. "Despite that pressed dress and expensive shoes."

"Maybe I am." Brakes, Willa. Brakes.

"Maybe you'll show me."

And that does it. Electricity sizzles in my veins. I feel that familiar impulsive urge. The one that says one night won't hurt anything. My hands react by reaching across the sofa and latching onto his shirt, pulling him toward me. Our lips meet. His hands find my hair, and we grope at each other like two people flailing for a lifeboat. Then Travis pulls away, his breathing shallow and fast. I tug my dress back into place.

"Wow," he says.

"Travis, I—" My face flushes with heat. Idiot.

"It's okay. That was just unexpected."

"Yeah. Unexpected, all right. I . . . I don't . . . Sorry."

"No, don't apologize. Look, we go way back. And I'm not going to lie. There's a lot of stuff I still think about. But I can't. I'm the one who's sorry."

I want to crawl into the corner and hide behind the curtains, like Mabry did every time Mama started yelling.

"I better go," he adds.

"Of course," I say in my professional I'm-the-one-in-charge voice. I cringe at its phoniness.

I walk him to the door, and he hugs me in an awkward embrace. He pulls back. "I'll call you after I talk to the chief."

As he drives away, I shut the door and bury my head in my hands. I release my hair from its tight ponytail and tug until my scalp starts to itch. What the hell is wrong with me? But I know the answer. Like eggs, our childhoods are fragile. If your keepers don't handle you with care, they can cause hairline fissures to snake through your shell. And they'll seem harmless, but they're not. Each crack has the ability to crack you. I'd worked hard on acceptance. Acceptance of having an absent father, of a mother whose best mothering included three-day benders and slaps across the face. Of a neurodiverse little sister who clung to me like I was a life preserver.

It's no wonder I gravitate toward men who won't be around long. Patterns can be hard to break, even for someone who gets paid to know better. I thought I could keep it all in its appropriate place in my mind. But tonight, I hear it scratching to get out.

It's this town. This house. That fucking car.

I'm learning, in more ways than one, nothing stays buried here.

February 2017

When the Cessna Citation II touched down at the FBO in New Orleans, the idiots surrounding Claire Fonteneau let out a whoop.

"Your dad's plane is awesome."

"It's actually my mom's plane," Claire said.

"Ooohhh. Senator wears the pants in the family."

Her brother's fraternity brothers high-fived and laughed as if this was somehow funny.

"You better not post anything tonight," her brother said. "Mom'll kill me if she knows I brought you."

"Yes, dear brother."

"Dude," one of his friends said. "Chill."

"*Dude*," her brother said back. "She's fourteen."

Claire flipped them both off, hopped down the jet's stairs and into her waiting Uber.

"Be back here by one a.m. Wheels up at two a.m.," her brother yelled.

Claire slammed the door and texted her friends, who were already waiting for her on Royal Street. **OMW bitches.**

The Uber dropped her on Canal because traffic was insane. Claire jumped out and walked the rest of the way into the French Quarter. Beads were flying from balconies down to moronic girls with their tops lifted. Bourbon was wall-to-wall costumes and masks and hammered tourists. It was perfect.

Until some drunk dickhead stumbled into the back of her.

She wheeled around and froze when she saw him. Not a drunk dickhead. Shit. Then he did something odd. He took her picture with a Polaroid camera.

"Not cool," she yelled at him over the roar of laughter and music. "Give me that." If that picture got online, her mother would kill her.

He smiled, held it over his head. "Come and get it."

She stepped closer, reached up, and in the next instant, felt something sharp jab her in the neck. Her vision blurred. She rubbed at the spot as the man leaned in and said, "I forgot to ask you to say cheese."

Chapter Ten

The next morning starts with a jolt. I sit up, startled. Some kind of noise woke me. My head pounds. Visions of last night click through my mind. Travis, the wine, the kiss. Oh God. And on top of all that are the remnants of my dreams. Dreams about missing girls and missing cars and small-town bullies.

Bullies had been the topic of my first podcast, inspired by the bullies who went after my little sister. She was an easy target. Her stringy blonde hair refused to cover her large ears, and the mean girls at school called her Mouse. One called her Rat. I waited for that one on the little school bus that took the kids home in the afternoon. Mabry and I always rode home in Mama's station wagon because she worked in the office, which got us a break on tuition, the rest of tuition covered by the current boyfriend. Somebody rich enough to have two refrigerators, Mama told us when we asked who he was.

That day on the bus, I waited. The leader of the bullies sat down by the window, and I moved up to the seat behind hers. As the bus rumbled into the driveway of its first stop, I pulled out a large pair of silver scissors I'd snagged from my homeroom. I snatched the bully girl's braids in one hand and snipped them off. She screamed. I dropped her braids in her lap. "Now who looks like a rat."

I was suspended for three days. It's the only time I remember Mama telling me she was proud of me.

Of course, that's not the advice I give out now. Today, a kid would be arrested for doing what I did. Probably sued. Rightly so. It was brutal, and I felt awful for that little girl who cowed away from me at school. And then I'd look at Mabry and feel awful for feeling awful. It's no wonder I found my way into psychology.

I swing my legs over the side of the bed, and something clunks onto the floor. Black VHS tapes litter the covers. I have a vague memory of emptying the box after emptying the bottle of wine that Travis left. I'd separated out a pile that was labeled. The others were unlabeled. There are so many. I open my phone and pull up my order. A screen informs me my order is still *In Transit*. No indication if it's actually going to show up today.

A loud knock sounds on the front door. The noise that woke me. I check my phone: 8:00 a.m. A little early for visitors, but I figure it's going to be Travis. I hope he doesn't apologize again. I'm the one who needs to apologize. Making a fool of myself is quickly becoming my new norm. Another knock. Or . . . it could be a package.

I jump out of bed and twist my hair into the neatest bun I can manage, slip into a pair of pants, and button up a shirt but don't bother tucking it in all the way. I trot down the front stairs, but when I open the door, I don't see Travis or a package. I see a caricature of a man with yellow-blond hair, rosy cheeks, and round rimless glasses. To top it off, he's wearing a bow tie with his tailored suit. And to his right stands a small towheaded boy who couldn't be more than three years old, dressed like his dad, right down to the bow tie.

The older one extends his hand toward mine. "I'm Charles LaSalle II of LaSalle, LaSalle, and Landry. And you must be Mrs. . . . ." He pauses with his hand outstretched between us to check a piece of paper in his other hand. "Dr. Willa Watters." He glances down. "This is Charles III. Charlie. He's making rounds with Dad today since it's summer and Mom needs a break."

I picture the young mother on the other end of that phrase and consider mentioning my podcast. Then my mind spirals to *if* I'll even still have a podcast to recommend. I clear my throat and shake Charles LaSalle II's hand. "Nice to meet you." I bend down and smile at his son. "And nice to meet you, Charlie."

Charlie hides his face in his father's leg, but something about him looks familiar.

"Son, don't be rude," Charles says, but Charlie only hides more.

"It's okay," I say, studying the boy. My antenna is up and telling me there could be more to Charlie than just being shy.

Charles clears his throat, studies me. "I . . . um . . . didn't mean to wake you. Hope it's okay we stopped by."

"It's fine." I glance down. Even though I'm dressed, I don't look like I've been up over ten minutes, which I haven't. The shirt is more wrinkled than I thought, and I've buttoned the pants but forgotten to zip them. I pull my zipper up. "Come on in."

Charles II blushes. "Again, sorry to bother you so early. I left a note saying I'd drop by. I popped over yesterday, but you weren't here," he adds quickly.

They follow me to the kitchen, and I notice Charlie is toe walking, like he's tiptoeing across the floor.

"Walk normal," the older Charles hisses under his breath, and my warning system wails.

I start a pot of coffee. Charles sets the piece of paper and an envelope on the kitchen table and sits. Charlie sits next to him, his legs dangling.

"Those aunts of yours were quite a hoot," Charles says.

I turn from the coffeepot with a tall mug. Hoot? Who the hell says *hoot* anymore? And this guy looks like he's barely out of law school. But he's right. The Aunts were a hoot. *Hoot* happens to be the perfect word for that pair. Twins who dressed like wild flamingos.

"Yes, they were," I say, sitting at the table.

An awkward silence creeps in, and I grasp for something to say. I see Charles staring at my large thermos, or maybe he's staring at the strange metal dolls leaning against it.

"Those made by Eddie Arceneaux?" he says.

I nod. "You know them? That family."

"Everybody does. Eddie's a good guy stuck in a bad place. I feel sorry for him."

"What about his brother Doyle?" Now that he brought up this subject, I want to see what he knows.

"Doyle's . . . well, he's an odd one. He's had a tough go too. Local kids call him Doyle the Boil on account of that complexion of his, but he's mostly harmless. He did some odd jobs for your aunts off and on." Charles leans in and whispers, as if Charlie can't hear, "He's been incarcerated before, but he's clean now." He leans back, clears his throat. "But I didn't come by to gossip. I came by to see if you found your mother's things. Our receptionist said you called, needing an attic key, so I brought one with me." He takes it from the small white envelope and slides it across the table.

I don't bother to tell him I already let myself in with a flathead screwdriver and a hammer. Besides, he could have left the key with the note under my wiper, but he didn't. He's here for another reason, and I wonder how long it will take him to get to it.

"I got in," I say. "And I'm happy to pay for any damages to the frame."

"Damages? Oh, well, okay then." When I don't elaborate, he says, "Do you need any help getting her stuff down? You've got two of us here to help."

"No, thank you." Another silence settles over the kitchen. "Would you like some more coffee?" I say.

"No. I'm good," Charles says.

I look at Charlie. "Would *you* like some coffee?"

Charlie doesn't giggle. He looks past me with a dull, blank stare. Listening is what I do best. But sometimes it's what I don't hear that gives me the most pause. And I haven't heard a word from little Charlie.

"What can I get you, Charlie?" I ask, studying him, trying to place how I know him.

Charles answers for him. "He doesn't talk much. Well, at all. He doesn't have his mother's gift for gab." He laughs, nervously. "Isn't that right, Charlie?" He tousles Charlie's hair, but Charlie stays unresponsive.

"How old is he?"

"Just turned three last weekend."

"Happy birthday," I say to Charlie, who still hasn't made eye contact with me, then to Charles, "Does he make any sounds at all? Has his hearing been tested?" I smile. "Sorry. This is my field, so I sometimes overstep."

"No, it's okay." Charles shifts in his chair, fiddles with his bow tie. "I think my wife saw you at Johnette's store the other day."

The boy at the Sack and Save. "Yes, she did."

"When she described the woman who helped her, I put two and two together."

This is why Charles is here. In person. With his son. And when I add little Charlie's behavior from today to the behavior I witnessed at the store, the picture becomes even clearer.

"His hearing is fine," Charles adds, glancing at Charlie. "Our friends say it's probably a speech delay. That's all."

Charlie needs someone to speak on his behalf. This is not a speech delay.

"Charles," I say in my professional tone. "Friends mean well, but they don't always know what's best. Do you want my opinion?" He nods, and I'm surprised by the amount of relief I feel. Despite my inappropriate behavior on live television, someone out there still trusts me.

As if reading my mind, he says, "For what it's worth, Dr. Watters, I don't think what you did on that TV show was that big of a deal. So I'd appreciate any advice you can give me."

I want to hug this man, squeeze him, and tell him thank you until my voice cracks.

This is why I wanted to work with children, to provide them with that advocate. Well, that and an excruciating stint as a research assistant in undergrad when I volunteered to help with court-appointed group therapy for sex offenders and child molesters. After that year, I knew my line in the sand, whom I couldn't work with as a therapist. I wanted to like my patients. I wanted my patients to like me. And I wanted to help the young.

I manage to restrain myself and say, "I'd suggest taking him somewhere for testing. At the very least, you need to talk to his pediatrician about his lack of speech."

Charles's cheeks go pink. "She recommended testing last year." He looks back up. "But his mother didn't want to label him. You know, not every kid is ADHD or whatever."

"That's right. But I'm not talking about ADHD. And I think you know that." I keep his gaze. "I'm just talking about exploring an option that may not have been explored yet. I'm happy to help if needed."

What I don't say is sometimes the hardest thing for a parent to do is admit their child needs psychological help. We live in a world where children need to be the best or else you hire tutors and coaches to make them the best. Not therapists. I've seen plenty of children fall through the cracks because their parents lived in denial. When I was practicing, it was the hardest thing. Watching parents get angry when I suggested genetic testing, or any testing for that matter. Some remained polite as they told me I was wrong. Others would slam the door on their way out. Neither type came back. And then there was the flip side. The parents who demanded testing. Were adamant their child was on the spectrum, and that's why he or she could not make an A in geometry. They were just as angry when I told them their child was a healthy, average child. I learned early on to strike the word *average* from my vocabulary.

"I read your book," he says, glancing at his son. "I want to help him."

My heart swells. There are no greater words I can hear. "Of course you do," I tell him. "I'll research some testing sites in Baton Rouge. Get the information to you. How's that sound?"

"Thank you." His smile is genuine. I can see the relief in it.

"Charlie's going to thank *you* one day."

My cell pings. I glance at the screen and gasp.

Your package is out for delivery.

"Well, we better be running along," Charles says.

I look back up, smile. "I'm glad you came to me."

"Me too."

At the front door, a private jet roars overhead, and Charles and I look up. "Don't see that every day," he says. Even little Charlie watches it. Then Charles hands me his card. "Let me know if you need anything while you're in town. Never know when a lawyer will come in handy."

I pace in the kitchen, in the parlor, and now on the front porch. It's not even ten in the morning, and it already feels over a hundred degrees. I check my phone again. My package is still coming today but no time is given. As I stare at my phone, I notice a missed call from my mother. Several missed calls.

I sit on the step and press her number.

Krystal Lynn answers with a deep wet cough. "Why haven't you been answering my calls?"

"Sorry, Mama. I've been busy."

"Where are you?" Mama says.

"I'm still in Broken Bayou."

There's a long silence, then in a quiet voice she says, "Did you find my things?"

"I did."

"You should just burn it all," Mama says. "There's nothing down there worth a damn." She wheezes into the phone, coughs.

A tightness forms in my throat. I never told her about that security tape. Why would I? I learned from her that lies protect your family. And Mama always needed protecting. The woman liked trouble, and

I was the one who was expected to get her out of it. Like the time she was drunk and wrecked her car into the front window of her boyfriend's neighbor's house. She made me swap seats with her. Bleeding from a gash in her head, she climbed over my lap and shoved me behind the wheel. I'm surprised she didn't drag Mabry from the back seat and try to pin it on her. More than once, after too many wine coolers, she'd allowed Mabry to sit in her lap and drive. When the police arrived, she was hysterical, screaming she'd begged me not to drive. I was thirteen.

I should have learned my lesson years ago. And yet, here I am.

"Mama," I say and pause. Ask her. "What happened with that old convertible?"

She clears her throat. "What convertible? What are you talking about?"

I stare through the moss in the oaks, through the shadows in the front yard. "You know what I'm talking about."

She's silent a moment, then says, "And you know what happened to it."

"Part of it." I swallow. "But there's another part, isn't there?"

Images of Mama that night with her swollen eye and cut lip flash in my head. Then it hits me. The empty safe I'd seen years ago when I went back to get the security tape. The stack of cash in the glove box as we left town. I had neatly tucked those two things into separate compartments and buried each deep in my subconscious. Putting them together now shows the full picture, and it doesn't take a wall of diplomas to figure out what that picture looks like. No more tiptoeing around.

"What'd you steal, Mama?"

"Well, that's a fine how do you do."

I rub my face a little too hard. "I remember you saying your boss that summer was some kind of hotshot, paid you cash. My guess is he had a lot of cash in that office." Sweat worms down my back. "Why'd you ask me to get rid of the car?" My voice cracks around the question. A blue jay darts from one of the limbs and alights atop another. The wind ceases. The moss hangs limp. But my heart is racing as I force out my next two words. "Answer me."

"Listen, sweet girl, I got no answers for you." Mama hacks into the receiver, and I hold it away from my ear for a moment. I hear her shallow breaths as she speaks. "Just come home, Willamena. That place is bad news."

"They found the car, Mama."

"What? Who?"

"The police. The divers that they brought in. That car's not in the bayou anymore. It's in a police impound."

A long silence follows. I let that knowledge sink in for her. Give her a moment to gather herself and finally tell me the truth.

She clears her throat. "Well, that's good," she says. "Maybe I'll finally get my insurance money."

And she hangs up.

I'm not sure what I was expecting from her. I'd learned years ago to stop expecting anything, but I needed to start a conversation with her about that car. And even though we didn't finish it, I have a feeling I know someone who might be able to fill in the gaps.

Chapter Eleven

No little silver bell rings when I open the door to Taylor's Marketplace. The air inside is cool and smells of old wood and pan-fried burgers. Other than the missing bell, Taylor's looks a lot like I remember. Warped wood floors, short shelves stacked with dry goods, homemade jellies, and canned vegetables. All sharing space with a bait shop full of live crickets, worms, and leeches. I'm not sure how the health department works down here, but I can't imagine a place like this in Fort Worth.

In the back sits a long counter with a grill behind it and a hovering scent of cigarette smoke. This place is less crowded than Nan's, but there's still a buzz in the air coming from the patrons sitting at the back counter. Ermine Taylor stands behind the cash register, which looks exactly like the one I used when I worked here years ago.

She glances up. "Willamena, you came by." She moves around the counter faster than I expect and wraps me in a hug. Then pulls back and studies my starched white shirt and pants. Her gaze stops at my feet.

I glance down at the orange boots. They're starting to grow on me. And they're much more comfortable than the heels I'd packed.

Ermine keeps her southern manners in check and says, "Don't you look good. Can I get you some breakfast?" She clasps her shriveled hand around my wrist and pulls me toward another counter containing bagels, muffins, and wrapped biscuit sandwiches. In front of it all sits a huge, fat jar filled with a green liquid and floating pale chunks. The sign next to it, **PICKLED PIGS' FEET**. I cringe and point to the biscuits. She pulls one out and hands it to me. "Coffee?"

"Yes, please. Large."

I follow her to the back counter and sit while she grabs a pot, a mug, creamer, and sugar.

"Here you go, sweetie," she says, pouring. She sits next to me and stares, shakes her head. "Except for those fancy-dancy clothes, you look exactly the same."

I don't, but I nod. "So do you."

"How's your mama?"

I don't tell her she asked me this already at the diner. It's the first question people seem to ask in the South. Hell, it's the first question I asked Travis. *Hanging in there* or *fine* or *great* are all the appropriate answers. Like the answer I gave her at Nan's. But she's staring at me with a look that says she knows good and well she asked me this question already, and this time she wants the truth.

"Mama is . . ." I sigh. "Still complicated."

Ermine nods. "Fair enough. And you? How're you?"

Her small hand touches my arm, and without warning, my eyes sting. I look down into my coffee, swallow the lump in the back of my throat, push aside the memories trying to escape. If Ermine's soft touch is that much of a trigger, I need to be careful about how many trips I make to this store. I look up. "I'm fine."

A man with a white beard at the end of the counter lifts his head above the small group of men beside him and says, "Ms. Ermine, Scooter Rees called me this morning. Said they called him to bring his tow truck back to the bayou just after sunrise. I bet they found something."

"Dixon Thomas," Ermine says. "Do not spread rumors in my establishment."

"No, ma'am. This ain't no rumor," Dixon says. "He told me hisself."

Ermine's brows crinkle. "Well, that could be anything. And keep it down. I'm trying to catch up with an old friend here."

Dixon nods and leans into his friends, animating his words but at a much lower decibel level.

Ermine looks at me. "Quite a time to be here. I've never seen anything like it. And I lived through Andrew and Katrina. We've got this missing schoolteacher, these barrels, a car coming out of the bayou. You ask me, this drought's uncovering things that probably should have stayed buried."

Amen, Ermine.

A throat clears behind me, and Ermine looks over my shoulder, makes a disgusted sound.

When I turn, Rita Meade smiles a blinding smile at me. Her thin hands rest on her even thinner hips. She's dressed casually for Rita Meade, crisp blue jeans and a yellow sleeveless shirt with a giant bow at the neck. "Good morning."

"No comment," Ermine says.

Rita turns to me. "I came by to say hello to Dr. Watters."

"Are you following me?" I ask.

She brings a manicured hand to her chest. "Of course not."

She doesn't even try to hide the lie in her tone. Ermine crosses her arms over her chest. Her feelings for Rita are quite clear.

Rita keeps her gaze on me. "I really would love to visit with you, Dr. Watters. In person or over the phone. I see an opportunity with you. And I never pass up an opportunity. You strike me as that type of woman as well. There's really nothing to lose. You can say *off the record* anytime."

"I'll keep that in mind," I say in the most professional voice I can muster.

Rita gazes down at me, her eyes bright and hyperfocused. "Please consider calling me. It won't be a waste of your time." She gives my shoulder a slight squeeze. "I promise." She straightens, points to the television hanging behind the counter, and says in a loud voice so everyone can hear, "You may want to turn that up in a few minutes." Then she clicks off on her stilettos.

Ermine stands, wipes her hands on her slacks. She starts to walk off, and I stop her.

"Ermine?"

"Yes?"

"Would you mind if I ask you some questions? I'm curious about a couple of things. Couple of people actually."

Her thin brows raise. "Who might that be?"

I swallow. "Do you remember the name of a man my mother worked for that last summer we were here? Had some sort of business where that antique store is now. Could have been a shady guy." I pause, then add, "*Probably* was a shady guy. Maybe a bookie."

Ermine looks to the ceiling for a few seconds in thought, then shrugs. "I can't say I do. That was a long time ago, and my memory's not what it used to be. Sorry about that."

"It's okay," I say, working to keep the disappointment out of my voice.

"So who else are you curious about?" she asks with a slight smile.

"I had a peculiar visit from Doyle and Eddie Arceneaux yesterday. What can you tell me about Doyle?"

She scrunches her lips up like she's tasted something sour. "Him I know. In and out of trouble his whole life. Petty larceny, disorderly conduct. Impersonating a police officer." She raises her eyebrows. "And then Travis is the one who bailed him out." She shrugs, but I get it. I know exactly what it's like to bail out your family.

Ermine continues, "Doyle's always been a little . . . off. Which isn't surprising given . . ." Ermine looks around, scratches at her neck.

I lean toward her. "Given what?"

Ermine straightens. "Now, hon, I don't wanna be the town gossip."

I need to be careful here. Like when I had patients, getting information is a dance. Sometimes you lead, sometimes you follow. Ermine might need me to lead. "I remember the Aunts never wanted me to go to their house. And I remember their father. He always scared me."

"Their father? Oh no, he wasn't the problem. That poor man did the best he could."

The men at the other end of the counter have moved on to fishing stories. Ermine glances at them. Taps her hand on the side of her leg. Now, I follow. I don't say a word.

Ermine studies her fingernails for a second, then sits back down on the stool next to mine. Here we go.

"It's the mother who's the problem," she whispers.

"How so?"

Ermine says, "You'll want to steer clear of Liv Arceneaux. Not that you'll have a hard time doing that. She's a recluse." She looks to the ceiling. "Praise Jesus."

"What do you know about her?"

"The rumors around her and that poor darlin' Eddie are tragic. Some say he was born the way he is, and others aren't so kind. Say Liv Arceneaux fed him all sorts of things like arsenic and rat poison, trying to *cure* him when he was a baby. Made him worse."

"Oh my God."

"I know. Who knows? She could've done that with Doyle too."

Nausea builds in my stomach at the thought of a mother doing that to her child. It's sickening. I hope Ermine is wrong.

"What about Travis's other brothers?" I ask.

"Now, that's quite a crew. Let's see. The oldest, I think his name is Thomas, lives in Houston. Divorced and in and out of rehabs. James the Jaybird, as they call him 'cause he got drunk and ran into a Piggly Wiggly naked as the day he was born, is incarcerated up in Monroe. Drugs. Hunter moved down to Houma, and last I heard, he was working on a rig out in the Gulf of Mexico. And poor Boone found himself on the wrong end of a shotgun when his girlfriend's husband came home. Tragic." I don't miss the glint in Ermine's eye. We've stumbled onto a topic she likes. "Then there was that sweet angel baby, Emily." Ermine shakes her head. "That family is cursed. Seven boys and one girl. And a mama I wouldn't trust to watch my cats."

Emily. If I remember right, she'd been a couple of years younger than me but looked closer to Mabry's age.

"What happened to her?" I say. "Travis told me she passed away."

"She was a sick little thing. Frail. Travis and Doyle were always the ones looking after her, getting her medicines, getting her groceries, but she was on a bad path too. Even Travis couldn't protect her. Ran away one night." She sighs. "Doyle found her. In the woods behind their house. Unconscious. Never woke up. After that, Eddie quit talking altogether."

I cover my heart with my hand, close my eyes. I had no idea how bad Travis's story was. But how would I? I left that summer and never looked back. I exhale as I look into Ermine's sad eyes. "Did they ever find out what happened to her?"

"Autopsy was inconclusive. I remember rumors, though, after." She takes a paper napkin and wipes away a coffee stain on the counter. Then looks back to me. "I'm telling you, whatever Liv Arceneaux was doing out there wasn't right. Who knows what really happened."

"Oh, Ermine." A lump lodges in my throat.

Ermine folds the paper napkin into a tiny square. She's upset. I need to wrap this up. "Ermine, thank you for telling me. It's absolutely tragic, but it does help me to understand some things." And of all the things Ermine just said, one phrase stands out: Doyle found her. Doyle, who was waiting for me at Shadow Bluff yesterday with a knife in his hand. I shudder.

"You know," Ermine says. "Travis moved back home a while back to try to keep the peace over there, but that didn't last. Too big of a job, even for a police officer. I think he still feels guilty about that. That he couldn't fix it."

A sharp pang ricochets in my chest. "I understand."

Ermine's sweet smile threatens to undo me.

"I know you do." She pats my hand.

"Holy shit!" The man named Dixon yells, and Ermine and I both jump.

"What in the world?" Ermine says, glaring at him.

His mouth falls open as he points to the television behind the counter. "They found another one."

The cook hits the volume on the television, and we all turn to watch. A familiar face fills the small screen.

Rita Meade stands on the levee in her yellow blouse, her shiny red smile beaming. "What started as a simple missing person story has escalated into something unfathomable for this small town. Locals here are in shock. So far, the West Feliciana Parish Sheriff's Office says four barrels have been recovered from Broken Bayou. The first one, over fifteen years ago in 2002. The last one, just this morning by volunteer divers. According to my source, this barrel contained human remains as well. Three of the four victims have been identified." Three pictures fill the television screen. One is an older woman, one a teenager, and one in her thirties. Rita continues, "Suzy Weatherton of Houston, reported missing in January 2002 after a trip to a St. Charles casino. Destiny Smith of Birmingham, Alabama, a fifteen-year-old runaway last seen in the New Orleans area the summer of 2015. And Teri Thompson of Biloxi, reported missing after a girls' trip to Jazz Fest in 2006. And there is some speculation the remains of the last victim have already been identified, although details on that cannot be confirmed." Rita squares her shoulders and stares down the camera lens. "Divers are back in the bayou this morning as this small Louisiana town holds its breath and waits."

Taylor's Marketplace sits in stunned silence. The old men aren't bickering. The fry cook isn't frying. Ermine reaches for my hand. Her touch sends a shiver through me. How many more barrels are there?

The image on the television cuts from Rita and the bayou to a one-story redbrick building with a glass door. A few feet in front sits a podium with microphones attached to it. Chief Wilson exits the building and approaches the podium. His hair is wild under the large Stetson, and his eyes are red rimmed. Several other law enforcement men and women enter the screen and flank his sides. Some in blue, some in brown, some in suits.

"Ladies and gentlemen," Chief Wilson says, "my statement will be brief; then I'll be handing the mic over to our lead investigator, Tom Bordelon, who will also make a brief statement." A man in the crowd raises his hand. "We will not be taking questions." Chief Wilson shuffles on his feet. "As you know, we are dealing with something unprecedented in our town. There are a lot of rumors right now, a lot of fear. I'm here to reassure you all and tell you we are working around the clock to get this solved. Your safety is our number one priority. I've asked the residents of Broken Bayou to please stay clear of our levees and the bayou at all times. I'm asking again. This is for your safety and the safety of our divers. We cannot tape off an entire bayou, so I'm asking you all to self-monitor and stay back. I promise we will keep you updated as often as we can. Thank you."

He steps aside, and the man in the khakis and white polo steps forward. "Good morning. My name is Tom Bordelon, and I'm a detective for the Louisiana State Police. I'd like to reiterate what Chief Wilson said and ask you to please keep away from the bayou at this time. It is of the utmost importance that we keep our crime scenes from being contaminated." He clears his throat. "As of this morning, we have recovered four barrels, each containing human remains. Also this morning, we were able to identify the latest victim, fourteen-year-old Claire Fonteneau. Daughter of Louisiana senator Ann Fonteneau."

Ermine gasps.

Dixon Thomas yells, "What the hell! That was fast."

The guy in the ball cap says, "Didn't she disappear about a year ago?"

"Shhh!" Ermine hisses and turns up the volume.

The lead investigator continues, "Senator Fonteneau was able to fly in from New Orleans this morning to make the positive ID based on items found with the remains. Mrs. Fonteneau has asked the media to please give her family time to process this tragic news." I think of the jet flying overhead this morning. Of a distraught mother on board, having to run the worst errand a parent could run. The investigator adds, "We have been working closely with the sheriff's department and local authorities and have narrowed down a person of interest. We will continue to question this person in the hopes of discovering who committed these heinous crimes. Thank you."

Reporters pepper him with questions: "Who is the person of interest?" "Are you calling this person a serial killer?" "What about Katharine Boudreaux?" "What about that car you found?"

Chief Wilson and the others walk back through the glass doors without looking back.

Ermine lowers the volume on the television. She looks to the ceiling and crosses her chest, mumbles a prayer under her breath. The room is deadly quiet. The men, the fry cook, and I all exchange a look. There's no more banter. No more gossip. It's like I can see the weight of reality settling onto their shoulders. Two barrels, then three, had been enough to get the town talking. Four has shut them up. I want to offer them some kind of advice, some way to navigate the feelings surrounding the horrific things bubbling up from their bayou, but I can't. This goes well outside my area of expertise. And the more things around me unravel, the more things *inside* me unravel. A thread has separated from the tight ball I've kept in place all these years, unspooling at an alarming rate, starting with that stupid interview and my ridiculous reaction to that caller.

My cell rings. It's Travis. "I need to get this," I say to Ermine.

"Hi," I answer as I walk away from the counter. "I just saw the news. Unbelievable."

"Willa, what the hell did you get me involved in?"

I stop midstep. "What?"

"When were you going to tell me?" His voice is quiet and calm, but his tone is clear. He's pissed.

"Tell you what?"

"Don't play me for a fool."

I think of the tapes. "What are you talking about?"

"I'm coming!" He yells to someone, then to me, "I'm talking about the trunk of your mother's car."

The ground shifts under me. Heat builds under my skin. What had Raymond said at the impound? *They must have found something good.* My voice shakes. "I have no idea what you're talking about. I don't know anything about the trunk."

"Jesus Christ, I'm coming," he yells again. Then he says into the phone, "We'll have to finish this later." He hangs up and leaves me in stunned silence.

I feel a hand on my shoulder, and I jump.

"Are you okay?" Ermine says.

"I don't know," I say.

"Can I help?"

I shake my head. "No. I'm good." I walk to the door, and Ermine follows me. A man wearing a cowboy hat comes through the front door, and Ermine watches him as he walks past us. When she looks back at me, her eyes sparkle. "I remember that fella now. The one you asked about first." It takes me a moment to realize she's referring to my mother's boss. That conversation feels like it happened days ago, not minutes ago.

Ermine continues, "He used to wear a big black cowboy hat. Drove some big, giant car. Ran with your mama." She squints and looks off for a moment. "Come to think of it, that fella just up and disappeared."

Chapter Twelve

I race into the driveway at Shadow Bluff, bound up the front-porch steps, unlock the front door, and take the inside stairs two at a time.

The boxes are where I left them in the front bedroom. I grab the one with the cowboy hat I assumed was Mama's. The image of her in bed that night years ago materializes. Her swollen and bruised eye. A cigarette between her lips. And a black cowboy hat perched on her head.

I rip open the box and dig through the musty clothes. The hat is still there. I extract it with a shaky hand and study the dry-rotted band above the brim, a decaying rattlesnake rattle wedged between it and the hat. I flip it over and search inside. No name. Just more rot. I drop it back in the box.

My mouth feels too dry. I stumble to the bathroom faucet and drink water from my hand. Then I splash it on my face. I grab a towel, blot the water off. I look behind my reflection and see Mabry in the tub after I came back from dumping the car. Steam rose from the water. Her eyes were bloodshot and swollen like she'd been crying.

I placed a warm washcloth on her chest. "Mabry, tell me what happened."

"I didn't mean it."

"Mean what?"

She opened her small mouth to answer but only spoke one word. "Okra."

Years before, I'd given Mabry a safe word. One Krystal Lynn didn't know about. Anytime Mabry felt unsafe, she could say that word, and then I'd get her out of the house. It was our secret. Not that we even needed a safe word. She could have just said she was scared, but I thought sharing a weird word was a smart way to hide our fear of Mama *from* Mama. The same word I thought I'd heard that caller say on *Fort Worth Live*.

I shut my eyes. When I open them, I notice my folding toiletry bag hanging where the towel was. I reach inside and pull out the silver object I can't seem to leave behind. It's cold between my fingers. Leave it alone, I tell myself. I drop it back in the bag and cover the bag with the hand towel.

I'm punching in my mother's number before I even make it back downstairs.

"Did your boss in Broken Bayou wear a black cowboy hat, Mama?" I say when she answers, slightly out of breath.

"What are you saying about a cowboy hat?"

She coughs, then a clatter, and the line goes dead.

"Mama?" I look at my phone, punch her number again, but this time, it goes straight to voicemail. She can be quite adept at seeming inept when she needs to be.

Blinding sunshine warms my face as I walk through the kitchen door into the backyard. I press Mama's number again.

"Willamena, what's going on?" she says instead of hello.

"We need to talk."

"Well, those are the worst words a person can hear. I haven't even had my lunch yet."

I gaze at the dry dirt in the backyard and remember the greenhouse that used to be there. Dolly Parton serenading the plants inside. The smell of fertilizer and soil.

"We need to finish our conversation about the car."

"I have no idea what you're talking about."

"What did we do?" My voice sounds steady, but my hands are starting to shake.

Several seconds tick by.

I stop next to what looks like the oldest oak on the property. The circumference of its trunk matches that of a corn silo, dried Spanish moss whipping from its branches.

When Mama speaks, her voice is a shrill scream in my ear. "We did what we had to!"

I press my hand on its bark, hoping to feel grounded. Krystal Lynn's conversations have a way of making me feel full of helium. "You don't need to yell. Just talk to me, Mama."

"Don't talk to me like I'm some project of yours," she spits. "I know how you are. I know your type. And I know if I tell you my story, you'll just call me a liar. You always call me a liar. Liar this, liar that. Liar, liar, pants on fire."

The old tree holds me up. If I had any doubt before that Mama had stopped her meds, I don't now. I'll have to call her doctor. But first, I need to calm her down. I may never find another moment when I'm ready to hear what she has to say about that night.

"I promise I won't call you a liar," I say in a soft voice. "I really want to hear what you have to say."

There's a long pause. I hear her labored breathing, like she's just come in from running. "I don't know where to start."

"It's okay, Mama. Just start at the beginning."

She clears her throat. "Mabry was upset that night you went out with that boy."

I lean harder into the old oak. I remember Mama being upset, too, more like jealous. The way she'd grabbed Mabry's arm. The cocky look she'd given me from the driver's seat. *Don't wait up.*

"Where did you go that night?" I say, my jaw tightening.

"A bar."

"With Mabry?" I try to keep my voice light, but it's starting to harden as much as my jaw.

"Yeah. She slept in the booth while my boss and I had drinks."

My stomach clenches. The picture in Mabry's sketchbook. Mama and a man. "What the hell?"

"Listen, it was harmless. I knew the owner."

I shut my eyes a moment. Harmless for her, not Mabry. I open my eyes. "Then what?"

"Then my boss says he needs a ride back to the office. So I gave him a ride."

"What time was it?"

"I don't know. That was a long time ago. Why are you dragging this up?"

I ignore her question. "So you gave your boss a ride?"

"Yes."

"At night to an empty office."

"Willa, I . . . yes . . . I gave him a ride."

"With Mabry."

"Yes, with Mabry."

"Why was your face bruised that night?" I say, hoping to throw her off and get an honest answer.

"Was it?"

"It was."

"I don't remember."

There's her first lie. I hear the stutter in her voice, the pause as she tries to think of what to say next.

"Okay, let's back up." I bring my hands to my eyes and squeeze. "What happened when you took him to the office? Did he run off? Did he go inside?"

"Well, no . . . yes. Kind of."

"Mama, I'm losing patience. You need to tell me—"

"He fell, okay?"

"What do you mean he fell?"

Mama coughs a loud wet cough into the phone. It takes her several minutes to regroup.

"Well," she says, "I followed him to the front door, and he unlocked it and turned off the alarm, then went to the back office. He was fiddling around with something back there when I heard a big thump. I ran back, and he was on the ground. Hit his head. Completely unconscious. And that safe was just sittin' there, wide open."

I inhale a long, slow breath and exhale into the phone. "So you robbed him." Not a question.

"Willamena, that man owed me. I saw my chance to get the money I was owed, and I took it."

Now it's my turn to be silent.

"Willamena?"

"Why did you leave the car there?"

"Mabry wouldn't get back in it. You know how she was. So on the walk home, I thought up the idea of the car and insurance. I really did think we could get some easy money for it."

Easy money. Krystal Lynn's city of Atlantis. Always talking about it. Always searching for it. Never finding it.

"And you sent me back to that office?"

"Right. For the car."

With an unconscious man inside the—I snap off the thought. "There was no man in that office, Mama."

"Oh. I bet he woke up and took off."

I want to scream. I want to pound my phone into the oak tree until it shatters. And most of that anger is at myself. How could I have agreed to do what my drunk, disheveled mother said? How come I didn't call the police when I saw her bruised face? How come I told myself all those years what I did that night was no big deal? None of it made any fucking sense. But Krystal Lynn had been out of her mind that summer. Her mania escalating to a height I'd never seen before. Any choice she made, made perfect sense to her. And I'd learned at a young age not to question her. Agree, go along, head down. That's what worked.

Mama stays silent.

My legs feel weak, and I stare at my orange boots and wish like hell for ruby slippers that wouldn't take me home but back to the past. But that's the wish of a child. I can make choices now that will make up for the ones I made back then.

"And that's the truth. I'm not lying. I'm telling you, I'm not lying. I am not lying."

She's lying.

"What's on that security tape, Mama?"

"What security tape?"

"You're not the only one who stole something from that office that night."

"Now, you listen to me, I don't know anything about a security tape. All I know is, I did what I had to do." Her voice sounds younger than it has in years, hints of the fireball she'd once been. Under different circumstances, her renewed vibrancy would give me hope. Instead, it pushes a rush of hot blood through my veins.

"What does that mean?"

"It means . . . none of your business."

"Thanks to you, this is very much my business. What about your old boss?"

"What about him?"

"Where is he?"

"I have no idea where that scumbag is."

"What's his name?"

"I don't remember."

And there's lie number three.

A sound floats to me in the backyard. Tires on the oystershell drive-way. I want to ask her why a police officer is asking me about the trunk, but I don't. I'm not up for another lie.

"Mama, I have to go. But this conversation is far from over."

I hang up and bolt back inside, through the kitchen, and up the hallway to the front door. Just as I open it, I see a delivery truck pulling away, and at my feet sits a large brown package.

Chapter Thirteen

In the kitchen, I pass up coffee for a glass and a bottle of Sack and Save wine. Drinking at noon isn't the best idea, but sometimes you make exceptions. Upstairs, I set the bottle of wine and glass down next to the box and television I'd already carried up. My hands tingle as I plug in the television. I sit on the floor in front of it and rip into the box. The VCR and cables are clearly marked, and it doesn't take as long as expected to hook them into the back of the television. Please work. I press the VCR's power button and hold my breath.

A green light comes on. My breath escapes with a small sound of disbelief. I power on the television as well, then grab one of the labeled tapes to test it. My mother's faded black scrawl reads *As the World Turns*. Mama's soaps were the sun in her universe. She immersed herself in their made-up problems instead of her own. How lovely it must have been. Little girls in my grade school played Cinderella and Snow White at recess, but Disney had been a foreign concept to me. I didn't grow up with princes and princesses. I grew up with Lucinda Walsh and Holden Snyder and Dr. Bob Hughes. Men cheated and lied and got slapped. They didn't kiss you gently to wake you up.

I shove the tape into the VCR slot and press play. My breath stops. Come on.

Wavy horizontal lines replace the white screen. Come on.

Electronic music starts.

"Yes," I say to the empty bedroom.

A shot of outer space appears, then a floating, rotating Earth glowing blue spins across the screen until it comes to rest as the letter *O* in the word *world*. A deep male voice announces "*As the World Turns.* Brought to you today by Ivory soap and Sure antiperspirant."

I sit back and shake my head. It actually works. I eject the tape and toss it into a trash bag I brought up from the kitchen. I study the pile of unlabeled tapes. The one I need is in there, so close I can literally touch it.

I grab an unlabeled one and push it into the VCR. My breath is so shallow that it feels as if I've been running. The tape is in bad shape; the images are barely visible, but I can tell there are actors on the screen, not my mother or my sister. I fill my wineglass and reach for another one. Then another. And another. The shadows outside the windows are long and getting longer.

After ten tapes, I start to worry Krystal Lynn's soaps could be all I find. I take a sip of wine and reach for another tape when my phone chirps behind me. I pick it up from the floor. It's an area code and number I don't recognize. I send it to voicemail. A second later it rings again, same number. I hesitate, then answer. A crisp female voice fills my ear.

"Dr. Watters?"

"Yes."

"This is Rita Meade. I'm sorry to bother you, but I—"

"How did you get this number?"

"I'm an investigative reporter. Finding a phone number really isn't that difficult."

My voice hardens. "*Why* did you get my number?"

"I'd like to visit with you."

I can think of at least one hundred things I'd rather do than visit with Rita. "I'm not sure that will be possible. I'm heading back home soon."

Rita charges on as if I hadn't spoken. "I think it's interesting that while I'm in this no-name town covering a sensational story, I run into a self-help celebrity who has ties to the very bayou I'm covering. Got me thinking, maybe there's another story I'm missing."

My eyes involuntarily fall on the piles of tapes. A cold, hard knot forms in my chest. "I hate to disappoint you, but there's no story." I take a large sip of wine.

Rita clears her throat. "Is it true you spent summers here with your family?"

"Well—"

"And that you and Officer Arceneaux had a little summer fling?"

"That's not—"

"Did your mother, at one point, drive a red convertible?"

My throat constricts, and my voice becomes a raspy whisper. "No comment."

I hang up before she can spit out another question. My cell immediately rings again. I send the call to voicemail, then block the number. I drain the rest of my wine and set the glass down hard. What the hell? This is not uncomplicating things, as Amy requested. I don't need a reporter stirring more up. I've stirred up plenty on my own. I want to handle that car quietly, with Travis and with the chief. Not splash it all over the news.

I tell myself it's okay. Rita's just hoping for an added spin on her story, and I don't plan to give it to her. I fumble through the unmarked tapes and grab another one. It's so badly decomposed I can't tell what's on it. I set it in the maybe pile.

The windows are dark now. I pick out a few more unlabeled tapes and set them aside. I grab the next tape and put it in. Another soap. Tape after tape, sip after sip, I wait, my anxiety reshaping itself into doubt. What if that tape had somehow been separated from the rest and thrown out? What if this is a fool's errand?

I let the next tape play. The scene on the television switches to a hospital. I should eject it, but the wine is pulling at my eyelids. Heels are clipping. Someone is arguing. Or is that in my head? I yawn. Shut my eyes for a minute. Just a minute.

I jerk awake with a screaming crick in my neck. The television screen has gone dark. I rub my neck, check my phone. It's four o'clock in the morning. I shift on the floor and knock over the empty wine bottle next to me. Shit. I get up, trudge down to the kitchen, and make a pot of coffee, then resettle in front of the television.

The coffee kicks in a few tapes later as I'm waiting to see more actors, but the screen shows something new. My heart bangs in my chest. Something flashes on the screen. No glowing globe. No preprogrammed '80s music. Instead, a scratchy, filmy black-and-white image appears. I inhale, lean in. Despite the grainy image, I can tell it's a parking lot, and long shadows extend behind the cars parked there.

Holy shit.

I touch the screen with my finger. I almost expect it to shock me or me it. The adrenaline in my veins is electric. I stay glued to the television as, one by one, the cars on the screen drive away. Day slips into night. The image I'm watching is dark now, but the back lot is lit by giant sodium-vapor lamps illuminating the parking spots. Mama's car may be in one of those spots soon enough.

I chew my fingernails. Minutes tick into an hour, but I refuse to fast-forward. I don't want to miss anything or risk ruining the old tape. Then I see movement on the edge of the grainy footage. A car whips into the lot. I scoot even closer.

The image may be in black and white, but the color of that candy apple red convertible is seared in my memory. A woman exits the driver's side, and a man in a cowboy hat climbs out the passenger's side. My breathing halts for a moment, then picks back up double time. The couple walks around the building toward the front. Even though I can't make out faces, I recognize Mama's swaying swagger immediately. And the cowboy hat tells me all I need to know about the man. Her boss. I watch the car as it sits askew in the parking space, knowing Mabry is in its cramped back seat.

I wish I could reach through the screen, through time, and pluck her free.

Several more minutes pass, and I wait. Then Mama trips around the corner of the building, the man close behind her. Her clothes are hanging at odd angles. Her hair wild. I can see her screaming at the car. A shadow in the car moves from the back seat to the front seat. Mama steps in front of the hood, and the man follows. They are arguing. Body language doesn't lie. Then he hits her.

I flinch and gasp.

On the screen, Mama falls to the ground and disappears from view; then the car's headlights switch on. Mabry.

The man starts kicking something. Oh Jesus, Krystal Lynn. I wait, but Mama doesn't get up.

Every muscle in my body tenses.

The man takes a step back, and Mama claws her way up the front of the car. She bangs her hand on the hood, yells something at the windshield, then runs sideways. The next thing happens so quickly that I would have missed it if I'd blinked. The man tries to run, but Mama's car lurches forward, straight at him, pinning him to the wall.

I smash my finger onto the pause button. A deep, guttural moan escapes my mouth.

Mabry. Twelve-year-old, innocent Mabry.

I want to turn off the television and be done, but my fingers have already pressed play again.

On screen, Mama runs to the driver's side and climbs in. The car backs up, and the man falls like a rag doll to the ground. Mama jumps from the driver's seat, and this time, Mabry exits the car as well. She looks so small. I pet the screen with my fingers. Mama grabs the man's feet and drags him to the back of the car and, with uncanny strength, tugs and pushes and hauls his body into a fireman's carry before dumping him into the trunk.

Mabry stumbles backward, away from the car, until she is no longer on camera. Mama slams the trunk closed and walks over to the discarded cowboy hat on the ground. She picks it up and props it on her head, then walks away from the car as if she's only out for a midnight stroll.

I stop the tape.

My head is swimming. My stomach knotted into a tight ball of sickness, wanting to be released. *I'm talking about the trunk of your mother's car.*

The house is quiet except for whispering cracks and snaps as if its old wood is settling under the weight of this macabre revelation. I stand. My legs feel stronger than I expected. I walk to the bathroom. My toiletry bag hangs next to the sink. I don't pause or contemplate my next move. I just act. Muscle memory. I slip my hand inside and extract the shiny object I had no business packing. A clean straight-edged blade.

The heart tattoo on the inside of my left arm, the pale skin around it, the scars underneath it mock me. I want to cut it from my arm. Dispose of it and all the memories locked inside. Instead, I nick the tattoo with one small precise movement. The cut releases a scream I'd been bottling for longer than I care to admit. Blood drips onto the white tiled floor. I stand still, my arm hanging by my side. I may have cut too deep. It's been a long time. Some people travel with one Xanax, like a security blanket, just in case they have a panic attack. Just knowing it's there can keep anxiety at bay. I travel with something much more toxic.

I put the sheath back on the blade, grab a towel, and apply pressure. Then I return to the television.

I'm not ready to keep watching, not ready to see myself come into the picture and get behind the wheel. I need to absorb what I've seen before I acknowledge my role in it. I can't go there yet. I pinch the towel in the crook of my arm and use my other hand to press rewind. While the tape whines in the player, I struggle to breathe, as if a rogue wave has slammed into me, knocking me off balance and holding me underwater. I have to get my feet back under me, press play again. And brace for another impact.

April 2018

Katharine Boudreaux steered her car the best she could down Main Street. She should have gotten a ride. Called a taxi. An Uber. Anything. She rolled down her window. The wind in her face helped. She turned onto Bridge Street. One more bridge and she'd be home.

Her cell dinged in the seat next to her. She reached for it, couldn't quite grasp it. She leaned over farther. Her fingers grazed the case. She looked down for a second, but when she glanced back up, she was headed not onto the bridge but straight for the side of it. She hit the brakes, or so she thought. The car lurched forward, hitting the side rail and catapulting Katharine's car over the side.

Katharine didn't know how long she'd been unconscious when her eyes fluttered open. Something had woken her. A flash of light.

Blood trickled down her face. It was quiet except for the sound of water lapping against the car. But her car was only partially submerged. She must have landed on the bank. She tried the door handle. It was stuck. She pounded on the window. And that's when she saw him. A man standing beside the car, staring in at her. She screamed.

"Hang on," he yelled. "Lean away from the window."

Katharine did as he said. A second later the window shattered. Katharine gasped as tears ran down her cheeks. "Oh my God. Thank you!" This man would know what to do. She couldn't believe her luck.

Katharine fumbled for her seat belt. The man leaned in through the window. "Let me help."

That's when she felt something sting the side of her neck. She yelped and raised her hand to the spot.

"What . . ." Katharine felt woozy. Her tongue too thick to form words. She was completely incapacitated.

Then the man held something up. "Let's do another one with your eyes open. Say cheese." A light flashed again.

Katharine's eyes fell shut. She heard her phone buzzing somewhere close.

But she never got to answer it.

Chapter Fourteen

Something heavy and hard settles under my ribs later that morning as I sit in the kitchen with Charles LaSalle's business card in my hand. *You never know when a lawyer will come in handy.* It's time to go to the police, but I'm not going without an advocate.

After showering earlier, I decided on pants and a T-shirt today. No more silk. No more pretending. I'm an accomplice to something horrific. No need to dress it up and call it something it isn't. I glance at the crease in my left elbow. The mark I left is small and red. No indication of the depth of pain it holds from knowing I helped my mother dispose of a body. I rub my face and try to stop my thoughts from unspooling, but they have too much momentum. And I'm too tired to stop them. I'm back inside Mama's cluttered car as I followed Travis from his house down a dark dirt road leading to the deepest part of the bayou. The Delarouxes' farm on the northeast side of town. A sprawling tree farm with an old farmhouse and several run-down shacks around the property. Travis stopped and turned off his lights. I did the same. We met in front of Travis's truck. The August night scorching, humidity so thick it was hard to breathe.

Travis pointed to the bayou. "Dump it there. Other side of the levee."

I set my coffee on the kitchen table with a shaky hand and will my last sip to stay down. The house is silent. The window over the sink shows a bright blue sky. My days in this town are longer than they should be. As if I really need another hour to sit and think about what I've seen.

I watched the tape more times than I should have, stopping it right after Mama hauled his body up into the trunk, then rewinding to watch again. Never watching far enough to see my younger self enter the frame. I should have. I need to see it. I need to own it. But I couldn't. I kept watching Mabry and Mama over and over and over. Maybe to make sure I saw exactly what I think I saw. Maybe to punish myself for thinking what I'd done for Mama all those years ago was harmless. I tell myself what I've told countless people: you were a child. But Mama wasn't a child. She knew. And she sent me there to get rid of it. Get rid of *him*.

Then a thought occurs to me that I hadn't considered yet. Its sharp and disturbing point piercing my throat, closing off my windpipe as I try to inhale. What if her boss wasn't dead?

I jump up from the kitchen table and release the contents of my stomach into the farm sink. I heave until all that's left is bile. I run the water, rinse my mouth, then lean back against the counter. Then the tears start. Slowly at first but building quickly into deep guttural sobs. After several minutes, I manage to catch my breath. He wasn't alive. There's no way. I saw what happened. If he'd been alive . . .

That's when I hear it. A car engine or a truck. An older model with a missing muffler. I race for the window in the front foyer and see tail-lights skittering down the drive toward the gate. It looks like Doyle's truck. He is the last person I want poking around here.

I race upstairs, skittish and shaky, for my handgun. It's where I left it, unloaded. I grab the cartridge box from my duffel and load it, then ease back down to the window. I flick on the giant chandelier in the foyer and look outside. The driveway is empty. I unlock the front door.

The late morning is as hot as every other morning. Not even a hint of a breeze. The sky above me shows no sign of creating a cloud anytime soon. Birds chatter through the oaks. The cicadas are already up and singing as well. The hotter it gets, the earlier they start. The humidity feels like a weighted blanket, and sweat starts on my neck even before I make it to the porch steps.

I sit and try to manage the river of emotions flowing through me. My fear morphs into anger, then remorse, then guilt. It's cycling through my veins like poison. And with it comes the memory of Mabry. Oh, Mabry. I cradle my head in my hands. Mabry was trying to protect Mama. Mama was trying to protect Mabry. And I'm still trying to protect them both. But that circle of protection is becoming more and more toxic.

No doubt, in Krystal Lynn's warped mind, sending her eldest child back to clean up her mess that night made perfect sense. But I can't stop my mind from reeling. Why? Why would she think that was the best option? A small sad laugh escapes me. I know better. I know you can't apply logic to an illogical person. I can't expect normal reactions from a woman who had no idea what normal was.

She wouldn't get back in the car. I saw the fear in Mabry's eyes that night. I assumed it was something Mama had done. In a way it was. But I had my hand in it too. I put that car in the bayou. I disposed of evidence. Of . . . I can't finish the thought. I harness every ounce of energy I have left to lock it away. No going there right now. And no calling Mabry. Even if she'd answer, I'm not sure what I would say.

As I stand back up, something brown and crumpled catches my eye at the bottom of the steps. Possibly trash. But it doesn't look like trash. It looks like a paper bag. And it wasn't there yesterday. I ease down the steps to it. The top of the bag is neatly folded down.

Part of me says don't touch it, but I give the bag a small kick. Whatever's inside is hard and sounds metallic. I think of the figurines and Eddie. If this is one of those, it's considerably bigger than the others. Whatever it is, it doesn't seem too dangerous based on my baseless assessment.

Slowly, I set my handgun down, pick up the bag, and unroll the top. I'm not sure what I'm expecting to find, but it sure as hell isn't what's inside. I drop the bag as if it's full of snakes. I stare at it several seconds before grabbing it and pulling out the metal object inside. A license plate. It's heavy in my hand. Cold. With a shaky hand, I drop it back in the bag. The old convertible was missing its plate. I roll the top back down. This isn't like the metal dolls Eddie made, the gifts he's given me. This is a message. A message from Doyle Arceneaux.

Nan's Café is not quite the clatter of activity it was a few days ago. Even though every table is full, some locals, some media, a heavy silence hangs over the room. The clink of silverware on plates is the loudest sound. Except for the orange boots and the fact I couldn't bring myself to fix my hair before I left, I still fit in more with the media, an outsider looking in. A few people study me. The locals look tired, their eyes turned down, their mouths in tight, straight lines. The media folks look hungry, not for food, for more death. Unlike the locals, their eyes are bright and focused. And most focused of all is a green pair staring straight at me. Rita Meade.

A text pops up on my cell, a new number.

The more you try to ignore me, the harder it will be. This is Rita.

I look over at her. The sides of her mouth curl up.

Great.

Even with Rita here, this is still better than sitting around Shadow Bluff, waiting for Charles LaSalle to call me back. I'd placed the license plate in the kitchen next to Eddie's dolls and stared at them so long my eyes hurt. Why would Doyle leave that for me? And when I take it to the police, will they believe that's how I got it?

If I stayed in that house one more second, I would have driven myself crazy with questions and eventually started on the tape again. Or worse, gone back to my toiletry bag. And I can't do that. So I decided, despite the fact I look and feel like a zombie, I needed to be in a public place.

A couple exits one of the booths by the bank of windows, and I slide in even though it hasn't been cleaned. A young waitress with blonde bangs and a mouthful of gum wipes the table with a wet rag, then sets a plastic menu in front of me. She disappears for a moment, then returns with a thick ceramic mug she clunks onto the table.

"Coffee, hon?"

A waitress half my age calling me *hon* manages to bring a smile to my face. But it's not a real smile. Nothing feels real at the moment. I feel like I'm an actor on a set, stumbling through a scene I'm not prepared for. Amy once did a stint in her early twenties as a production assistant in Los Angeles. She told me how, when she was on set, she lost all perspective. Her world would shrink to the actors, the director, the gaffers, and grips, and that would become her new world.

That's how this town feels. Except no one is yelling "That's a wrap."

The coffee is strong, and I don't bother with creamer or sugar. I don't need it diluted right now. My nerves are crackling under my skin, and although caffeine may intensify it, I don't care. I need fully loaded.

I feel someone staring at me from across the room. I look up, expecting Rita again. Worse. It's Travis. He's a few tables away, sipping coffee and watching me. I nod. He nods back. I don't like the way he's studying me. He wads his paper napkin into a ball and drops it on his plate; then he scoots back from the table and heads my way.

I sit up straighter, push the hair off my shoulders.

"Morning," he says. He's smiling, but the smile is too pinched, too static.

"Hi."

"We need to finish our conversation."

I think about the license plate. "Yes, we do." I shift in my seat.

The look he's giving me has me breathing a little faster than I should be. Recalling everything I watched on that tape isn't helping.

"Not here, though," he says.

I nod.

He looks down at me like he's waiting. Maybe he wants me to get up and follow him, but I'm not quite ready. "I'll call you later," I say.

"Willa."

"I promise."

He sighs and exits Nan's. I watch him climb into his truck and pull out of the lot. I need to tell him I'm going to the police. Tell him what's on that tape. But even thinking of saying that out loud has my throat closing off.

The waitress returns to take my order, but I have no appetite. I tell her I'm sticking with coffee only, and as if in a choreographed dance, chairs begin scraping on the diner floor, and suited patrons start sliding from booths, adjusting ties, and applying lipstick. All race for the door, including Rita, who pauses at my table. "Information flows both ways," she says.

In seconds, the place is cleared out to the point I wonder if I missed a fire drill of some kind. Rita's cryptic words ring in my head.

"Did I miss something?" I say to the waitress as I motion around the now empty diner.

She chomps her gum. "Nah. This is what they do when the sources tell them something's up. It's like a horse race to the bayou."

The internal magnet that pulled me back to this town in the first place vibrates. I ask for my check.

Outside, it's hot. Surface-of-the-sun hot. And humid to the point I can't catch my breath. But even with all that water in the atmosphere, it still hasn't rained. Everything around me looks dry and dusty and shriveled up. The water in that bayou is going to continue to evaporate, and the more it does, the more likely it is something else will surface.

The news vans back out of the lot and turn left onto Main. Before I can think about it, I'm in my car following them, heading east onto Bridge Street, then crossing over the bridge to the opposite side of the bayou from where the car was found. They turn onto an unpaved dirt road. This side of the bayou is wilder, more trees and scrub brush, less grass. I park behind the vans. Reporters jump out and hustle to the top of the levee with their camera operators chasing them. I am not in my right mind. I have no business being here. I need to turn around and leave, go back to Shadow Bluff, and try to reach Charles again. But as I slip my car into reverse, I see Rita on top of the levee, motioning for me to come up. My car idles. It's risky. She knows about the convertible. But she also said information flows both ways. And I need all the information I can get. I put the car in park. No risk, no reward.

As I walk up the levee, Rita leans into her cameraman, hands him her mic, and teeters her way to me on stick-thin heels. Most of the crowd hovers on the opposite side of the bayou from where I'm standing. Only a few people huddle below me, whispering and pointing. Like Nan's, the levee is much quieter than the last time. No loud conversations. No hum of energy. The tragic circumstances surrounding this bayou are real now. And reality has thrown a wet, heavy blanket over this town.

When Rita reaches me, she holds out a hand. "Dr. Watters."

I stare at it. Rita stares at me. Even though manners weren't at the top of Krystal Lynn's list of things to teach her daughters, I take Rita's soft hand and shake it.

"Enjoy your breakfast this morning?" she says. When I don't respond, she adds, "I was serious about what I said at Taylor's. Anything can be off the record. I just want to talk."

"What did you mean by 'information flows both ways'?"

She ignores me, glances over her shoulder, then back to me. "Pretty crazy. Right?"

I stay stoic, nod again. I know to watch what I say with this one. She can spin shit into gold. A modern-day Rumpelstiltskin.

Along the bank, divers dressed from head to toe in black wet suits and carrying large divers' flashlights slip under the opaque water for brief periods of time, then resurface. Officers try to hold back the press as they try to push forward. All in a weird slow dance that gets them both nowhere.

I look around for Travis. He's talking to Chief Wilson as the tow truck driver from the other day leans against his now silent truck, smoking.

"Pretty crazy," I say.

My instincts tell me to wait, that Rita will answer my question. So I don't fill the silence.

Finally, she says, "Look, I'm not going to lie to you, Dr. Watters. I'm interested in your episode on *Fort Worth Live*, but that's not all I'm interested in. I'm curious why you're in this small town at the same time bodies are coming out of the bayou. I'm curious about that old convertible that came out too." She stares at me with a steady gaze. "I know a lot about that car. Things I think you should know."

My feet feel as if they are covered in cement. I can't move. I'm stuck, staring at her, and hoping she hasn't noticed how difficult it is for me to swallow. What the hell was I thinking?

"Give me a chance, Dr. Watters," she says. "I'm only asking for one conversation."

Before I'm able to respond, a loud horn slices through the humid air and cuts Rita short. We whip our heads toward the small boat of divers. The sheriff's radio crackles. Travis yells, "They got it!"

Rita shoves a card in my hand and in a breathless voice says, "I really do think it'd be good for you to tell your side of the story." She swivels on her heels and sidesteps back down the levee before I can even begin to respond. I study the card and slip it into my purse. The only story Rita wants to tell is the one that'll get her the best ratings.

I watch the tow truck driver stomp out his cigarette and fire up his diesel. As the truck backs to the water's edge, Rita's cameraman ignites the light on his camera. I can see Rita's mouth moving as the scene unfolds behind her.

The flat-bottom divers' boat floats closer to the edge. Two divers come up from the water, take the chains from the tow truck, and disappear again. Just like with the car. But this time when the chains grind forward, something else comes out of the murky water. A large black steel drum barrel.

Barrel number five.

◆   ◆   ◆

I park in front of Shadow Bluff and leave the engine running. My thoughts slide from Rita's comment about that car back to Mama. All of it revolves around her. It always has. If the soaps had been her sun, Mama had been ours, a hot ball of fire pulling my sister and me along in her orbit. My aunts did what they could to help us, but a few months in the summer wasn't enough to combat Mama's gravitational pull. Even though I became successful and self-reliant, the threads tying me to Mama are tough and harder to break than I realized. And they're no longer buried deep. Here they're exposed, like the roots on the old oaks surrounding me, twisted and gnarled and easy to trip on.

I turn off the car and check my cell. I've missed a call from Charles LaSalle. Shit. I punch his number, but it goes straight to voicemail. Then my phone rings. It's Amy. I consider not answering, then decide avoidance isn't going to do me any favors. I need to know what's going on at home.

"Hey," I say, stepping out of the car.

"What's wrong?"

"Wow. I only said one word."

"And that's all it took. What's up? You on your way home?"

I ignore her last question as I head for the porch. "I'm thinking about all this stuff with Christopher is all. Have you heard anything?"

"The rumors about him being married have died down. His divorce papers are a matter of public record. You were right. He was divorced a year before you went to work with him."

I exhale. "At least that's some good news." I climb the porch steps. "But the attack on my competency is still gnawing at me."

"One thing at a time," she says.

"I'll probably need to call Christopher at some point." It's been years since we talked. It's a miracle we separated as amicably as we did, given the fact he admitted to not only falling out of love with me but also falling in love with someone else . . . a much younger and completely enamored version of myself. My admiration for Christopher had worn off when I came to finally understand I didn't want him to take care of me. I wanted to take care of myself. I figured his affair was the bad thing that finally showed up, and it was almost a relief. No kids. I'd kept my maiden name, my own bank account. Nice and tidy, like I like it.

At the top of the porch steps, I stop. A small metal object is propped against the door.

Things aren't so nice and tidy anymore.

I bend down and retrieve it. Definitely one of Eddie's. It looks like a tiny metal voodoo doll. But this one, instead of somewhat normal-looking arms and legs, has small knives shooting off a round body and a misshapen head welded to the top. It's rudimentary and certainly creepy but still quite well made. I look around the front drive and the trees flanking the house. I'm alone.

"Amy," I say, glancing at the newest doll Eddie has left me. "Tell me this is all going to work out."

"This is all going to work out." A pause. "Come home, Willa."

"There's something else," I say as I take the doll inside to the kitchen.

"Oh God, what?"

"Rita Meade is here. And she wants to talk to me." I add the doll to the collection on the kitchen counter, by my thermos and the license plate. Quite the menagerie.

"The national-news-reporter Rita Meade?"

"The one and only."

"Damn. You did go viral. Stay away from her. No comment."

"I know."

"No comment, Willa," Amy repeats.

"Got it." But as I stare at the odd collection of items, I wonder. As much as Rita and her knowledge about the car frighten me, there's something about her that intrigues me as well. Good or bad, she's honest. "Amy, I've got to go. I'll call you later."

I hang up before she can protest and sink into a kitchen chair. The car, the tape, the barrels, my mother's lies drown out the other issues I need to be focusing on. The ones that pertain to my future, not my past. But my past is where I live now, like it or not.

Chapter Fifteen

I lie in bed wide awake the next morning. I'm not sure how long I've been awake. Long enough to watch the sky lighten. My body and my mind ache for sleep, but neither get their wish. Every time I close my eyes, I see that tape playing over and over again.

I sent Charles a text before falling asleep, and he responded he could meet me at the police station today, this afternoon, after the sheriff's news conference at the bayou. I'm not sure if I'm relieved or terrified. And those feelings continue to fight each other as I scan the other messages waiting for me. Three are from Rita, and the last one says she's on her way over. It was sent twenty minutes ago.

I trudge to the bathroom and splash water on my face. What the mirror shows is not kind. Dark circles float under both eyes, which are red and puffy. My hair is wild and tangled, and the long T-shirt I chose is starting to stink. I realize I haven't done any laundry since I've been here. Which is how long? I count backward. Five days? Six? A week? I glance in the mirror again. It looks like I've been here for years.

A loud knock sounds downstairs, followed by an even louder voice. "Dr. Watters? Hello? Is anyone home?"

As I reach the bottom of the stairs, Rita knocks again. "Dr. Watters, are you home? I want to visit for a minute. I promise I won't take up much of your time."

I weigh my options. The smartest would be to stay quiet and let her move on. But I have a sinking suspicion she'll be back. Rita doesn't strike me as the type of woman who will tolerate being ignored. Besides, I've already toyed with the idea of talking to her. But I wanted it to be on my terms, not hers. Maybe I can keep this on my terms. Control the narrative. Maybe Rita, as frightening as it is to offer myself up to her, might be able to help me. *Information flows both ways.* And this woman is full of information.

Another knock, and I open the front door to a sticky morning and a wide-eyed Rita Meade. She is glossy to the point of reflecting light. Her face looks airbrushed. Her hair blown into silk. Her smile blinding. A few days ago, I would have been jealous. I can't imagine what she's thinking of me.

As she studies my face, she says, "You didn't get my messages."

It's a statement, not a question. I smile the best I can and shake my head.

"I told you I was stopping by." She smiles her full-wattage smile. "Thought I'd take a chance." She's wearing all black today. She must be sweltering. As if she's read my mind, she glances over my shoulder and adds, "Do you think we could talk? Inside?"

It's not too late. I can say no and shut the door. Tell her I'm not interested and to leave me alone. But a part of me is interested, or maybe *intrigued* is a better word. And if I'm being honest with myself, I've reached the point where all I can think to say is *fuck it.*

I shrug and leave the door open as I walk back to the kitchen. I hear Rita's heels behind me.

"This place is beautiful," she says. "And thankfully air-conditioned." She laughs, but I keep walking in silence.

When I reach the kitchen and scan the room, I realize my mistake. The license plate is still propped on the counter next to Eddie's dolls. I turn to redirect Rita back to the front of the house, but she's already moved around me and pulled out a chair at the table. Her eyes dart around the room as she sits, and I'm sure she's seen the plate, but she doesn't acknowledge it.

I pour us each a coffee, setting hers in front of her with the creamer and sugar. I sit opposite her and run my hands through my knotted hair.

"Thanks for letting me in," she says.

I nod, look down at my chipped nails, then back to her polished ones. I exhale what little energy I have left. "I'm not sure I'm up for a long visit."

She plucks a cell phone from her purse and sets it on the table. "I won't be long. I promise." She points to her phone. "I'd like to record this. Make sure nothing gets misconstrued." She straightens her narrow shoulders. "At any point, you can say *off the record.*"

"Off the record."

She squares her shoulders, her long red fingernail hovering over the record button. I stay silent. She stays silent. Finally, I exhale and lean back in the chair. She wins.

"Fine. This can be on the record." Then I add, "To start."

She presses record. "Please state your full name."

"Dr. Willamena Pearl Watters."

She looks down at her phone. "Broken Bayou interview. August nineteenth, 2018."

I gasp. "Today is August nineteenth?"

Rita looks up. "Is that a problem?"

A memory flashes so hot and bright in my mind that I want to shield my eyes from it. Mama flitting into the upstairs bedroom at Shadow Bluff, holding a lopsided chocolate cake with at least two tubs of Betty Crocker chocolate frosting sliding off it onto the giant silver serving platter. Seventeen bright candles burned on top. "Happy birthday, darlin'." She pointed an acrylic nail at another candle off by itself. "One to grow on." Mama popped her hip out to the side. "Now, hurry up and make a wish before my arms fall off."

A soft hand touches mine. Rita clears her throat. I blink, shake my head. "You know what. Now may not be the best time for me after all."

Rita pauses the recording. She drums her nails on the table, then sighs. She shows me her phone screen, exits out of the recording, and drops it back in her purse.

"I think you and I have more in common than you know. Two southern girls who made right, despite having the odds stacked against them. We both deal in media, just different aspects of it. We've both been accused of sleeping with a man in order to advance our careers."

I think of Christopher and the rumors. "I—"

She holds up a hand. "I know it's bullshit." She leans onto the table and adds, "And who cares if it isn't. See, what I care about is a good story. When I saw you the other morning in that shitty diner, I knew I had one." She straightens again. Her eyes dart to the license plate on the counter, then back to me. "You've definitely got a story."

"Yes, I do." I'm too tired to argue with her, and I'm way past needing to practice what I preach. Honest healing isn't as easy as I make it sound in my book or on my podcast.

Rita says, "That was your mother's convertible, wasn't it?"

Instead of answering, I clear my throat and force myself to sit up straighter.

"I've done my homework, Dr. Watters."

"And what has that homework revealed?"

"That many years ago, a man named Zeke Johnson bought a red convertible and gave it to a woman who worked for him. That a few weeks later, Zeke went missing." I keep my face neutral, but my insides twist into a knot. My breathing quickens. I have to get her out of this kitchen. Rita continues, "Not a huge shock to most people who knew him. He was a bookie and running bets through his business. He was into all kinds of things. Some people even claim he had connections to the Marcello family in New Orleans, but my guess is he started that rumor."

"I don't know . . . I think . . . maybe we should do this later."

She continues as if I've said nothing. "I'm pretty sure Zeke disappeared that summer because he got busted running drugs through his office."

Tell her to leave, I prod myself.

"Hope your mom wasn't hung up in all that."

Tell her to leave now.

"That guy's been in and out of jail ever since and now serving time in a federal pen for tax evasion."

Rita keeps talking, but her words are indistinguishable from the rushing sound in my ears. The entire kitchen feels as if it's tilted sideways. I plant my bare feet on the floor under the table to steady myself. "Wait," I say, interrupting her. "Did you say he's in prison?"

"That's right," she says.

I spring up from the table so fast that Rita recoils. I want to hug her, thank her, but I say, "You need to go."

"What?" Rita blinks at me.

"I . . . I forgot I have to be somewhere," I lie. "I'm late." I grab her purse from her chair and push it into her arms.

She fumbles with her bag. "Well, when can we pick this back up?"

"I don't know. I'll call you." I lead her back to the front door and practically shove her through it.

She stumbles onto the porch but recovers quickly and smooths her shirt. "I'm going to hold you to that. I can be your best friend or your worst enemy. It's up to you. Personally, I think we'll be friends. You're a smart woman. You know I can help you. Share your story the right way." She points her long finger at me. "Between that car and those barrels, I see a George Polk Award in my future."

"Sounds good," I say in a rush and slam the door in her face. I spin around and take the stairs two at a time up to the second floor and don't stop until I'm in front of the television, fumbling with buttons on the VCR. I tap my hand on the side of my leg as I wait for the television to spark to life. He's alive, I keep repeating to myself.

The tape starts to play where I left off. Mama and Mabry are no longer on screen. Just the car. I stare at the image and minutes tick by. Come on. As I wait, I force my mind backward again, to the night on the Delaroux property. Travis and I were near the bayou. He handed me his keys and was about to leave when he looked in the window of the convertible.

"What about all this other stuff? You dumping that too?"

I followed his gaze to the piles of crap behind the front seats, items moved from the old car to this one. "Maybe we could put it in your truck."

"Fuck that. I'm not putting anything in my truck."

"Come on, Travis. We'll take it right to my aunts' house. I can't just leave it all in the car. It's our stuff."

He ran his hands through his hair. "I'm starting to freak out."

"*You're* freaking out? What about me?"

"I told you I'd help you, but I don't want to know anything else. I want to leave."

"Please, Travis."

His eyes darted around the property. He looked back at me. "Willa."

"Please."

He sighed. "Fine. I'll see if I can find something to put it in. But you're going to have to deal with it."

He returned a few minutes later, dragging garbage bags. "Here," he said. "Found these in one of the shacks." He handed one to me as I leaned behind the front seat.

We emptied everything from the car to his truck; then I turned to him and said, "Time for you to leave."

A loud bird whistles outside the upstairs window. My breath catches in my throat. The trunk. The trunk was *empty* that night. We emptied it. The bags I dragged home after leaving Travis's truck at his house.

Oh my God. Rita's right.

The screen changes in front of me. I concentrate on my breathing. I'm afraid if I don't, I'll hyperventilate. The car is moving. Not moving out of the parking space but moving side to side, like it's rocking in place. It's subtle, but it's definitely moving. Something moves in the cramped back area behind the driver's seat. A shadow under the industrial lights overhead. Then the driver's door flies open, and a man falls out onto the concrete. He lays on the ground for several seconds. Then he scampers up, looks around, and runs.

I stop the tape, hit rewind, and watch again. And again. And again. Until I'm convinced my eyes aren't playing tricks on me. He got out of the trunk. A wild laugh builds in my throat but comes out sounding more like an animal's cry.

Then I think of Travis mentioning the trunk to me. Raymond at the impound. *My guess is, they found something good.* Something was in that car when the police hauled it from the bayou, but it wasn't my mother's boss. *Thank you, God.*

I check the text from Charles LaSalle again, then check the time. The press conference at the bayou is about to start. I race downstairs to the kitchen, shut the door that's ajar again, grab my tote from the table, and head for the door.

◆ ◆ ◆

It's not hard to find the spot where the press conference is taking place. News vans fight for space along the dirt road adjacent to the levee. Same spot where my mother's car was pulled from the bayou. I park and follow the crowd to the top. A podium is set up below, by the water. A few reporters start to gather, Rita among them. She applies a fresh layer of lipstick. A cameraman hands her a mic, and she adjusts an earpiece in her ear. As I watch her, I think she was right, maybe we aren't so different. At least we wouldn't have been so different a week ago. Today, I'm not so sure.

Locals hover close, whispering. I look from group to group. A few I recognize: the woman from the antique store, Ermine and her group of friends, the missing teacher's parents; others I don't recognize. But all look concerned. Except for one. He's off by himself, watching from a distance. Doyle Arceneaux.

A blinding light assaults Rita's face from the top of a camera, and she beams in its harsh glare. She's speaking into her microphone, but

I'm unable to hear her words, only seeing the animated way she moves her face as her mouth forms those crisp, unaccented sound bites. The light extinguishes. Rita rolls her neck and looks around. She finds me in the back of the crowd and motions for me to come forward. I stay where I am. A slight shake of my head.

"Ladies and gentlemen." Chief Wilson's voice echoes in the podium microphone. The mic squawks back, and Travis steps forward, adjusts it, and steps back. His face is blank, unreadable, and he doesn't catch my gaze. He keeps his eyes trained on the television crews who are pulsing inward.

"Ladies and gentlemen," the chief repeats. "As you know, we have made an arrest in the case involving the barrels found in Broken Bayou. Also this morning, we have some new developments, and the lead investigator with the Louisiana State Police, Tom Bordelon, is here to discuss those details further. Tom."

The chief looks to the man standing next to him. A man I'd seen on the television at Taylor's Marketplace a couple of days ago. He steps forward. He's wearing tan cargo pants and a crisp white shirt with a shiny badge attached. Today he is also wearing a large brown cowboy hat, which brings to mind the images I'd seen on that old videotape. A tape I purposefully left at home today. I don't want to give up the only evidence of what really happened. So I'll make a copy first, before I hand it over to the police.

Then my mind turns to Mabry. She and Mama didn't know the man Mama heaved into that trunk had survived. I reach for my cell as a voice booms through the microphone.

"Good morning, everyone. Thank you for being here with us today. Since the first barrel was found here, we have utilized volunteers, watercraft, and diving teams to conduct a methodical search of Broken Bayou. To date, five 55-gallon steel drum barrels have been recovered, all containing human remains. Thankfully, and miraculously, four of the victims have been identified. Those four were in the missing persons registry. As you can imagine, it has been extremely hard on the families of these victims. I ask that we continue to give these families space." He pauses to look at each reporter, pausing at Rita a little longer than the others. "Also, Walter Delaroux from West Feliciana Parish has been arrested in connection with these barrels. He's been in police custody since Tuesday and was formally charged today."

Chills dance across my skin despite the heat. The man whose property I snuck onto that night I dumped Mama's car.

The lead investigator continues, "Mr. Delaroux lived in Broken Bayou most of his life before moving recently. Each barrel found has a removable bolt-lock lid. Each lid contains a hole, and all were open when found. We believe this is how the barrels filled with water when submerged. Also, sand was found in two of the more recent barrels. We believe it was also used to help with submersion. In addition to the barrels, we have also recovered two vehicles from the bayou." I straighten. Two? "One vehicle was recovered last Sunday. The second was recovered just this morning." A murmur ripples through the crowd as Tom Bordelon continues, "Based on clothing and items found inside, as well as the description of the car, we are confident the body discovered behind the wheel is Katharine Boudreaux, whose parents reported her missing back in April. Currently, we do not believe she was the victim of foul play." I search the crowd and see the Boudreaux couple huddled together off to the side. The mother is crying, and the father is stoic, exactly how they looked when I saw Rita interview them on the levee. The father had seemed off to me. Unattached. And as I watch, he pulls something from his pocket, puts it in his mouth, and swigs from the water bottle in his other hand. He's not stoic. He's medicated.

The investigator continues, "We will continue with our investigation and keep the public informed of any new developments. Thank you."

"Is it true the plates were missing from both vehicles found in the bayou?" Rita yells.

"That's correct. We identified Ms. Boudreaux's vehicle by the VIN number."

"But the other car hasn't been identified?" she adds.

"Correct. It was in the water much longer; therefore, the VIN eroded."

Another reporter shouts a question. "What evidence do you have that Walter Delaroux is a suspect? And are you considering him a serial killer?"

"A tip was called in, and that tip led to Mr. Delaroux's arrest. There are also records indicating Mr. Delaroux reported several barrels missing from his property, starting back in early 2002. Claims we now believe to be false. And, yes, we are certain these crimes are serial offenses."

"Why are you so sure Katharine Boudreaux's death is not foul play?" Rita says.

"There are clear indications it was an accident."

Another reporter says, "What are the dates the barrels were dumped in the bayou?"

"As of now, we can only go off when the victims were reported missing. We have sent all the remains to the forensic pathologist at the state crime lab in Baton Rouge for further analysis. We are also grateful to Senator Fonteneau for all of her help in expediting this investigation." He nods toward a somber woman on his side, and she nods back.

Chief Wilson steps up and holds up his hand. "That's all the questions for today. Thank you."

"Chief," Rita yells. "What's the license plate number for the car pulled out this morning?"

The investigator checks his notes and reads off a license plate number from the sheet of paper. I choke on my next breath.

Rita shouts, "Is it true human remains were found in the first vehicle as well?"

I switch from choking to not breathing at all.

"No comment," Bordelon says. "Thank you, folks."

Human remains. As much as I don't want to believe it, there's no way Rita would offer that up without a damn good reason. Besides, Travis's reaction over the trunk and Raymond's comment at the impound back up her statement. That sickening reality also tells me Travis and I were not alone on that property after all. Someone had been there, lurking, watching. Waiting to hide something of their own.

People file past me. The press conference is over. But I stay rooted to my spot, scanning my memory of that night. I'd pushed the car into the water with Travis's truck, then backed out and drove off as fast as I could, leaving the car to sink. I fix my eyes on the muddy water of the bayou below. What if the car hadn't sunk? What if the back end had been left exposed? An opportunity created for the man who lived on that property.

I pull out my phone as I turn away from the bayou and head back over the levee. I check the time.

No more waiting.

Chapter Sixteen

Cold stale air greets me inside the small front room of the Broken Bayou police station. It's still brown. Still outdated. The same woman still sits behind the big brown desk, her bouffant a little messier than the first time I saw her. She looks exhausted. Holding up one short finger, she motions for me to have a seat. The options for having a seat are a row of brown plastic chairs. And in the last one sits Charles LaSalle II. He rises when he sees me, straightens his pale suit. It's time to get this errand over with.

"Ms. . . . Dr. Watters," Charles says, holding out his hands.

I hope calling him was a good idea. He's not a criminal lawyer, but at least he can be a presence if I need him. I told him everything. About the car, the supposed insurance money, about who helped me dump it. The license plate and who I believed left it. I did not tell him about my mother's boss. Or about the videotape. Not yet. He explained how my coming into a police station with a lawyer will not look good. I'll look guilty. I told him I still wanted him there. So he asked for one dollar to retain his services and told me to let him talk first so he can neutralize that from the start.

I watch Charles wringing his hands and hope to God he can actually do that.

"Willa?" I look up and see Travis standing by the front desk. His eyes dart to Charles. "What's going on?"

"I came to talk to Chief Wilson."

"And you brought a lawyer?"

"Just to be safe."

Travis shoots Charles a look of utter bafflement, then refocuses on me. "Can I talk to you for a minute?"

"I don't think that's—" Charles starts, but I cut him off.

"It's fine."

Charles looks wounded, like he was denied a moment to shine.

Travis leads me to the far side of the room. Margie has finished her call, and she watches us with hawk eyes.

His voice is low in my ear. "What the hell are you doing?"

"I need to talk to the chief."

He shakes his head. His voice is steady and smooth. "I want to help you, Willa. But you showing up with him"—he points to Charles—"doesn't look good. Is there something you're not telling me?"

"No, I just thought it would be best to have someone with me. I've never done this before."

"All right. I get it." Travis's eyes are accented by dark circles. His skin looks sallow and more wrinkled than I remember. But mostly, it's his voice that's different. I hear the stress in it. "But help me here. We cleaned out that trunk. Right? Remember?"

"Yes, we did," I say, glancing at Margie, who seems to be engaged in stacking papers. "That car was empty when I put it in the bayou."

"Well, the trunk wasn't empty when it came out." He releases a long breath.

"Travis, what if that car didn't sink all the way? What if someone else had been there? Seen an opportunity and took it. I don't remember seeing anyone when I left, but that doesn't mean I was alone."

Travis studies me. "The only person that would have been there is Walter Delaroux, but something's not adding up for me."

I glance at the brown paper bag I brought in with me. "There's something else that doesn't add up."

"What?"

I point to the bag on the chair next to Charles. "Someone left that teacher's license plate in a bag on my front porch."

What little color he had in his face drains away. "What the fuck? When?"

Margie darts a look in our direction.

"Yesterday."

"And you didn't call me?"

"I thought it was my mother's plate."

"Either way, you should have called me."

I realize now I probably should have. But so much has happened since yesterday, the plate got lost in the shuffle. "I'm telling you now."

Travis looks up. "Walter Delaroux has been in custody since Tuesday. We pulled him in on some outstanding warrants to get him off the streets, then charged him this morning."

"Then someone else had that license plate," I say.

"Shit."

"Also, I saw an old truck yesterday morning, before finding the bag."

He rolls his neck. "You didn't happen to get the license number on that truck, did you?" I hear the dejection in his voice. He already knows the answer.

I shake my head. "But . . . it sort of looked like Doyle's truck."

"Christ." He closes his eyes a moment, opens them. "Are you sure? I mean, really sure? Did you see him actually set a bag on your porch step?"

I shake my head. "No. But it sounded like Doyle's truck. You know, missing a muffler."

"Hell, Willa, half the trucks in this parish are missing mufflers." He frowns. "No way. No fucking way."

"Travis." I tread lightly. "Maybe you could just talk to him."

"Fine."

"And," I add carefully, "maybe I could be there when you do. I'd like to talk with Eddie too."

He tilts his head. "I get it, Dr. Willa. You think you can analyze those two? Good luck. Many have come before you and failed. Do yourself a favor and save your energy for people you can actually help."

I understand his cynicism. The trickle-down of mental illness is toxic to families. I see he's getting uncomfortable, but if uncomfortable bothered me I wouldn't have a job. A thought is shaping itself in my head. It could have been Doyle's truck in the driveway yesterday morning, but Doyle may not have been driving it. Eddie seems the more likely person to leave something for me. Eddie likes giving me gifts. But why would he give me that one? And I'm not even sure Eddie can drive. "I'd still like the opportunity to visit with them. Especially Eddie."

Travis glances at his lap and sighs. "Oh, Willa, you and I are not so different. We both come from fucked-up families where our job was to protect our siblings. But don't bother with my brothers. I can handle them. Okay?"

I nod. He's still protecting them. But my instinct says he shouldn't be protecting Doyle. I can't quite put my finger on it, but I sense it. It's triggering a skill I learned as a child, watching my mother. I could sense her mood shifting, feel the energy coming off her body like a radio frequency. I could time it almost to the second when she would snap. Doyle is like that. Close to breaking. I see it in his body language. His eyes. Something bad is coming.

"Dr. Watters." Chief Wilson waddles into the room, holding a cup of coffee and a stack of papers. "Ready?"

Travis sighs. I can see he's worried. He should be. Because of me, he may lose his job today. But I have to do this and do it without protecting Travis. I'm already protecting too many people as it is.

Charles jumps from his seat and walks to the chief's side. I grab the bag from my chair and follow them down the hallway, feeling Travis's stare on the back of my neck like a hot poker. I say a silent apology to him, but if I'm going to talk about the night I dumped that car, his name has to come up. Raymond walks up the hallway toward us. He grins at me, then gives me an odd look as Chief Wilson escorts me into a side room.

I expect an interrogation room like the ones I've seen in cop shows. Gray metal chairs, one-way glass, a swinging light overhead. Instead, Chief Wilson leads us into a neat, organized office. The papers on the desk are stacked in precise piles next to a laptop computer. The room almost seems sterile. Travis follows us in and drops into the chair behind the desk. I see the nameplate on the desk. Shit. We're in his office. My guess is the chief knows Travis and I have history and thinks this would be a more comfortable setting for me to open up. What he doesn't know is this will make it even harder. I sit in the one chair opposite Travis while the chief stands and sips his coffee. Charles lingers behind me since there are no more chairs in the room.

Chief Wilson says, "Can I get anyone some coffee or water? It's going to take a few minutes to get the state investigator here. Thought it'd be better if we wait for him to get started. Margie called him when you came in."

Charles and I say yes to coffee, and the chief returns with two cups.

The four of us stare at each other in the quiet room. Even though no words are spoken, an electric current courses through the air, and my skin tingles. The longer we sit, the more I want to say forget it. I made a mistake. I sense Chief Wilson knows what I'm thinking, and he starts up a conversation about Shadow Bluff and the Aunts and how the old house could be refurbished into something grand again. I nod and play along, but my mind is racing.

Finally, the door swings open, and the man I saw at the news conference steps in, wearing a button-down shirt, khakis, and dusty cowboy boots. He extends his hand to me. "Tom Bordelon. I'm the chief investigator for the state on this case. I'll be visiting with you today." He looks around the room. "Chief, Travis." He stops at Charles and nods. Charles nods back. Tom Bordelon pulls in a chair from outside the room and settles next to Travis beside his desk.

"Gentlemen," Charles says, "I have instructed my client to tell you everything she knows. She's here to provide information only. And I'm only here to make sure she gets immunity if needed."

The chief sets his coffee down. Travis gives me a slight nod. He knows what's coming.

The investigator puts a recorder on the table. "I'll be recording this and taking notes." He says the date, August 19, all our names, and then asks me to start at the beginning.

"Before I start, I want to make sure my mother and I . . ." I glance at Charles. He nods. "Get immunity."

"Well, I can't guarantee that until I know what you're going to tell me," Tom says. "You just have to trust me. I'll do what I can."

"I dumped a car in the bayou almost two decades ago. I was a stupid teenager and dumped it so my mother could get the insurance money. That car was the first one you pulled out of the bayou."

Tom nods, leans forward. "Dr. Watters, I don't care one bit about some insurance scam from almost two decades ago. That's off the table. You don't need to worry about that." He cocks his head to one side. "What you do need to worry about, however, are the human remains found in that car's trunk."

My body goes cold. I feel Charles staring at me. "I had no idea about that. I promise you that car was empty when I pushed it in the bayou."

"Do you have proof?"

"Yes," I say quickly. "A videotape."

"I'd like to see it," Bordelon says.

Charles clears his throat behind me. Travis raises his eyebrows. So much for my plan to keep that quiet for now.

"Of course," I say to Bordelon, straightening. "I'm sorry, I didn't think to bring it with me."

Bordelon looks to the chief, then back to me. "Well, we'll need you to bring it in as soon as possible." He adjusts his chair. "For now, tell me about when you dumped the car."

I readjust in my chair, shoot a quick glance to Travis, who nods. "I was seventeen. My mother, sister, and I were visiting our aunts here in Broken Bayou. My mother got a new car. A convertible. I've since learned it was a gift from her boss, Zeke Johnson. A guy she worked for part time while we were here." I forge on. "One night, my mother asked me to get rid of the car. She said we needed money, and she could claim the car was stolen and get insurance money for it. So I got rid of it."

Tom says, "Why would your mother ask you to get rid of it? Why wouldn't she get rid of it herself?"

I look him in the eyes. "Because I was a minor. She said if I got caught, I'd just get a slap on the wrist."

He nods. "And did your mother report the car stolen? Did she ever receive insurance money for it?"

"I don't think so. She said she did, but Mama said a lot of things. She's bipolar and, at the time, a serious alcoholic." Images come back to me. The open and empty safe in the back office. The wad of cash in the glove box of the old station wagon she got back. "What I actually think is she stole from her boss."

Tom scratches at his face, rubs his chin. "Okay, let's fast-forward. She's asked you to get rid of her car. You've agreed. Now what?"

This is where it's going to get tricky for Travis. I sneak a peek at him but can't read his expression. I look at Tom. "I walked to where my mother left the car, and then I went to a friend's house and asked for help. Then I drove the car to Walter Delaroux's farm."

Tom leans forward. His eyes widen. "Walter Delaroux who's in custody for the barrel murders?"

I nod.

"Who was the friend?" Tom says.

I rub my brows, take a breath. Sorry, Travis. "Before I say his name, I want you to know he had no idea what I was up to. He was only helping me because I begged him to. He left his truck for me to use to push the car in, and he walked away before I ever dumped the car." I add, "And we cleaned the car out, even the trunk. There was nothing in that trunk. Nothing. I swear."

"What's his name? Your friend."

I swallow, then point to Travis. "Travis Arceneaux."

The chief whips his head to the side. "Travis?"

Travis nods. His eyes find mine. I mouth the word *sorry*.

Tom looks at the chief. "Maybe you better take Travis down to your office. I'll be down in a minute."

As Travis follows the chief out, his hand grazes my shoulder. A light touch, a simple squeeze that tells me it's okay.

Once he's gone, Tom turns his attention to me again. "Were either of you ever alone with the car?"

"Only me."

"Did you see the car sink?"

I shake my head. "I don't think it had sunk all the way by the time I left. I could only push it so far. There's something else." I place the brown bag I've had in my lap onto the desk. "It could be evidence."

Tom excuses himself and returns wearing gloves. He opens the bag and pulls out the license plate. Studies it a minute, then looks at me. "Where did you get this?"

"Somebody left it on my doorstep yesterday."

He returns the plate to the bag. "Did you touch it?"

I nod.

"We'll need to get your prints then," he says. "So we can keep them separate from any others on here."

I nod again.

Tom sits up straight, rolls his neck, removes his gloves. "Okay, we're going to start over. From the beginning. I want every detail of the night you dumped the car and the morning you found that missing license plate at your door. And anything in between you think is relevant. Hell, even if you don't think it's relevant."

I start talking again. I repeat the story of the night I dumped the car. I tell him about the videotape, about what I saw on it. Then I fill him in on the morning I found the plate. The truck, the missing muffler.

"It sounded like Doyle Arceneaux's truck," I say.

Tom leans back. "Travis's brother?"

I nod.

"Why do you think he'd do that?"

"I have no idea, but something about him scares me."

"I'll keep that in mind," he says, but I can hear in his voice he's blowing me off.

Charles clears his throat behind me. I jump. He's been so quiet I'd almost forgotten he was in here with us.

"My client," he says, "is highly trained in human behavior. She does not mention Mr. Arceneaux for no reason. I've done a little digging, and I can confirm he has a long history of trouble with the law. Everything from drunk and disorderly to impersonating a cop. A person who dons a police uniform and pretends to be a person of authority is a problem."

I glance back at him and smile. Nice job, Charles.

"Hang on." Tom excuses himself again and returns with a thick tattered folder. He sits back down and places his hand on it. "Colorful guy."

I look back at Charles again, then to Tom Bordelon. "Do you think I need to be concerned for my safety? Should I have someone watching the house or something?"

"Look, Dr. Watters, this is a small town with an even smaller budget. We have all of our resources focused on this case. We don't have the manpower to provide protection. All I can recommend is if you find yourself in trouble, call 9-1-1."

"Or I could leave town," I say, and the expression on his face tells me that won't be an option.

"I'm going to need you to stay put. You understand, don't you?"

After all I've said, I'm thankful he's not putting cuffs on me right now. I sound guilty or, at the very least, involved. Asking me to stick around at least indicates he's going to let me walk out of here.

"Of course," I say.

He asks for my cell number and all possible ways he can find me if he needs me. I give him Shadow Bluff's address, and Charles gives his number as well. Then we're allowed to leave.

I thank Charles and walk to my car. I pull out my cell to text Travis but stop myself. He'll call me when he can. Until then, I wait.

◆ ◆ ◆

Night has finally fallen on this day. Cicadas and crickets and bullfrogs create a symphony around the house. The porch creaks under the rocker as I rock slowly back and forth, sipping on tea this time instead of wine and feeling the memories of Broken Bayou wrapping around my neck like a noose. Has it only been hours since Rita Meade showed up on this porch?

I stare at my cell. Travis hasn't called. The avalanche that's been coming for me feels like it's finally landed. Another sip, and I close my eyes. I allow myself to go back in time again, away from the present. To my last birthday here. That day started and ended so differently. Mama's mood shifting from light to dark like an eclipse. It started with cake and laughter and ended with her asking me to cover up a crime. A crime that, thank God, didn't happen.

The day after, the Aunts dragged Mabry and me out of bed early. Said we had to go to the bayou to meet the reverend. Like they knew a sin had been committed and needed atoning. We wore handsewn white dresses, mine way too short because Pearl forgot I was seventeen, not seven. Reverend Beaumont Delaroche waited for us in the hot muddy water with his bulbous nose and tattered Bible, promising he'd save our souls as we waded out to him. He held our arms a little too tightly as he muttered some strange words, then shoved us below the surface. I thought on the walk home I'd feel different. I only felt confused. Then I delivered Mabry back to Mama's room like she requested. The television blaring drama and scandal. Mabry climbed into her bed still dripping bayou water and curled into Mama's side.

Mama turned her almond eyes to me. "I told those crazy aunts of yours baptizing y'all was a bad idea. It's all a bunch of hogwash. They're trying to make y'all something you ain't. No saving you two. Y'all got my blood in your veins." Mabry whimpered, and Mama pulled her closer and went back to staring at the television, a plume of smoke snaking from her lips. "Get cleaned up, Willamena. Pack y'all's things. When preachers get involved, it's time to get the hell out of Dodge."

I open my eyes, set my cup down, and cover my face. A lump lodges in my throat, and I breathe in hot night air in order to dislodge it. After several breaths, I open my phone and punch Mabry's number. Her laugh. Her voicemail. I hang up and say out loud to the darkness in front of me, "You did nothing wrong, Mabry. I know the truth now."

I hang up. Happy birthday to me.

November 2014

Mary Duncan searched the crowd at the Louisiana Renaissance Festival for her husband. He'd told her coming to Hammond would be fun. Big fun, he'd said. So far, she'd ruined her new sneakers in a huge mud puddle, been briefly trapped in a horrendous Port-O-Let, and accosted by a court jester juggling flaming sticks. She'd seen enough feathered hats, jingling scarves, and Irish wolfhounds for one day. This was not her idea of fun. It was time to go home.

A large crowd filed through the sloppy makeshift street toward the back of the expansive property. Mary joined them, opening the pamphlet in her hand. The joust started in ten minutes. Of course. That's where Harold would be. She fought her way through the bottleneck of people at the crystal tent, then came to a complete stop by the food court. Turkey legs and odd selections of meat were being advertised from every booth. Gross.

Mary searched for a way around the crowd.

"Excuse me, ma'am," a man beside her said. "There's a way through just over here."

She looked where he was pointing and saw a gap between the sides of the tents.

"Thank you," Mary said, relieved.

"Follow me," he said.

But when she followed him, she found herself on the outside of the festival.

He stopped and faced her. "Say cheese."

He took her picture with a Polaroid camera. "What are you doing?"

He leaned in like he was going to tell her a secret, and that's when she felt something sting the side of her neck. She yelped and rubbed the spot. A wasp sting was exactly what she didn't need right now. Her head swam; her legs started to shake.

"Here, let me help you."

Mary leaned into his shoulder. Her vision blurred. And right before she passed out, she managed to say, "Thank you, Officer."

Chapter Seventeen

I start the coffee and check my phone. 6:00 a.m. My back aches from the small bed upstairs, and I wonder how many more nights I'll be in it. The investigator asked me to stick around. But he didn't say for how long. Still no calls or messages from Travis. But there is a voicemail from Bordelon. He needs the tape. I release a slow breath. Even though I know there's nothing incriminating on it, actually the opposite, I still feel the need to keep it safe from others. But that's the animal-instinct part of my brain. The part that still believes I'm protecting something. Today I let it go.

Back upstairs, I slide the video into the slot, rewind it, and press play. At the same time, I aim my cell phone at the screen and start recording. I sit through it all again, thankful I know how it ends. When it's over, I eject the tape and slip it into my tote. Then I return to the kitchen, to my coffee.

I push my tangled hair off my face and wind it into a messy knot and check my other messages. Amy's called and left a text message. I need to call her, fill her in. But the thought of trying to explain all this to her makes me even more tired than I already am. I open her text and exhale a loud breath.

Christopher's ex isn't pushing it any further. Especially after this was posted. Take a look. When are you coming home!

At least something good has happened. I click the link and watch an amateur video of a woman and a screaming child in a grocery store. The Sack and Save. Charlie. The stock boys who'd been videoing. Charles LaSalle had reposted their reel, tagged my podcast's account, and captioned it: This is the real Dr. Willa. Something shifts inside of me. The knot of anxiety around my career loosens slightly.

I pour another cup of coffee and turn to the sketchbook I snagged on my way downstairs. I woke up thinking about it, about Mabry's sketches. My subconscious at work while I slept.

I pull the cover open and thumb through the drawings, stopping at the last picture. The one I saw when I first opened this book. The little girl with a finger over her mouth, like she has a secret. The boy with her. Looking at it now, with less anxiety to cloud my view, it hits me. The eyes, narrow, set far apart. The jawline. This little girl is not little at all. She's frail, sick. And she's an Arceneaux. I run a finger over the sketch. Emily.

The image is so lifelike that it feels like something Mabry saw. A moment captured. But what moment? From the looks of the drawing, a secret one. Maybe, like me, Emily snuck out to see a boy, more than once. And on this occasion, Mabry was there as well, watching them. A little mouse in the shadows. It seems she was out of my sight more than I remember. I wasn't as in control of her as I thought.

Ermine mentioned Emily's illnesses and rumors of Liv Arceneaux feeding poison to Eddie. Just rumors, but that type of thing is not unheard of. MSBP. Munchausen syndrome by proxy. Caregivers who create illness in the one they are caring for. Sometimes they go too far. I look at the sketch again, and goose bumps cover my arms.

I rinse my mug in the kitchen sink and catch my reflection in the window above it. Wild hair and sad eyes, like Mama looked on our last full day at Shadow Bluff. It was the day after our baptism. Mama's room was quiet and dark and smelled like cinnamon and cloves with an undercurrent of smoke and booze. Two lumps slept under the covers, one larger, one smaller. Mabry lay on her side, hugging a pillow. No way I'd let her get sucked into the vortex of a Krystal Lynn spiral. Only one family member was allowed to come apart at a time. That member was always Mama.

Mabry stirred and opened her large eyes. She blinked at me and immediately started to cry. Then she whispered, "Okra."

"Shhh." I patted her small shoulder. "Come with me."

I pulled Mabry's hand, but Mama's long slender arm snaked from under the bedspread and wrapped around Mabry's waist.

"Don't you take my baby." Mama spoke with her eyes still shut.

"Something's scaring her," I said.

Mama opened a crusty eye. "*You're* scaring her." She wormed her way into a seated position, snatched her cigarettes from the bedside table, and balanced one in between her lips. She flicked her lighter and inhaled.

Mabry started to cry harder.

At the exact same time, Mama and I said, "Oh, stop crying."

Mabry blinked.

"Get up," I said to Mama. I pulled Mabry from the bed. "We're getting the hell out of here."

"Look at you gettin' all bossy."

"You're the one who said when preachers get involved, it's time to leave."

"Yeah, but I'm tired now." She fell back onto her pillow.

"Too bad."

I flung the sheets off her, and she yelled, "Hey!" The tops of her legs were as bruised as her face.

"Get up, Mama. It's time to start acting like a grown-up."

She shuffled into this very kitchen, barefoot and wearing a robe, her hair a greasy tangle, her eyes puffy slits.

"Well, lookee who decided to grace us with her presence?" Petunia sniffed at Mama.

"You know, you girls should have been in church with us today," Pearl said to me. "Reverend talked about Proverbs eleven. 'Whoever troubles his own household will inherit the wind, and the fool will be the servant to the wise of heart.'"

Mama plopped into a chair. "Got any coffee?" Her voice came out like that of a raspy lounge singer.

I placed a cup in front of her.

Mama looked up at me. "Creamer?"

"You can drink it black."

Mama rubbed her nose and sipped.

Pearl and Petunia looked at one another. Pearl said, "We've been talking. Petunia and I."

Petunia said, "We're concerned."

"For the girls," Pearl finished.

"We . . . ," Petunia started.

"We . . . ," Pearl said.

Mama's eyes narrowed. "Oh, for Christ's sake, spit it out already."

"You need to clean up, Krystal Lynn," Petunia said. "This is why those girls don't have a daddy."

I studied Mama as she fished a cigarette from her robe pocket, lit it, and blew smoke into Petunia's face. No one mentioned our father. Ever.

"Of course," Petunia said, "you're just like her. Your mama was just as troubled as you are."

Mama's face hardened. This is another topic we never discussed, our grandmother, my aunts' sister. From the look on Mama's face, it was going to stay that way.

Pearl scowled. "If you don't watch out, someone's gonna take these girls from you."

"That right?" Mama said. "You wanna take 'em? Go ahead." She swirled her cigarette around. "You can have 'em." Mama laughed.

Mabry whimpered and looked at me with wide eyes.

I studied Mama. If she ended up like her mother, did that mean I'd end up like mine? Something hard in my stomach said there was no way I'd let that happen. "We'll be fine," I said to the Aunts.

Mama stopped laughing. Mabry tried to crawl into her lap, but Mama pushed her away.

"We need a car," I said to Mama.

"What happened to that fancy red car?" Pearl said.

"Got rid of it," Mama said, never breaking my gaze.

"Go get us a car," I said. "Now."

I exhale, turn away from my reflection in the kitchen window, and head upstairs. I can't stay in this house, waiting for Travis to call. There are too many things to think about here. I need to move. And there's someone I want to talk to.

Upstairs, I start to brush my hair, then realize how long it's been since I washed it. It's time to clean up. I shower, work leave-in conditioner through my hair, then detangle it, pulling a little harder than I should. When I'm done, I hop out, brush my teeth, and slide on the ugly orange boots. I forgo the silk shirts, though, for the wrinkled and stained T-shirt. Where I'm going, no one will give a shit what I'm wearing. Then I spot the VCR. The police station. I'm heading there after my stop. I glance down at my outfit. They won't give a shit, either, as long as I take them what they need. I grab my tote, checking to make sure the tape is still in it.

In my car, I open my phone and search a name until I find the address. Not that I really need it. Even though I've only been there a couple of times, I know exactly where it is.

I wait in front of Ace's Hardware until they open. I run inside, grab what I need, then pull back onto Main and follow my GPS to a potholed dirt road on the north side of town. It winds through dense woods until it dead-ends into a rutted dirt driveway. I stop and kill the engine.

The Arceneauxes' house is a sagging heap of bricks. A blue tarp covers part of the roof, and old cars in different states of disrepair fill the yard. Trash and weeds fight for dominance. Off to one side sits a grassy area covered in large pieces of playground equipment, sand piles, and discarded tools, and I remember Travis telling me Doyle's job involved building playground equipment for schools. Next to the equipment is a dilapidated shed that looks like a metal shop, a place Eddie could make his little metal dolls. I slide my car into park and stare at the dark house in front of me. This could be a stupid mistake, but I can't get the brothers off my mind. I debate again if I should have called Travis. But it's a little late for that now. I'm here. I need to follow my momentum.

The curtains on the front window move slightly. I make out the outline of a face before it disappears. They know I'm here.

My boots crunch across the dead, dry grass on my way to the front door. I pull the screen door open and knock. Nothing. I wait, knock again. The front door creaks open, and a waft of cigarette smoke assaults me. I pull back and stare at the tall thin woman in front of me. Her hair is stringy with sections of her pink scalp showing through.

"Mrs. Arceneaux?"

She inhales through withered, pale lips, exhales. "Yeah." She ashes her brown cigarette onto the floor. "Who are you?"

"My name is Dr. Willa Watters."

"We don't need no doctor."

She starts to shut the door, and I prop my foot against it. "I'm a . . . friend of Travis's. I wondered if I could talk to you and to Eddie?"

"No," she says and slams the door in my face.

A crow caws in the distance. I stare at the front door. Decision time. I can keep pestering these people and run the risk of having the cops called on me, which is definitely not the path I need to pursue. Or I can back off this porch and go back to Shadow Bluff and mind my own damn business.

"I want to talk about your daughter," I yell. Decision made. "I want to talk about Emily."

The door remains shut. I tell myself I'll count to twenty slowly, then I'll leave, but my mouth and brain seem to have disconnected. I yell, "I'm not leaving!" I give up trying to convince myself I'm going to do anything that resembles sane. My phone buzzes in my tote. I check the number. Mama's doctor. The front door opens again. I send the call to voicemail and look up, but Mrs. Arceneaux isn't standing there; Eddie is. His eyes are as dim as the space behind him. He moves his large frame away from the door, and I take this as an invitation to come in.

The living room, if it can be called that, is filthy with rotting food and overflowing cardboard boxes. The stench is sweet and thick and coated in cigarette smoke. Stacks of magazines lean in every corner. A torn leather sofa faces a giant television. Gaming controls cover the floor in front. The television looks as if it cost more than the entire house. I cover my nose with my hand and follow Eddie through the mess to the small kitchen.

Liv Arceneaux sits at a card table in a folding chair. The kitchen is only slightly neater than the living room. The sink is full of dirty dishes, and the walls are streaked with grime, but the card table is spotless. My mind scrolls through diagnoses, like someone flipping through an old-fashioned Rolodex. I land on several, OCD, hoarding, and depression among them. I wonder when those started. I wonder if losing her husband, her daughter, and if Ermine is right, a son, triggered it. Or was the state of this house a reflection of something that started long before? A slow-moving avalanche she couldn't escape from.

"Offer our guest a chair, Edward," Liv says.

Eddie pulls a folding chair out from the table and presents it to me like we're on a date. He smells like boiled cabbage. My stomach clenches as I sit.

Liv trains her gaze on me. "Why you talkin' about my little girl?"

I look at Eddie. He stands behind his mother and stares at the ceiling like it holds all the answers.

"I'm an old friend of Travis's. I came back to Broken Bayou to get some things for my mother, and we reconnected."

She scowls, lights another brown cigarette. A curl of blue smoke rises in front of her face. "Travis tell you he was a bed wetter?" The smirk on her face begs me to react, but I keep my composure.

Body language, vocabulary usually let me know who I'm dealing with pretty early on in a conversation. Liv has set a record. She let me know in only a matter of seconds. Thankfully my previous conversation with Ermine has me prepared for this woman, and I'm able to listen without flinching.

When I don't respond she says, "Travis never did right by this family. He left when we needed him most. He only thinks about himself."

I heard that same phrase before, from my own mother, when I finally got up the courage to move out. She railed on about how I made them follow me to Texas, and now I was abandoning them. If I hadn't had Christopher, I probably would have stayed. But good or bad, marrying him got me out of that house. Travis found his way out, too, and it's obvious he's not Liv Arceneaux's favorite child because of that.

"I'm here because I found a sketchbook of my sister's, and one of her drawings interested me." I reach into my tote and extract the sketchbook. I lay it on the flimsy table and open it to the sketch of the girl and boy. "Is this Emily? My sister drew this."

The sound that erupts from Eddie's mouth can only be compared to a suffering, dying animal. I jump, and my hand hovers near the opening of my tote for the other item I'd tucked in there. Mrs. Arceneaux's face contorts into a mask of grief.

"My baby," she wails. Her arthritic hand pets the picture. Tears well up in her eyes. She pulls the sketchbook closer. Her finger traces Emily's face, then stops on the drawing of the boy. Eddie snivels and wipes his runny nose. Liv studies the sketch. Then with one quick movement, rips the drawing from the sketchbook.

"You can't have her," she says, her voice full of venom. Then she tears the picture in half, separating the boy and Emily. She slides the half with the boy's image back to me.

A seed of anger blooms in my gut. Mabry drew that. It's not Liv's to take and destroy. I will myself not to react. "I would have offered it to you. All you had to do was ask." I take the sketchbook back.

Liv drops her cigarette onto the kitchen floor and crushes it with a filthy slipper. "The boys were all so jealous of her," she says, tracing the sketch. "She was perfect. Sometimes I pretend she's just run away and she'll be back."

"I'm sorry," I say. Even though it's been decades, her grief is still palpable, etched in every line on her face. Losing a child is the worst grief of all. Not that I've experienced it. But I've come close.

"Mrs. Arceneaux, I'm a child psychologist, and I have access to a lot of books that can help with grief. If you'd like, I'd be happy to send them to you."

Her face hardens. "It wasn't my fault."

I straighten, lean back. "I never said anything was your fault. I was just trying to help."

"I don't need your help." Her tone has changed to defensive and sharp. "You don't get to come in my house and start talkin' about Emily. Telling me I need help. Showing me pictures of my dead daughter. Who do you think you are?"

The kitchen grows silent except for a scratching noise somewhere down the dark hallway. I can picture the rat that's responsible, and I shiver. Time to wrap this up. I swallow, hold my hands up.

"I'm leaving." In the corner of my eye, I catch Eddie moving closer to me. I ease my chair back. "Well, thank you for—"

In a swift move, much swifter than I thought him capable, Eddie reaches my side and clamps a meaty hand on my shoulder. The weight of it speaks to his strength.

"Stay," he says.

I look up at him, keep my voice as steady as I can. "Take your hand off me, Eddie."

"Edward, don't scare the lady," Liv says, a smile on her lips.

He removes his hand but hovers close.

"I'm sorry about him." She points a finger at him, but nothing in her voice says she's really sorry. "Dumber than a fiddler crab. Show this nice lady out, Edward."

I look at the torn picture Mabry drew. Liv Arceneaux looks at it as well. Then she slides it toward me. I tuck it back in the sketchbook and follow Eddie to the front room. At the door, he rocks on his massive feet, and his eyes keep darting down the hallway. I follow his gaze. The air around me sizzles with a strange, unseen energy. Part of me is yelling to run and the other part is yelling to stay. I don't want to leave him alone with that woman.

"Do you want to tell me something, Eddie?" I say. He chews his bottom lip. "Have you been leaving gifts for me at Shadow Bluff?" I add.

He nods.

I smile. "Right. Tell me about the gifts."

He looks down the hallway again. "Show."

"You want to show me?" I say.

The air in this house is hot and sticky, but a shudder works down my spine as Eddie points to a closed door. I glance at the front door, then back down the hall. I slip the sketchbook into my large tote and fumble inside until I feel the cool handle of my handgun. Then I feel for the other things I stopped for on my way here.

"Show me," I say.

He does his best to tiptoe down the hallway. I follow. He slides a dead bolt open on the outside of the door.

"Keep her safe," he says.

The chill I felt earlier magnifies into a cold steel blade as Eddie opens the door and a whoosh of air sucks outward from a small bedroom. Like a seal has been broken. The room is clean. So far, the only clean room I've seen. A twin bed with a ratty pink blanket occupies one wall. On top is an old baby doll missing one arm and clumps of hair. A few of Eddie's metal dolls keep her company. There's one window on the back wall. The other walls are empty. No closet. No bathroom.

I walk in, past the door with the lock on the outside, my pulse quickening with each step. They'd locked Emily in here. Eddie barely fits inside the room with me. His towering stature reminds me to keep my distance. He could snap my neck in one move.

Eddie turns in tight circles next to me.

"Eddie." He stops spinning. I pull out the handful of metal trinkets I purchased from Ace's. I present the metal parts and pieces to him, nuts and bolts, screws, and scrap pieces Ace was happy to part with. He reaches for them, and I close my hand. "I tell you what. Every time you answer a question, I'll give you one. Okay?"

He nods.

I need to start simply. I look around. "Was this Emily's room?"

He nods. I hand him a metal piece. He slides it in his pocket.

"Do you miss her?" I say.

He nods again and gets another piece.

"Why did you want to show me her room?"

He covers his ears and lowers his head to his massive chest and starts to rock. I've gone too fast. "Eddie? Eddie?" He looks up and stares at me. "What was Emily's favorite color?"

"Pink."

I hand him a small metal bolt. "I like that color too." I point to the metal figures on the bed. "Did you make those dolls for her?"

He nods, and I drop a screw into his hand.

"You're very talented." I pause. "And thank you for sharing them with me." He smiles, and I swallow. "Why are you sharing them with me, Eddie?"

Eddie cocks his head to one side. He starts to rock again. "It's a secret." His voice is a childlike whisper. I hand him a bolt. Go slow.

"Can you drive, Eddie?"

He shakes his head no. Another bolt.

"Do you still ride your bike?"

A nod yes.

"Do you know where I'm staying in town?"

Another nod, another bolt. So Eddie could've ridden his bike to Shadow Bluff to leave the last doll on the porch, but whoever left the license plate was driving a truck.

"Do you know about something else left for me? A license plate maybe?"

He stops rocking. "It's a secret," he repeats.

"Do you know where the license plate came from?" I say.

It happens so quickly I almost miss it, but I'm studying him, looking for it. And there it is. His eyes dart to the far window. He backs away from me, and I walk over to the window and look out. Across the dry, dead grass, several yards away, is the discarded play equipment and the shed I saw when I pulled in. And behind that, jutting from the ground in the wooded area surrounding their land, is a single white cross. Maybe for a pet, maybe a memorial for where Emily was found. I shiver.

Something creaks behind me, and I turn. Eddie sits on the small bed, the frame groaning under his weight. He shakes his head. "She don't want to be alone," he says in a soft mumble.

"It's okay. I can help you, Eddie. I'm a doctor."

His body sways. "No help."

I study the metal dolls on the bed beside him, and an idea comes to me. Like the ones propped in the kitchen at Shadow Bluff, they remind me of a little family. And I've used dolls before in therapy with children who won't speak about their abuse. It's safer, less threatening. Play therapy is also very revealing. Children can only play things they know.

"Eddie." I glance at the dolls. "Would you like to play something? Maybe we could play house and family." I point to each individual doll. "One could be a boy. One could be the mother. One could be the brother."

Eddie shakes his head and doubles over. I think he's sobbing again until I see his hand fishing under the bed for something. I back up a step.

"Eddie?"

He falls to all fours on the floor and reaches deep under the bed, struggling to get to the darkest part. I bend over and watch. He drags a shoebox out and leans over and smells it. A deep, long inhale.

"What's that?" My pulse quickens.

"A gift."

I hand him another metal scrap. "Who gave it to you?"

"Brother." That's worth two bolts.

He opens the box, and I lean closer to see what's inside. Eddie jerks his head up, slams the lid on, and shoves it back under the bed. He starts to moan and rock.

"Eddie?" I bend down next to him, and he strikes out so quickly I can't avoid his hand. His open palm smacks the side of my face and knocks me to the ground. I'm used to patients slapping and lashing out when they get stressed or overstimulated, but they are children with small hands. Eddie is a very grown man, and his slap is something I've not experienced before. My cheek radiates pain, and I rub my jaw as I stand.

Eddie lumbers toward the bedroom door. "Hide."

"Hide?"

He shoves me out of the way with a straight arm, blocking the exit and looking into the hall, then back at me. "You hide."

"Me?"

"He won't like you here."

"Who?"

"Brother."

The front door slams shut. A man's voice carries to the back bedroom. "Looks like we got ourselves a visitor."

I know that voice. The inflection. Doyle is home.

I hear an exchange of voices in the front room. Eddie looks at me, terrified. "Hide," he says again. He leaps toward me, and the floorboards shake. He grabs my arms and tries to shove me behind the door. His fleshy paws dig into my shoulders.

"Eddie, stop!" I yell, trying to pull from his grip.

"Hide. Hide. Hide."

"No! Stop it." I manage to twist from his grip as Doyle knocks on the doorframe.

"Hello? Anyone home?" he says with a wicked grin.

Eddie freezes. I rub my arm as I work to steady my breathing.

"What we got here?" Doyle says, his eyes traveling from his brother to me, then to the tote where my hand is now once again on my gun.

"I was just leaving," I say.

"What're y'all talking about in here?" He stays in the doorway. He shoots a sideways glance at his brother.

"Emily," Eddie says.

Doyle turns his attention back to me. "You shouldn't be here."

"I said I was leaving." I try to move past him, but he blocks me again. "Doyle, let me leave," I say slowly. My heart rate is pounding as I think of him on the porch with that knife, as I watch him staring at me like I'm prey. I grip my gun tighter.

"What you got in there?" he asks, looking at my tote.

"You don't want to find out," I say.

I see his Adam's apple move as he swallows. He opens his mouth to say something, closes it, works his jaw back and forth. Whatever he was about to say, he keeps to himself. Instead, he moves only enough to let me by, and when I sweep past him, his hot whisper fills my ear. "Be careful."

I cross the filthy living room. Mrs. Arceneaux is on the front porch, still smoking. The sun is high and the humidity smothering.

Mrs. Arceneaux says, "Find what you were looking for?"

I don't answer. I make it to my car and fling open the door when the reed of a woman by the front door yells, "If you see Emily, tell her it's time to come home. You hear?"

I slam my SUV into gear and pull away from the Arceneaux house. Doyle, Eddie, and Mrs. Arceneaux stand by the door, and I watch them in my rearview mirror until they're nothing but ghosts.

Chapter Eighteen

The smell of the Arceneaux house lingers on my clothes as I park in front of the small police station. Margie looks up when I enter the front door. I called her on my way to let her know I was coming.

"He's waiting on you," she says, pointing down the short hall.

Tom Bordelon and Chief Wilson are sitting in the chief's office when I walk in. I place the security tape on the desk. Tom picks it up, and a part of me wants to grab his hand and stop him. Tell him to be gentle. Mabry's on there. Sweet, innocent Mabry. A fissure in my chest is starting to reopen.

"Anything else you need to share with us?" Tom asks.

"I'm worried about staying here. Is there any way I can go back to Fort Worth? If you need me, I promise I can get back here quickly."

Tom Bordelon shakes his head before I can even finish. "We need you to stay put. There's nothing to be worried about. We have a suspect in custody."

"What if that's the wrong suspect?"

"Dr. Watters," the chief says, disregarding what I said. "Thank you for bringing this tape to our attention. If we need you for anything else, we'll let you know."

In other words, shut up and get out.

"I don't feel safe here," I say to them.

The men exchange a look that tells me they are tiring of me.

"Lock your doors," Tom says. "Call 9-1-1 if you need us."

◆ ◆ ◆

As I sit in my car with the engine running, I pull out my phone and text Travis to please call me, then see my mother has called, many times. I haven't talked to her since watching the rest of the tape. She has no idea how that night ended.

Mama coughs in my ear when she answers.

"Hey, Mama."

She coughs again, and this one sounds deeper and full of phlegm. She moans after the fit passes. "Are you home?"

"Not yet." I glance at the police station. "We need to talk about someone. Zeke Johnson."

"Who?"

"Don't do that. We're way past pretending."

She clears her throat. "Well, what?"

"He's alive. He's serving time in a federal penitentiary."

A long silence fills the line. I wait.

"This sounds like a conversation we need to have in person," Mama says.

"That's not an option at the moment, so we're going to have it right now."

"You know people listen in on cell phone calls."

"The only person I need listening is you." I lower my voice even though it's just me in the car. "That night, and you know the one I'm talking about, your boss got out of the trunk. I watched the security tape. The whole tape. I saw it. I saw him get out of the car. And I saw who was driving, Mama. I know what happened. And I know you *knowingly* sent me there, as a child, to clean it up." That familiar hard-edged anger starts to worm its way into my gut, but instead of choking it down, I let it burn. Maybe it's time to feel that anger, set it free. Holding it inside may be good for my mother, but it's eating away at my core. Consuming me. I think of what I've told so many parents: It's okay to be angry.

"You sent me there to dispose of a body," I say, each syllable coming out in bitter spurts. "Your daughter. Your child. You were supposed to protect me, not send me into harm's way. What kind of mother does that?"

A deep, still silence follows. My breathing is ragged. I expect to feel slightly better, but I don't. I feel the same. Except now a new emotion creeps in, anger's twin, sadness. When Mama doesn't answer, I forge on. "The police down here know that car was yours. I went to the station yesterday with a lawyer."

"Good God, Willamena. Only guilty people hire lawyers." The phone shuffles as she works to cough something up. After everything I just said to her, that's all she can think to say back. I rub my face. Several seconds pass before she adds, "If what you told me is true about *him*, then sounds to me like there's nothing to talk about."

"Oh, there's plenty to talk about. Human remains were found in the car's trunk when it was fished out of the bayou."

I hear her wheezing across the miles. "But . . . what? You're confusing me. This doesn't make any sense."

"That's why I'm still here. That's why I'm staying here."

"Sweet girl, I'm tired. Whatever they found in that car has nothing to do with us. And the police are nothing but troublemakers, if you ask me. They've got a lot bigger fish to fry than you and me. I watch the news. I see what's going on down there. It's sick, and you need to leave that dirtbag town before you find yourself up in that bayou too. Who knows what other sickos are roaming around? It's not safe there."

Mama's right. It's not safe here. But here is where I have to stay. "I'll be careful."

"Willamena, this might be bigger than you." Her voice has lost its luster, its energy.

"Mabry thought she killed a man, Mama."

My mother gasps. "Shut your mouth. Don't say things like that."

"It's true." My chest tightens under the weight of that truth.

"I can't do this anymore, Willamena. Come home. I'm tired."

She sounds tired. She's come down. The lows are hard, no fun. I'll bet she's having a hard time getting out of bed in the mornings. I've got to start thinking outside of this zip code. Life is going on back at home. And like it or not, children aren't the only ones who need advocates. Sometimes parents do too.

"I'm going to call your doctor, Mama. Okay?"

It's like I can hear her nodding. In a sad whisper, she says, "Okay, sweet girl, you do that."

She hangs up. I immediately punch in her doctor's number. He's given me his cell, the saint of a man. I leave him a message and then back out and head toward Main. Nan's catches my eye, and my stomach growls.

The patrons inside Nan's all look shell shocked. I fit in nicely. I find a table in the back corner and settle in. A waitress arrives and turns over my coffee mug and pours coffee.

"Know what you want?" she says in a tired voice.

"Something greasy."

"Well, you come to the right place." She points to the plastic menu. "Special this morning is buttermilk biscuits with crawfish gravy and a side egg with hollandaise. Sound greasy enough?"

I can almost hear my arteries clogging. I hand the menu back to her. "Sounds perfect."

I study the room. Everyone has their heads down. Some are whispering as they look at their phone screens. I think about Travis and what he said yesterday about us not being so different. He's right. We'd been on parallel paths. Then the bayou spits up its carnage, and I come to town, and our paths collide again. I foolishly thought I could bury something and keep it buried. What a joke. Travis and I had both been so naive. He probably more so than me. I knew who I was dealing with. My mother. I understood, somewhere in the back of my mind, I shouldn't have helped her. Travis trusted me. And now his job is in jeopardy. And miraculously, mine isn't.

Broken Bayou has surpassed my on-air tirade. To the rest of the world, my moment in the social media glare is gone. Just like that. The notifications have slowed. The voicemails have stopped. Yet here I am involved in something much worse than viral videos.

I pull out my phone and type "Emily Arceneaux, Broken Bayou, death" into the search engine. The waitress tops off my coffee on her way to another table. I stare at my screen. Several hits come up, most for social media accounts. I scroll until I find an old newspaper article that grabs my attention. But it's not about Emily. It's about a man who drowned. I click on it. A picture of Travis's father pops up. As I read, I discover he'd been fishing with Doyle the day he died. Doyle said his father was drunk and slipped on the dock, hit his head, and slid into the water. Doyle jumped in after him, but it was too late. The drowning was ruled an accident.

Seems the sticky web surrounding this small town has another thread, and Doyle has my full attention. What if he knew I dumped that car years ago? Travis could have told him, or more likely, Eddie could have followed us and told him. But then what? Why would Doyle go to a half-sunk car in the middle of the night? I sit up straight and clank my coffee mug onto the table. To hide something.

In college when I worked with the sex offenders' group, I'd briefly studied forensic psychology. I knew enough to know serial killers get better with each kill. The first one is usually messy. Then they learn. I glance down at my phone. Emily was found in the woods. By Doyle. Their father died in the water. Doyle was there. Now, bodies, long buried, are coming out of that same water.

Someone clears their throat above me, and I jump and look up to see Charles LaSalle II. He's exchanged his bow tie for a purple-and-gold necktie today. He grins down at me.

"I saw you come in and wanted to say hello. How are you?"

I clear my throat, refocus on where I am. "Pretty good, I guess."

"I'm glad I was able to help you yesterday."

I'm not sure I'd call what he did helpful, but at least I had an ally. I nod.

"Listen, I really just wanted to come over and thank you."

"For what?"

"For little Charlie. What you said about him stayed with me. I called his pediatrician and got a recommendation for a testing center in Baton Rouge. We go next week." His pink cheeks grow even pinker.

I smile a real smile for the first time in days; then I frown. "Oh, Charles, I told you I'd help you with that. I'm sorry. I've been . . ."

"Busy," he says for me. "It's okay. We got it handled."

"I'm so glad. For you and for Charlie."

"Me too." He looks around, then back at me with sad eyes. "You know, my wife is talking about moving. Says little Charlie can't grow up in a town like this. I just . . . can't believe this is happening . . . here." He points to the floor. "I grew up here. My parents grew up here. My grandparents grew up here. Small-town living is in my blood. It's safe. You form relationships; you raise your children in a world where they can ride their bikes to the store without you thinking they got kidnapped. And now this." He looks around at the throngs of people crammed around us. "Makes me sick to my stomach."

"I understand. It's a lot to absorb."

He rubs his hands together. "Well, I didn't mean to go on and on and interrupt your breakfast. I just wanted to say thanks, and be sure to call me if you need any more legal help. I'll do what I can."

"Thank you as well, Charles. For reposting that video."

He smiles. "That's the least I could do."

I finish what I can of my breakfast, and as I exit Nan's, I freeze. A car is parked in the spot next to mine, the engine still running. Rita Meade sits behind the wheel, staring at me through the windshield. She smiles and waves. As if she's been waiting for me.

I let Rita follow me back to Shadow Bluff. I've seen the tape. I've talked to the police. Talking to Rita again pales in comparison. Besides, the last time we visited, she gave me more information than I gave her. Maybe she'll keep sharing.

I steer off Main onto the road to Shadow Bluff. The oak-lined path feels more like a rabbit hole. One that's swallowing me up. The lack of sleep recently isn't helping, but it's more than that. It's a sadness for the young girls and women murdered and dumped in the bayou. For their loved ones who have suffered through the constant news coverage along with their grief. A sadness that is finally settling in after days of being distracted with my own problems. And then there's Walter Delaroux. The police obviously had enough evidence to arrest him, but what if they're wrong? Someone left that license plate for me, and it certainly wasn't Walter Delaroux. Rita may be able to shed some light on that. Not that she's the overwhelming expert, but she may have the answers I need. And in return, I'll give her the answers she needs. The first step toward unburdening myself.

Bright patches of sunlight dot the oystershell drive. My head feels as full of shadows as the front yard. My heart feels dark. My body aches from the inside out. Memories of Mabry and Mama float through my mind like dandelion seeds, and I let them glide by without grabbing on to any. Even the sweet ones. I'm too fragile for them at the moment.

At some point, I'll tie this all up and go back to the life I left in Fort Worth. But what is that life going to look like? Me coiffed and smiling and ready to dole out advice to the masses? I can't see it. And of all the frightening things I've encountered over the last few days, this one frightens me the most. For years, decades, I pictured it. I saw myself climbing the ranks. I saw myself being my own boss and helping as many people as possible. Being successful and in complete control. But those visions are starting to drain of all color and clarity. Success at this point would be getting out of this town without being arrested.

I park in front of the house, and Rita follows me up the front-porch steps. Inside, I direct her to the right. She finds a seat on the sofa in the front room.

In the kitchen, I start a pot of coffee and study Eddie's metal dolls on the counter. Something dances on the edge of my memory, but I can't quite grasp it. Something about that house, about the shoebox clutched in Eddie's massive hands, about Doyle in the doorway, telling me to be careful.

I pour two cups and take them with me to the front of the house. I settle in next to Rita and set our coffees on the table. The room is warm and full of light, but I still feel a chill. She's looking at me with eyes that know more than they should.

"Thanks for letting me in," she says. "Again." She smiles.

Rita is a mixed bag for me. Some salty, some sweet. I need to be careful with her, but something feels genuine about her. I hear it in her voice. "I figured if I didn't, you'd just be back tomorrow."

"And the next day," she adds with a smile.

We sit for a minute in silence; then I say, "Look, I don't know where to start."

Rita crosses her legs and leans forward. She takes her phone from her bag and sets it on the coffee table. "I know where to start." She glances at the recorder on her phone, then to me. I nod.

"I like you, Dr. Watters," she says. "I like your podcast. I like your book. I don't want to hurt your career in any way whatsoever. I only want to cover this bayou story. And even though you're not the whole story, you're part of it."

"Yes, I am."

"Let's start with why you're part of it, and then, after, I'd like to talk about something else. Something that may be a lot more uncomfortable for you."

I'm not surprised. I know what she really wants to talk about. I've been questioned about it before. I can do this. I *need* to do this. I swallow the knot forming in my throat. "I'm ready."

Rita straightens her shoulders. "I know you spoke with the lead investigator yesterday. Had that lawyer with you."

"News travels fast here."

She tilts her head. "I make sure of that."

I remember her saying she had a source at the police station, and a vision of the woman at the front desk pops into my head. Margie. "Margie makes sure of that," I say.

Rita shrugs. "I know you dumped that first car in the bayou a couple of decades ago. But I don't believe you dumped it with a body in the trunk. I've spent my entire career talking to guilty people. You're not guilty of that. But you are hiding something."

"Aren't we all," I say, brushing aside the image of the videotape.

"Will you tell me about the car?"

I sip my coffee. I've already told the police. Telling Rita is second fiddle now. The words I spoke to my mother circle back to me: *Start at the beginning.*

I rewind the clock to that summer and replay the same story I told the investigator. Rita listens intently, without interrupting. I finish with the license plate left on my porch steps. She looks off a minute, then says, "Do you have any idea who left it on your porch?"

"I have an idea."

"Interesting. Someone is either trying to scare you or send you some type of message, and I doubt it's the man they have in jail. He's not the type of guy to have connections on the outside to do dirty work for him. The cops have had a hard time tying Walter to your car. Knowing it was dumped on his land will help, but the license plate showing up here creates a problem connecting him to the teacher's car."

"I thought the investigator said the teacher's death was an accident. At the press conference by the bayou."

Rita's eyes brighten. "No way she's a coincidence. She could have had an accident, sure. But something about it doesn't sit right with me. And it doesn't sit right with the police either. They're just not ready to say why."

"What do you know about Walter Delaroux?"

Rita shifts on the sofa. "Who's interviewing who here?"

I raise my eyebrows.

She takes a sip from her coffee, sets it down, and continues, "Old Walter has been in and out of jail since he was eighteen. Mostly petty stuff. And even though the police haven't connected him to all the victims, they have connected him to the actual barrels. They're his. He claimed they were stolen years ago, but there's no proof. And Walter's been caught dumping in the bayou before. Fertilizers and chemicals from his farm. The problem at this point seems to be motive. Some of the remains go back over a decade. Then there's your mother's car, which you dumped on the back of Walter Delaroux's property. And now that missing teacher's car. I keep getting the feeling your car and that teacher's car are like bookends. The barrels in between. They must be connected somehow." Rita sets her coffee on the table. "What I know so far is they've only tied Walter Delaroux to one of the victims, the senator's daughter. He had beef with the senator over some nonsense about regulations on tree farming and had written her all kinds of rambling letters. The evidence is weak at best, but because that victim is high profile, the police moved fast. Whomever you have an *idea*"—she air quotes—"about might be worth discussing."

I stay quiet.

Rita threads her long fingers together and rests them on her lap. "Who?"

"Doyle Arceneaux."

Her eyes narrow. "Is that who you think left the plate?"

"I heard a truck that sounded like his that morning, in the driveway. But I didn't get a good look. Something about Doyle doesn't sit well with me."

She nods. "Interesting family."

"Do you know about his sister?"

Rita nods again. "Oh, I know about them all. And Emily Arceneaux has a strange story."

"I've heard some of it. Not sure what's local gossip and what's the truth, though."

"Did you know her?"

I shake my head.

Rita opens her phone and scrolls. "Emily Arceneaux. Youngest. Only daughter. Sickly kid. Lots of medical records but mostly just her mother bringing her to doctors, insisting she was ill. The jewel of her mother's eye." She looks up from the phone. "But people in this town talked. Turns out there are several complaints on record about the Arceneaux mother, especially in regard to Eddie and her only daughter."

"Munchausen syndrome by proxy," I say.

Rita taps the end of her nose with her slender finger. She opens her phone and scrolls again and looks up. "Emily attended school until she was eight or nine. The teachers and even the school principal noted the little girl wasn't ever sick, but the mother kept insisting the daughter was indeed ill. They said in a statement in her file that Emily was a happy, healthy little girl. For a time. There's even a complaint from a local doctor about finding no evidence of illness, yet the mother insisted to the point the doctor had to call the police to have her removed from his office. Then her mother pulled her out of school. There's a note about homeschooling but no proof Liv actually did it. After that, Emily really was sick. There were a sprinkling of doctor visits where it was charted Emily had lost weight and looked malnourished. I even found a child protective services visit to the Arceneaux house about a year after she was pulled from school. A welfare check. Nothing came from it. Everything checked out."

Everything checked out. I sigh. I've heard countless stories over the years about welfare checks to homes where everything checked out, only to hear later of a negligent death in that very home. It happens all too often with a broken system, exhausted state workers, and parents who can lie their way out of trouble. I find it hard to believe that anything in the Arceneaux home would check out, but maybe back then, the house wasn't so chaotic and messy. Maybe back then, Liv had a better poker face.

Rita continues, "Rumor was her mother kept her locked up at home, treating her for illnesses she didn't have. Some say the woman was overprotective and fearful, some say she was negligent, and others say she was just plain crazy. But whichever one she was, the fact remains, sick or not, that girl died in October of 1999." Rita pauses. Her eyes lock on mine. "And she was buried on her family's property."

"What?" I gasp.

"Yep."

The cross I'd seen outside the window of Emily's bedroom. I shiver. "Is that legal?"

"It is. Thing is," Rita adds with a sly smile, "she may not be buried there anymore."

I gape at her. "What?" I repeat. It seems to be the only response I can say.

"The neighbors behind their property think Emily was dug up and moved at some point."

"Why?" I think again of Liv and how she talked like Emily had disappeared. What if she had?

"Who knows? Could be a rumor. Nothing to back this one up but some nosy neighbors." She crosses her legs and leans in. "I'm still working through it."

"You've thought about Doyle Arceneaux too," I say.

"I've thought about everyone. Unlike the police, I'm exploring every lead."

She rolls her neck, checks her phone. It's still recording. "Okay then," she says, locking her gaze on mine. "Shall we change gears?"

I don't answer her. My mind is reeling with the information she just shared, as it filters through what I know about that family. I need to talk to Travis sooner rather than later.

"Dr. Watters?" Rita says.

I refocus. "Yes?"

"I'd like to talk about you now."

Any importance I placed on myself and my public humiliation has been overshadowed in a big way. It takes me a second to understand why Rita even cares about me anymore. But this is Rita Meade. She cares long after others don't.

Sometimes I wish I could freeze life at one moment in my childhood when Mabry and I were happy. Ironically, that moment would be in Broken Bayou. One of the summers we caught fireflies or bobbed in the bayou, splashing water on each other, smelling the sunscreen in her hair the next morning.

Other times I want to skip over my childhood entirely, pretend it never happened. The sweet pain too much to bear. But my pain is what Rita wants, a twist to her story. And for reasons I can't explain, I want to give it to her.

A story with a twist is the best kind.

Chapter Nineteen

"The *Fort Worth Live* interview?" I say.

"We'll start there," Rita says in a soft voice. "What happened?"

I exhale a long breath. Cross my arms over my chest. "You know what happened."

"I mean, *why* did it happen? What triggered you to come unwound enough to rip off your shirt on live television?"

The heat in the front room feels suddenly unbearable. I rub the back of my neck.

"One minute you were fine," Rita continues. "Then that caller came on, and"—she snaps her fingers—"a switch flipped. I've watched it several times." I cringe, and she keeps going. "Was it the caller's voice? Was it what you thought she was saying? There's obviously something there. And I have a feeling I know what, or rather who, it pertains to. I live for stories, Dr. Watters. I live for research. And Emily Arceneaux isn't the only person I've been researching lately. I know you've suffered. And I have a great respect for people who turn their suffering into success."

I let out a sharp laugh. "Success? I'm not sure I know what that is anymore." I look down. I don't feel strong enough to go where Rita is leading.

I look up, sigh. "The caller. She sounded like my sister."

Rita gives me the slightest nod. "I thought so. Do you want to talk about your sister?"

I weigh the question. My knee-jerk response is hell no. But I remind myself I've done it before, talked about her before. Rarely, but I have done it. And these questions are bound to come up again. I've made sure of that by my stunt on live television. Maybe if I lay it all out for Rita, I can somehow control the narrative. I glance out the front windows at the large knotty oaks. Birds flit through the limbs. Squirrels scamper up their thick trunks. Everything is as it should be. And yet, in this room, everything feels completely off kilter. But I can't keep running from the topic of Mabry. It's too exhausting.

I meet Rita's gaze. "Where do you want to start?"

Rita's hand lights on my arm. "The day you found her."

I turn from the window and face Rita and say out loud what I've thought every day for the last five years. Since I discovered Mabry, lifeless and floating in my mother's tub. "I couldn't save her."

The house is warm and still when I shut the front door behind Rita. I'm alone again with my heavy heart in a place where every wooden slat holds a memory of my sister. I press my back against the door and slide down to the floor. My eyes sting as tears course down my cheeks. I managed to tell the story to Rita without a tear falling. Now that she's gone, they won't stop.

Sweet Mabry. Saying it all out loud to Rita has weakened the wall I constructed to protect myself from that day five years ago. Now, the images break through, and I can't look away. Mabry's doe eyes frozen open. Her wet hair. The weight of her body in my arms as I grabbed her and tried to force life back into her mouth. The last thing she said to me was to leave her alone. She was angry at me for getting married, deserting her, leaving her to fend for herself with Mama. I tried to reconnect so many times. When my marriage failed, I thought I could win her back, convince her to come live with me. I left her pleading messages, promising I'd take care of her again.

And she took every last prescription pill in Mama's bathroom, crawled into the tub, and left forever. No note. No closure. Nothing.

I push off the floor and make my way to the kitchen. A fresh bottle of wine awaits. I open it, pour a glass. Drink it standing. It was so hard to accept what Mabry had done. To accept my part in it. I failed her. I help children every day, but I couldn't help my own sister.

I fumble through my tote on the counter and pull out my cell.

Here I am at the top of my game, a successful podcast, a new self-help book, and a phone full of calls to my dead sister's voicemail. I even kept her phone. It has become some sort of talisman. Another unhealthy thing I'm not ready to let go of. Every year I swear I'm going to throw away her phone and quit paying the bill. But then her angel voice would be gone, too, her laugh. Something else I'm clinging to.

I gulp another sip of wine. Of course, that caller on the show wasn't my sister. I knew it wasn't. But she sounded so young, so helpless. When I watched the clip, the voice sounded nothing like Mabry's. But that morning, in that moment, I heard *her*. I heard the silly safe word I gave Mabry. Like how a crack of sound can trigger an avalanche, that word triggered me.

My eyes fall on the thermos next to the metal dolls from Eddie. I didn't tell Rita all my secrets. The saddest one still exists. Hidden in plain sight. A hard knot forms in my throat. The tears build again. I lock my jaw to try to stop them, but again they fall. This time for me. For my foolishness. My toxic fucking foolishness.

The high-rise condo, the podcast, the kitten heels. Those are the things I've presented to the world. But becoming a therapist, helping others, lecturing the masses, writing a book called *Honest Healing* hasn't snapped me out of my delusion. If anything, it's made me justify it.

I grab my cell, the wine, Mabry's sketchbook . . . and the thermos and plod upstairs.

After Mabry's memorial, a man in a nice suit handed an urn to Mama. She said it was too heavy for her to carry, so I carried it, feeling like all my important parts had been sliced off and incinerated alongside

Mabry. And as Mama drove us back to her house, I promised Mabry I'd protect her, keep her safe. She'd always be with me. That night, Mama and I climbed into the same bed, and she held me tight and kissed my head and sang in my ear until I finally fell asleep.

I promised Mama I'd find the perfect spot for Mabry's ashes. A place she could always be free and happy. Bright light filters through the old windowpanes in the front bedroom. I haven't found that place yet.

But then again, maybe I haven't been looking.

My duffel and the stack of attic boxes sit by the door in the bedroom. The old television and VCR are turned off. Trash bags of VHS tapes piled next to them.

I wanted Mabry with me. She should have always been with me. If she had, maybe she wouldn't have . . . I swore to myself it was temporary. A way to keep her close until Mama and I could decide where to put her. A container no one would question.

No vase. No urn. Just a simple thermos, sitting on my kitchen counter.

I drop everything I've brought upstairs onto the bed and walk into the bathroom. My travel kit is open, and among the face lotions and toothpaste sits the sharp reminder of my pain. I pull the straight razor out, and before my breathing can even change, I deliver a quick surgical slice to my left arm. The sting is immediate, but it's just a nick. I wait. Nothing happens. No relief. Of course there's not. Once you confront and understand the reasoning behind your toxic actions, they lose their power.

I grab a towel from the side of the sink and press it onto my new wound.

Stupid, stupid, desperate woman.

I climb into the twin bed with the wine and sad array of items. I pull the thin sheet up to my chin and rewind to the day I broke into the attic to get to those boxes, the tapes. I think back to the letter on my kitchen counter in Fort Worth, back to the show and Harper and ripping my shirt off on live television. Then I think back to the week before all that, when absolutely nothing had happened. What I wouldn't give to go back to that week.

A fresh shudder rolls through my body. Mabry. She will never know she didn't kill a man.

I pull my phone from under the covers and press Mabry's number. A laugh. *Leave a message.* I end the call and punch the number again and again and again until tears blur my vision. I throw the phone across the room and cover my head with the sheet. My back heaves as a flood of pent-up sadness bursts through the crack in my dam. Tears for Mama and Mabry. Tears for a little girl named Emily. Tears for my failed marriage. Tears for all the people who thought I actually helped them. I can't even help myself.

The Aunts' ghosts whisper in my ear about salvation. Mama returned that morning I told her to get us a car, smeared red lipstick on her face and the keys to our old station wagon in her hand. Mabry and I hugged the Aunts goodbye as Mama leaned through the passenger window and shoved something in the glove box.

I slid behind the wheel. Mabry climbed in the front seat and Mama lay across the back. I glanced in the open glove box. A stack of cash sat inside. I slammed it shut, telling myself it was the insurance money, even though a part of me knew better.

As much as I wanted to get away from the bayou and what I'd done there, I still had an urge to fling open my door and run for Travis's house, but the precious cargo next to me kept me put.

Pearl yelled, "I pray for y'all's salvation."

No Hank Williams Jr. or Loretta Lynn songs blared as we pulled away from Broken Bayou. Only cicadas and whip-poor-wills and the golden sun on the bayou. Mama passed out with her cigarette still between her lips before we even made it to the Atchafalaya Basin. I motioned for Mabry to get it. She reached over the front seat and plucked it from Mama's mouth. Then she brought it to her own lips and inhaled. Coughing and scowling at Mama, she lowered the window and flicked it out with her little twelve-year-old hand. I held my right arm out over the back of the seat, and she scooted across to my side, placed her small head on my shoulder.

"Love you, sissy," she whispered.

I stroked her hair with my hand. "I love you too."

Then I slammed down on the gas and got us the hell out of Dodge.

Chapter Twenty

Ermine is behind the register at Taylor's Marketplace when I walk in the next morning. She takes one look at me and escorts me to a table away from the others, snapping her fingers at the waitress to pour me some coffee. The coffee is strong and hot and helps my hands stay steady. Ermine slides into the chair next to me. She doesn't speak. She only pats my hand.

My eyes are dry and salty from all the tears, and my chest feels like it's full of sand. I bite my lower lip to keep the tears from coming back.

"Do you want to talk about whatever this is?" She scans my face, my knotted hair, the dirty clothes I'm wearing.

I shrug.

"Honey, what happened?"

"Mabry." Her name is thick on my tongue.

"Oh, sugar. We were all just heartbroken when we heard of her passing. It's tragic. When your mama called your great-aunts and told them, they were beside themselves with grief."

"Mama called them?"

"She did. But it was a good bit after. There'd already been a memorial. I wanted to say something to you when I first saw you the other morning, but you looked so good, and you seemed fine, so I thought I should leave well enough alone."

I meet her gaze. The tears fall. "I'm not fine."

A few locals sit at the back counter, eating their breakfast, a heavy silence hanging in the air along with the smell of frying bacon.

Ermine squints back at the counter, then to me. "My place is upstairs." She points to the ceiling. "Why don't you go on up, and I'll bring up some breakfast to you."

The back staircase is steep with uneven boards, and I wonder how Ermine can manage these every day. At the top is a small landing and a door. The door is unlocked.

A small living room greets me. Light pours in through the large window on the far wall. A small sofa faces the window, which has two recliners in front of it. And each recliner has a cat curled into it, asleep in the patches of sun falling on them. One lifts its gray head, looks at me, lays it back down. An open kitchen sits on the right, with a counter separating it from the living room. Pictures cover every inch of it. Pictures of her with what looks like a team of grandchildren. Not a posed moment among them. In these shots, Ermine and the kids are in different stages of laughing, on a beach, in this living room, at Taylor's counter. There's a photo of her and Mr. Taylor behind the cash register downstairs. I saw their love firsthand, the looks they gave each other. Even Mabry captured it. I shut my eyes. Swallow. Open them.

I choose one of the barstools at the counter. The space is quiet and warm. No televisions. Only the sounds of the birds outside.

Ermine opens the door and enters, holding a tray. She sets it on the counter in front of me.

"Eat," she says. "No withering away on my watch."

A plate of fluffy biscuits and gravy and two pieces of crispy bacon await. My stomach growls. Ermine grabs a glass from the cabinet and fills it with water, sets it in front of me as well.

The first bite of food lodges in my throat, and I think I won't be able to oblige Ermine. But once that bite is down, the flavors spark my appetite even more than the smell. It tastes like a hug. Comfort food.

I take several more bites, and Ermine says, "There you go."

She speaks to me like a child, and in a way, I feel like one. Completely unequipped to handle my emotions. Of all the things I'm equipped to do, that one should be my specialty. I set down my fork, and my chin drops to my chest.

Ermine walks around the counter and touches my shoulder. I collapse into sobs. She wraps her frail, thin arms around me and squeezes me tight. "Let it out," she says. "Let it all out."

And I do. I let Ermine hold me and rock me like a baby and whisper to me that it will be okay. I release every tear, every barb I want to direct at my mother, every barb I want to direct at myself. Then I release my secrets. I tell Ermine about Mabry's phone, paying the bill so I could still hear my little sister's laugh, keeping the phone itself. Then I tell her about keeping the ashes, and when I do, Ermine's arms lock around me even tighter.

After several minutes, I pull my head up and wipe my face. I gasp, catch my breath, exhale. "I'm sorry," I say. "I didn't mean to unload all of that on you. It's just . . . I've been holding on to something I can't hold on to anymore. Maybe saying it out loud to you is my first step."

Ermine pats my hand and says, "Let go or be dragged, honey."

Ermine makes two cups of tea, and I accept the mug. It smells like roses. She leads me to the small sofa. Both cats are up now and curious. They pounce off the recliners and wind themselves around Ermine's thin ankles. She bends and scratches their ears.

"This is Frank," she says, pointing to the black-and-white one. "And this is Beans," she says, still scratching the gray one.

I laugh a real laugh for the first time in a long time. "Frank and Beans?"

"Now, stop," Ermine says, giggling herself. "They'll know you're laughing at them."

But Frank and Beans don't seem to know any such thing. Frank is now in my lap, purring and making bread on my leg with his little paws, and Beans has settled next to Ermine on the couch.

"Thanks, Ermine," I say. "For letting me come up here. For listening without judgment."

She pats my knee. "I'm glad I could help."

A low rumble rattles the panes in the living room window. Ermine eyes me, then leaps off the couch. Beans runs down the hall on my right. The sound comes again as Ermine makes it to the window.

"Well, forevermore." She looks over her shoulder at me. "It's raining."

Thunder booms as Ermine and I scramble downstairs. We wedge our way onto the front porch of Taylor's, past several patrons and the fry cook. Rain plinks off the roof. One lady behind me claps.

"Praise the Lord," Ermine says.

Cell phones come out and weather apps are illuminated. The bright day turns dark, and a crack of lightning zigzags above us. Then the sky opens and unloads a torrential downpour. We all stand on the porch, watching the rain come down in sheets.

"Months without a drop," the fry cook says. "Now, we gonna have a flood."

Ermine grins over her shoulder at him. "I'll take a flood."

I tell Ermine thank you again and run into the rain to my car. Once inside, I shoot off a text and wait for the response. My phone dings almost immediately.

Let's meet at Shadow Bluff.

It's still raining when I open the door and invite Travis into the house, and I'm still wearing the *Fort Worth Live* tee. The formal wardrobe in my bag feels like even more of a joke now. Travis shakes the rain from his hair as he steps inside. He's not dressed in his usual uniform. He's wearing jeans and a simple T-shirt and cowboy boots. His expression matches mine. Sad.

In the kitchen, I pour him a cup of coffee, and he accepts but doesn't sit. He leans against the kitchen counter, and I stand next to him.

"I'm on administrative leave," he says, staring into his coffee cup. "But only because Chief arranged it. Which is pointless really." He meets my gaze. "I'm being fired, Willa. I've lost their trust. That's a nail in the coffin for a cop."

"Oh, Travis. I'm so sorry." I had a feeling this would be the consequence, but hearing it from him is gut wrenching. "I never meant for that to happen. Please know, I would've kept your name out of it if I could've."

"I know."

"I feel awful." I reach for his hand, but he pulls it away.

"Chief said if I'd have come forward at the beginning of this, he might could've saved my job. But I didn't want to drag you into it." I sigh and start to talk but he continues, "This is going to take a while for me to process. Being a cop is all I know. It's everything to me. And now it's gone. One stupid thing I did eighteen years ago, and it's all gone." He tries to look casual, but I see his jaw harden. "Why the hell did you have to call me that night?"

I know what he's doing. He's deflecting. It's a natural response. He could have said no when I called that night or after he realized what I was asking of him, but he didn't.

"I wish I hadn't called," I say.

"There's something else we need to talk about." He shifts on his feet. "I heard you stopped by my mother's house yesterday."

Shit. I start to reply, stop, and regroup. "I did. I just wanted to visit. I didn't mean to upset anyone."

"Willa, didn't I ask you to leave my brothers alone?"

I hug my arms across my chest. I'm sleep deprived and emotionally drained, and I don't feel like a lecture. So I throw out a question to distract him. "How sure are you that Walter Delaroux is the right suspect?"

He shuts his eyes a moment. "What are you doing? Why are you harassing my family?"

"I'm not harassing anyone. I'm simply asking questions."

"You a reporter now too?"

"I'm just looking for answers."

"To what?"

"To whatever's happening in this town."

He sighs. "And you think I'm not looking for answers? To what's happening in *my* town? We—" He stops, takes a breath. "They have a suspect in custody. For a reason."

I decide to switch gears on him, to the topic that won't leave me alone. "Tell me about Emily."

"What?"

"Your sister. I found a sketch of her in Mabry's old sketchbook."

"What does she have to do with this?"

"I don't know. I'm just interested. I don't really remember her. And you never talked about her much. How long was she ill?"

He studies his boots. "As long as I can remember."

"Why was she ill? What did she have?"

"Willa, what are you doing?"

"You know what I'm doing. Children, especially those who may need extra care, capture my attention, and I can't let go."

He sets his mug down, turns to face me. "She wasn't sick in that way. In *your* way. She was unhealthy. It happened before your last summer here."

I reach for his hand again, and this time, he lets me touch it. "Travis. Why didn't we ever talk about her?"

"My mother forbid us from talking about her. My father was drinking too much by then and went along with it. Then my mother refused to let the coroner take her. Got my dad's gun and said she'd kill anyone who came for her girl."

"That must have been terrifying for everyone else in the house."

"It was." Travis continues, "My mother petitioned the Louisiana Cemetery Board for a family plot on our land. The local registrar issued a permit. And my sister was buried. And we all went on about our lives, without saying a word. Just how my mother wanted it. Then a few weeks later, she started in about Emily again and insisted she ran away. Kept saying Emily was coming back. It was really messed up."

"I'm so sorry." I pause, then ask, "What about your father? Is he buried there too?"

Travis barks a laugh. "No. My mother said the ground where Emily is is sacred. No drunks allowed."

"Oh, Travis."

Travis's face is a blank canvas, but he can't fool me. Underneath, he's hiding an immense sadness, and I wonder how he keeps it hidden. Then again, of course, I know how he does it. I've done it my entire adult life. Years of practice.

"Maybe we can talk about your brothers for a minute." I keep my voice low, nonconfrontational. "Specifically, Doyle. Do you think there's any way he could have followed us that night? When I dumped the car? I've got good instincts. It's part of my job, my career. I think Doyle is hiding something."

"What?" He laughs. "Are you kidding me? Doyle has nothing to do with this, Willa. That's out of line."

He's right. I am out of line, but something Rita said is nagging at me. "Why did your mother start to talk about Emily like she ran away?"

Travis looks around the kitchen, then back to me. "Because Emily did run away. Many times." He rubs his face. "But I always brought her back." He looks away from me and sighs. "Except the last time."

"The last time Doyle found her," I say.

"Who've you been talking to?" he says.

"What was her cause of death?"

His jaw moves side to side as he studies me. "Look, I know the rumors, okay? About my mother. But they're just rumors. And now you want to start rumors about my brother."

"Travis, we need to talk about this."

"No, we don't." He pushes away from the counter, and I follow him to the front door. I stop on the porch as he runs down the steps into the rain. He stops, looks back at me. "Please, Willa. Leave my family alone."

I park alongside River Road and kill the engine. It's dark. The rain has stopped. I told myself not to come here. It isn't safe. Yet here I am, ignoring my own common sense, sneaking into the night to finish something, purge myself while I have the momentum to do so. And this is the best place. Not to mention the best time. No witnesses.

I check my tote. My gun is tucked inside along with two other objects. I scan the levee as I climb out of the car. It's as empty as I hoped. No news vans. No people scouring the banks. Seems everyone is listening to Chief Wilson's orders to stay away. Everyone but me.

I find a grassy spot to sit on. The murky bayou slugs by below. So many secrets buried in there, now exhumed.

My head throbs. A gust of wind blows through my hair, and a stray raindrop falls on my face. It runs with the tears that started again at some point as my thoughts of Mabry and our mother tangle and twist into a knot with Emily and her mother. Two young girls with two troubled mothers who died too soon.

The memory of Mabry's memorial slams into me like a fist to my stomach. I see her large photograph and the pink and white flowers. I see Mama throwing herself onto the floor of the funeral home, wailing. I watched, numb. Mama insisted Mabry would never want to be buried, so she had her cremated. I was glad. I wasn't ready to give Mabry up either. In a sad way, I understand what Liv Arceneaux might have felt. Letting go is brutally hard.

I look down at the thermos in my lap. I wonder what Amy would say if she could see me right now, sitting on this levee in the dark, losing my grip on whatever it is I had my grip on in the first place. But I know what she'd say. She said it to me so many times. "Set Mabry free."

Something snaps on the levee behind me. A twig. I jump and turn around. No one's there. But the sound's got me edgy, reminding me I don't need to be alone out here long. I need to get this over with.

I pull my cell from my pocket and punch in a twenty-four-hour 800 number I memorized years ago. A recording answers and asks what I need help with. I answer with the words I've needed to say for so long: cancel mobile account.

The woman who finally helps me does everything in her power to keep me from canceling Mabry's account. She doesn't know. She doesn't understand. She just wants to keep a customer. Finally, I say, "She's dead."

Seven minutes after punching in the number, the account is canceled. Mabry's voice is gone. Forever. A gaping fissure opens in my chest, and I want to release the pain coming from it. I want to yell into the stale, humid air. I want to slice my skin and let the pain spill out onto the wet grass around me. I want so many things. I rub the small heart tattoo on the inside of my forearm, next to the fresh cuts. Mabry's heart. I press my lips together and choke down the acid in my throat. And somewhere, deep beneath the pain, another feeling fights to the surface. Something I haven't felt in a long time, if ever. Relief. Sweet, unburdening relief. And with that relief comes another feeling. Forgiveness. The relief I expect. I always tell my patients that when it hits, it will feel like someone who's been twisting your arm finally releases it. It's instant. But forgiveness I didn't expect. Yet it's even more important. Forgiveness can offer freedom.

I glance at the thermos in my tote but remove the other item I brought with me. An outdated cell phone. The battery's been dead for years. I used to charge it regularly but then realized it didn't have to be charged for me to hear Mabry's voice.

With the phone clutched in my hand, I ease down the backside of the levee to the bank of Broken Bayou. It's sloppy, and mud sucks at the orange boots. Dark water churns from the heavy downpour. My hand is shaking, but before I can change my mind, I throw the phone as hard as I can into the warm night air. A splash, then nothing.

"Nice throw."

I scream and whip around. A flashlight beam blinds me. I hold up my hands to protect my eyes, gauge the distance between me and this stranger and if I can run. I picture Doyle, standing there with one of his knives.

"Oh. Sorry," the man says, and the light lowers.

My eyes adjust again to the darkness. I can tell it's a cop standing there, and I exhale as I think of Travis. Then I remember Travis doesn't have a uniform anymore. And even when he did, it didn't look like this man's. The officer steps closer, and I see his face. "Raymond."

"What the hell are you doing out here?" Raymond St. Clair says. He scans the bank with his flashlight.

"Taking care of something I should have taken care of years ago," I say.

Raymond glances at the bayou, then back to me. "Well, you shouldn't be out here alone."

"I know."

"I saw the car parked by the levee. Got worried."

"I was just about to leave." I manage a smile even as I close my tote to hide the large silver thermos. My talisman.

Raymond's eyes dart in every direction, then land on me. "You need to be careful out here."

I glance at the bayou, then back to Raymond. "At least you have a suspect in custody."

He lets out a quick laugh that holds no humor. "Everybody knows Delaroux's not the guy. He's just a way for the DA to look good." He shakes his head. "No. Our guy's too smart to get caught."

Smart isn't exactly the word I'd use to describe Doyle. Sly is more like it. Maybe even lucky. But not smart.

"And the whole town knows you've been talking to that reporter," he continues. "I don't think I'd be advertising my involvement, if you know what I mean."

"I'm not a threat to anyone."

"I know that. And you know that. But . . . still. Be careful. So many people come close to danger and never even know it. It's crazy." He nods toward the water. "Like those women. One minute, they're having fun somewhere; the next minute, they're incapacitated." He rubs the side of his neck. "We all gotta watch out for each other now. You know?"

My skin prickles. I nod. Something about the expression on Raymond's face looks familiar, but I can't quite place it.

"C'mon, I'll walk you back," he says, nodding to the top of the levee.

"Just give me a minute," I say.

Raymond nods, doesn't question me. He walks to the top of the levee, stops a moment, then turns his back to me.

The bayou gurgles below me, and I picture myself grabbing the thermos and walking down to it. I see myself opening the lid and releasing Mabry's ashes into the wind, into the water where we were baptized. So many awful things have come from that water. Something pure and good needs to go back in.

But my muscles boycott. I gather my things, and instead of walking to the water, I walk away from it, past Raymond, and back to my car.

It's late. I'm tired. And it's not time.

October 1999

Emily Arceneaux checked her bedroom door. Still locked. Good. They'd think she'd gone to bed. Emily waited. She just wanted to be normal. She wanted to be like the other girls in town. She wanted to have fun. She couldn't remember the last time she laughed. Well, that's not true. He had made her laugh. And now he wanted her to leave with him. That made her smile. And Emily didn't smile a lot.

A sound came from her window. A pebble hitting the glass. Emily raced to it and opened it. He would be out there, waiting for her.

She grabbed a small bag from under her bed, next to the pile of meds she'd been secretly stashing. For once, she felt like she could think clearly. It'd been his idea to stop the meds. He'd been right. He'd also been right about something else. She had to get out of this house. Away from her mother.

She raced back to the window. The drop down wasn't awful. She'd done it before, plenty of times, but this time she knew she wasn't coming back. Her brothers wouldn't find her this time. No one would.

She dropped the bag, and it landed on the ground with a quiet thud. Then she slipped out into the night, grabbing her bag and racing for the woods. Racing to her sweet Raymond. The boy who promised to save her.

Chapter Twenty-One

Hot water from the shower washes over me until steam fills the entire bathroom. It loosens the knots in my shoulders. Despite what happened at the levee last night, or maybe because of what happened at the levee last night, I feel better. More in charge. I rub a spot on the glass and look out at the thermos on the bathroom counter. Well, maybe not completely in charge. At least I slept. The first full night of sleep I've gotten in days, exhaustion finally catching up to me.

The water loosens my mind as well, and my thoughts travel to the month after Mabry's funeral. Mama was in bed. I had to force her to get up. I leaned her head over the kitchen sink and washed her hair, put fresh clothes on her. Then she hugged me. Pulled me in tight and sobbed into my neck.

"I'm so sorry," she said, between sobs. "I shoulda done better."

The shower water runs cold, and I yelp and duck away from it. But I can't duck away from the memory. The raw truth in Mama's voice. That moment of clarity when she was honest and vulnerable, not hiding behind her huge persona. A dull ache spreads through my chest. A voice deep inside me, one I want to ignore, says, Sound familiar? I step out to dry off, and that's when I hear it. A sound outside the bedroom. I freeze with my hair dripping and the towel wrapped around me. There it is again. A creak. Like someone walking on old floorboards. Then the sound is gone. I stay put for another minute and, when I don't hear anything else, ease into the bedroom.

The room is empty. The bed still unmade. Everything is as it was when I went to sleep last night. The boxes and my duffel are in their same spots. The old television still on the floor. The security tape, thankfully, gone. I have a strong feeling it would have taken the place of Mabry's voicemail if I'd let it.

The sound doesn't come again, but I still grab my gun off the nightstand and take it with me downstairs. The house is bright and full of light. The storms have gone. Nothing looks out of place down here either. The front door is still locked.

My cell trills in my hand and I jump. "Holy shit." I look down and see my mother's name.

I swipe it open.

"Are you home yet?"

I look around the front foyer of Shadow Bluff. "Not yet."

"Sweet girl, you'd better get on out of there."

I want to tell her about my breakdown over Mabry. About the ashes. About all of it. I really want to talk. But I can't seem to form the words. "I'll be leaving soon," I say.

"My doctor came by the other day."

I walk onto the front porch and sit on the steps. "Oh, Mama, I left him a message and forgot to follow up. Things got a little . . . hectic . . . here." Squirrels scamper through the puddles in the front yard and frogs croak from every shadow. Hot, salty air sits over the porch like a wet blanket.

"He wants me to try a new medicine."

I don't hear anything in her voice that sounds bitter, but I stay cautious. "I am concerned. I worry when you stop taking your medication. I want you to stay healthy is all."

"Well, I told him I'd try it."

This makes me sit up straighter. "You did?"

"I did. You know you're not the only one who worries. I worry too."

I let out a long breath. This is the clearest she's sounded in months. I have a feeling she's already started whatever he prescribed. "You sound really good, Mama. More alert."

"Maybe not this morning. That friend of yours came by early. Woke me up. I've had all kinds of visitors."

"Who? Amy?"

Mama coughs in my ear, clears her throat. "No. The other lady."

My blood turns to cold sludge in my veins. "What other lady?"

"That fancy one who dresses like you. Rita Meade."

"What!" I jump up from the steps. "What the hell?"

"That one's quite the busy bee. She's got lots of questions about my old car and you and some little girl named Emily."

"Holy shit, Mama. What did you say?"

"I told her to get her fancy pants the hell out of my room."

I smile. "Of course you did."

"Who is that woman?"

"I'm sorry. She's . . . I'm not sure what she is. We've been talking about some things. She's a reporter."

"We've already had this talk, Willamena. You don't need to be talking to anyone. This is nothing to do with us. That idiot got out of the car. You said so." Mama coughs again, and this time, it lasts until she coughs something up. I hear her spit.

"I hate that Rita came up there. She's digging for her story, that's all. But she should have told me she wanted to talk to you."

Mama is talking about Rita in my ear, but I'm not listening. I open my text messages and type one to Rita.

What the hell are you doing?

The response is quick:

Almost back. Will explain. Meet me at Taylor's in an hour.

I'm at Taylor's Marketplace, sipping coffee, when Rita walks in. She waves to me as she clips to the back counter. She orders a coffee and sits next to me. She still looks perfect even though she must have driven nonstop to get back to Broken Bayou so quickly.

I face her. "My mother? Really?"

"Sorry. I should have told you." Her coffee arrives, and she takes a giant sip. "I like your mother. Fiery, that one."

"Start explaining."

Rita leans in. Her eyes are bright, pupils dilated. This story is her drug, and despite her smooth hair and shiny lips, I see it's getting the better of her. Something about her seems off. She's too put together, too intense. "I had to talk to her. Your mother. I had to talk to the woman who owned that car. I wanted to hear her side of what happened the night she told you to get rid of it. I wanted to see her face when she told me, experience it with her."

"And how'd that go?"

"Not well. She told me to march my fancy ass to the door." She laughs.

"I could have saved you the trip."

Rita sips more coffee even though, judging from her shaking hands, that's the last thing she needs. "I just want to make sure I look under every stone. This story is a monster. A whale. And I'm reeling it in."

I study her hands again. "How many hours have you slept in the last few days? Seems to me, the story may be reeling you in."

She smiles, but the smile looks manic, unhinged. I know the feeling. The last two times I saw my reflection, that's what looked back at me. This place has a way of doing that to a person.

"Nothing's reeling me in," she says with a glazed look. "I've had a lot of time in the car, driving. A lot of time to just think. And something's not sitting right with me."

I lean in.

"Doyle," she says.

"What about him?"

"I don't know. But something's not right. I keep going over everything the investigator has told me and our talks, and everything points to him. Now, there's the sand thing."

"What sand thing?"

She fidgets with a stray hair in her face and tucks it behind her ear. "Some of the barrels, the newer ones, had sand residue in them."

I vaguely remember hearing something about that from one of the press conferences.

"I did some digging," Rita says with another smile.

"Shocking," I say.

"Did you know there are dozens of types of sand? There's river sand, desert sand, sea sand." She ticks them off on her fingers. "So many types, it's crazy. But do you know what type my source says was in some of those barrels?"

Then it hits me. Doyle's job. I think of the piles of sand I saw from the bedroom window at his house. "The kind used to fill playground sandboxes?" I say.

"Bingo. And on top of that, guess what I just found out?" She doesn't wait for me to say *what*. "Doyle's prints were all over that missing teacher's license plate."

My pulse quickens. Doyle left that plate for me. When I asked Eddie about it, he said it was a secret. He knows his brother is up to no good. I sit back in my chair. "Then what's not adding up?"

"The police are keeping something quiet." She leans in. "There's talk at least some of the victims were drugged."

"How would they know that? Based on the . . . condition of the victims." I shake the thought away.

"The schoolteacher." Rita's eyes are wide and bright. "Her autopsy is providing some interesting information."

"They can't possibly have that information already."

Rita nods. "You'd be surprised how fast you can get information when a senator is involved." She lowers her voice. "There's something else. That investigator is questioning the way the sheriff's office handled that stolen barrel report back then. Apparently, the paperwork was filed incorrectly, possibly on purpose. Like someone deliberately filled it out wrong to create problems later on if it ever got brought up again."

I think of all the law enforcement swarming the bayou. All wanting a piece of this pie.

Rita sips her coffee. "Anyway," she says. "There's something else."

"Christ. What?"

"Really, *someone* else. Emily."

"What about her?"

"After we talked, I contacted Tom Bordelon about her. Like you said, she seemed important. Could be, she is. My source called me this morning. They want a DNA sample from Liv Arceneaux or one of the brothers."

"For what?"

Rita rests both her arms on the table and leans closer. "To compare to the bones found in the trunk of that car you dumped."

The air in Taylor's Marketplace suddenly feels too thin to breathe, like I've elevated to an altitude well above sea level. My chest heaves. My stomach constricts into a knot. "Please, no."

"Look, no question little Emily was buried on her family's land. The question is, did she stay buried? They're working on a warrant to find out."

If Doyle followed us the night I dumped that car, and saw where it was, he could have relocated Emily to that trunk. But *why* would he do that?

"Walk me through this again. The dates. When did she die?"

"October 1999," Rita says.

"And my mother asked me to get rid of her car in August of 2000. I decided to put it in the bayou. I clean out the car. Travis leaves. I use his truck to push the car into the water. That's it."

"That's definitely not it," Rita says. "That's why I'm still here. The pieces are starting to reveal themselves. Time to put them together. And I bet I'm a lot closer than that Podunk police chief *and* that investigator."

"Rita." I lower my chin, study her. "Slow down."

She drains the remaining coffee in her cup and stands. "No room for *slow down* here. I'm rolling on this."

"You're scaring me a little bit."

She releases a loud laugh, and the other two customers in Taylor's turn to stare. "Good."

I don't bother to tell Rita exactly what my mother told me, that this could be bigger than her. She's beyond listening. Whether it's her that puts all this together or not, I hope it gets done quickly. Despite the good night's sleep, despite the coffee, I feel something ominous hovering close.

Rita gazes down at me. "I've got something I'm checking out this afternoon. Somebody I want to interview. Possibly a secret boyfriend of Emily's. My digging uncovered that gem as well. Then I'm heading over to talk to Tom Bordelon."

The drawing from Mabry's sketchbook comes to mind. Like the pictures she'd drawn of Ermine and her husband, Travis and me, even Mama and her boss, Mabry was capturing what love looked like to her. Emily and a boy.

Rita points a long manicured nail at me. "Keep your phone on. I'll fill you in when I'm done." She clips to the front of Taylor's and is out the door before I can yell after her.

Ermine slips up beside my table. "That one's a real piece of work."

"Indeed."

"She bothering you?"

I shake my head. "I actually think I'm starting to like her."

Then Ermine says to me what I intended to yell to Rita. "Be careful."

◆ ◆ ◆

I text Travis and ask him to please come by again. When I get back to the house, I go through each room, with my gun. Although, I'm not sure what I would have done if someone had been here. I didn't think that far into my plan when I started looking in rooms. Thankfully, it hadn't mattered.

I set my keys and gun on the kitchen table and look at the kitchen door. The chair I wedged under the knob before I left is still there. I hear tires on the oystershell driveway, then someone calling my name out front.

Travis sits in his truck with the windows down. I walk up to the passenger window. He looks as if he's been up all night. His hair is scattered in all directions. His clothes are wrinkled. He looks at me with sad eyes. "Doyle's missing."

"What?"

Travis tilts his head. "I figured that's why you texted me."

"No, Travis. It's not. I texted you because I just had a very interesting conversation with Rita Meade and—"

Travis scoffs.

"And," I continue, "she mentioned something that got me thinking."

"What's that?"

"Did Emily have a secret boyfriend?"

"What? Why?"

I hold up my finger. "I'll be right back." I race to the kitchen and snag Mabry's sketchbook from the counter. I fumble through the pages until I find the loose sketch Liv Arceneaux ripped in half; then I race back to Travis.

I hold out the drawing, slightly out of breath. "Mabry drew this. The other half is a drawing of Emily."

Travis's jaw goes slack. "What the fuck?"

He grabs the picture and holds it closer. His throat moves as he swallows.

"Do you know who that boy is?"

Travis's jaw is no longer slack. It's tensed so hard I can see the muscle in it. Travis looks up, and the answer dawns on me even before he says it. The expression on the boy's face. I'd seen it last night, by the bayou. On Raymond St. Clair's face.

"It's Raymond," I say.

Travis nods and thrusts the picture back into my hand. "Yeah. I always suspected."

Then something else comes to mind, and the sketch shakes in my hand. "Rita also mentioned there may be evidence at least some of the victims were drugged."

"Jesus. Y'all had quite the chat." He rubs his face.

"Is it true?"

He nods.

The fine hairs on the back of my neck prickle. Last night by the bayou comes back into focus. *So many people come close to danger and never know it. One minute, they're having fun somewhere; the next minute, they're incapacitated.* "And Raymond was an EMT before he was a cop."

"How do you know that?"

"He mentioned it when I was at the impound."

Travis raises his eyebrows. "What were you doing at the impound?"

I hurry on. "It doesn't matter. But listen, last night I was out by the bayou."

"Alone? Willa, I wouldn't do that right now."

"I wasn't alone. Raymond was there, too, and he told me—"

He interrupts me. "What do you mean Raymond was there too? Raymond's in New Orleans. Said he had to follow up on a lead."

My body goes cold. "Raymond wasn't in New Orleans last night." Raymond who works for the same sheriff's office that possibly falsified a report years ago. A report that pertains to this case. *Our guy's too smart to get caught.*

But what about the sand? I'd seen piles of it from Emily's bedroom window the day I visited. It's possible someone else had seen it. Doyle may not be smart, but he's smart enough to know that could lead back to him.

"Travis," I say. "What if it's him? Raymond?"

Travis shakes his head, incredulous. "No way. No fucking way."

"You told me you know when it's one of your own. What if you didn't know?"

"I'd know."

I look down at the sketch. "How sure are you Emily died of natural causes?"

"What?" He shakes his head again, then stops. A harsh breath escapes. "Wait a minute. Just wait a minute." He holds a finger up, sits a few seconds, and says, "I used to see Raymond, back then, in the woods behind our house. Sometimes I'd run him off. I thought he was there to torment me but . . ."

"But he wasn't interested in you," I say.

Travis's jaw clenches again. "He was interested in Emily."

"Travis." I glance behind me. "It sounded like someone was in the house with me this morning. Tiptoeing around."

Travis is out of the truck before I can say another word. I follow him up the front steps and into the foyer.

"Travis, I—"

"Stay here."

I wait on the porch, tapping my foot, but I can't stay still. I catch up to Travis as he's coming down the stairs to look around the first-floor rooms. All the rooms are empty.

Back at the front door, he says, "This all just keeps getting more out of control." He runs his hand through his hair, stalks back to his truck, and jumps behind the wheel. I follow him to the driver's side door.

"I don't know what the hell is going on, but when I find Raymond . . ." His words trail off as he slams his truck in gear.

"I don't know if that's a good idea. You need to let the investigators handle this."

"This could involve my family. I'm handling it."

"Because it's family is exactly why you shouldn't handle it."

He looks at me with a cold stare. "If you see him, call me. And don't go near him." Then he swerves out of the driveway before I can say anything else.

Chapter Twenty-Two

I step back into the foyer and lock the front door. Take a minute to breathe. I'm too on edge to be here, in this house, in this town. My mind is swirling. I zeroed in on Doyle to the point I missed other cues. I mentioned Doyle not only to Travis but to Rita and the investigator as well. I was so sure. I squeeze my eyes shut and rub my face. Oh my God. What am I doing? I've gotten so tangled up in this, I've lost perspective. I thought I had it all figured out. And last night . . . my throat constricts. I was alone with Raymond, who just happened to find me on the levee. Who lied to Travis about being in New Orleans.

Would a chair wedged under a broken door really deter an intruder? A killer. I don't want to sit around, waiting to find out.

I'm googling hotels in Baton Rouge even before I reach the landing on the second floor. There are several options. And Baton Rouge is close enough that I could get back if the investigator needs me. Had Tom Bordelon said stay close or don't leave town? I convince myself he said stay close. Baton Rouge is close.

In the front bedroom, I cram my things into my duffel: toothbrush, skirts, heels. I zip it shut and study the room. Nothing has been forgotten. I pull the sheets off the bed and pile them up with the towels I used. I can't remember any cleaning instructions. I'll call Charles II and offer to pay for a service to come in and clean. Add it on to the damage tab from the attic door. A cold stone drops in my stomach. The attic. I didn't look in the attic when I came in. Maybe Travis did. I caught up to him as he searched, but we stayed on the first floor. I tell myself it's okay. I'm being paranoid. But still, I look to the bedside table for my gun. Shit. I left it in the kitchen. Next to my keys.

I sling the straps of my duffel onto my shoulder and start heading for the hallway when I hear it. This time it's not some indistinct creak or snap. It's a very clear sound. Footsteps. And they're coming from above me, from the attic.

I race for the stairs. The attic door squeaks open. My heart thuds in my chest as I clamber down the front steps and run for my keys and gun. Footsteps sound on the stairs behind me. I smack my duffel into the doorframe as I turn into the kitchen, let out a moan, and drop it in the hall. The chair is no longer under the doorknob; it's at the kitchen table. I lunge for the table, grab my keys, and—

My gun is gone.

"I'm gonna need you to not move." The voice behind me is a slow drawl. Possibly drunk. Definitely one I recognize.

I don't move.

"Now, real slow, turn around," he says.

I turn and stare down the barrel of my own gun. And behind my gun is Doyle Arceneaux. His eyes watery. His hands shaking. "I don't want to hurt you."

I swallow, keep my eyes on his. Breathe. "I know you don't."

"You're in trouble."

"Doyle, please lower the gun."

He looks at it like he's surprised to see it in his hand, hesitates a moment, then lowers it. I exhale. He glances at the kitchen door. "That chair didn't work. I knew you had something that needed fixin'."

"What are you doing here?" I rub the phone in my hand and wonder if there's any way I can dial 9-1-1 without him noticing.

"I needed a place to hide. It's not me."

"I know," I say even though I don't know any such thing. Just as the facts point in one direction, something happens to completely upend my theory. Like Doyle showing up in my kitchen, holding my own gun on me. My heart pounds against my ribs. I decide to gamble on a question. Maybe it will get me the answers I need. "Doyle, why'd you leave me that license plate?"

His eyes widen. "Where is it?"

"I gave it to the police."

His shoulders relax a little. "They know."

"Doyle, all they know is your fingerprints are all over it."

"I didn't do anything!" he yells.

I hold up my hands. "Okay."

He looks around the kitchen. He looks like a child who's been caught doing something wrong. "I was in one of the bedrooms earlier. Then I moved out to the shed." He points through the open door with the gun. "Then I saw Travis pull up and ran to the attic. He's looking for me." He glances at my gun again. "I thought this might be handy."

His voice is different from the last time I saw him. He sounds more like a child. Less threatening. Like he finally understands his toughness is actually bravado.

I keep my gaze on his, my voice steady. "You don't need to hide anymore."

He swings the gun in my direction. "Yes, I do!" His voice is shrill and defensive.

I keep my hands up. "Okay. It's okay."

Doyle's breathing is shallow. He taps his leg with my gun; then his eyes widen as he notices the phone in my hand for the first time. I take a step back. He jumps for me so quickly I fall backward, and he snatches the phone from my grip. The kitchen door clicks open.

We both stare at it as he puts my phone in his back pocket. Every fight-or-flight instinct in my body screams *run*. Doyle may not plan to intentionally hurt me, but his voice tells me he's afraid. Desperate.

That's a dangerous combination. I wheel around and race for the open door.

I burst into the backyard, but Doyle gains on me fast.

"Stop," he yells.

I keep running. I hear his breath close to me; then I feel him grab my hair. My neck jerks back, and I scream. Despite his skinny frame, he's strong. Stronger than me. I fight and kick at him, but he gets on top of me and straddles my chest. I scream again; he slaps me, open palmed. "Shut up!"

I'm stunned for a moment. My cheek burns. Then my adrenaline kicks into overtime, and I twist an arm free and claw for his eyes, but I can only reach his cheek. My nails dig into his face and leave red, bleeding marks as I drag them across his skin. He cries out like an animal and raises the gun. I see the butt of it coming for my head.

That's the last thing I see.

I come to with a blinding headache. Something sticky covers my right cheek. I try to touch it but realize my hands are tied behind my back. I smell cabbage and body odor, and as my eyes adjust, I wish I was still unconscious. I'm on my side on a small bed in a room with bare walls and one window. The window is dark.

I'm in the Arceneauxes' home. In Emily's room. In her bed, under her sheets, with a broken, one-eyed baby doll tucked in next to my head. I moan a low throaty sound as I move away from the doll. My breathing is stilted, and I work to keep my heart rate under control. Hyperventilating will not help here, but I'm having a hard time keeping my head clear. I remember being at the house, in the kitchen. Doyle with the gun. Me, running.

Another moan escapes as I manage to push myself into a seated position. My head swims. My arms burn. I try to judge the time from the night sky through the window, but the darkness tells me nothing.

A ripped piece of paper, however, with scrawled handwriting tells me plenty. *I want to help you. This is for your own good.*

I cannot be here. Doyle may or may not be guilty of the heinous crimes at the bayou, but now, he's definitely guilty of kidnapping. And although, in his warped mind, he seems to believe he's helping me, there's no way being in this room is helpful.

When I stand up, black dots dance across my vision. I sway but somehow stay upright. I walk to the door and turn around so I can try the knob. It's locked. I release a heavy breath, thinking of the lock on the outside of the door. I inhale and exhale slowly. Panicking is not an option.

I scan the room. Eddie's metal dolls are lined up against the opposite wall; most look like the ones he gave me. One looks half-done, like he's still working on it. Some look sharp. I move my feet across the dusty floor. That's when I notice I'm not wearing any shoes. I wonder where the boots are I had on earlier but decide it makes no difference. I have much bigger things to worry about. Then I notice my clothes. I'm no longer wearing the pants I had on earlier either. I'm not wearing pants at all. I'm only wearing my underwear and a huge gold T-shirt with LSU written on the front in purple. Eddie's T-shirt. I remember it from when I saw him on the levee with Doyle. I cringe at the thought of Doyle changing me into this, but I won't dwell on it. I have to get moving.

I walk over to the metal dolls, sit on the floor next to them, and find what looks like the sharpest one. I turn my back to it and grab it in one hand and try to manipulate it to cut at what's binding my wrists. But I can't get my hand to bend in the right way, and I end up dropping it.

"Shit."

I feel for it behind my back and, in the process, realize the knot does not feel as tight as I thought. If I work it hard enough, I might be able to slip my hands out. I start slowly rubbing my hands together. The friction from the rope burns my wrists, but I keep rubbing, keep pushing to make the hole bigger. My hand slips a little, and I cry out. I keep my eyes on the door. The Arceneaux house is quiet.

After several minutes, I feel the rope give, and one of my hands pops free. I release a hard exhale and bring my hands around, massaging the bright-red marks left behind. I touch a finger to the goose egg on my forehead where Doyle hit me and wince. Then I knock the rope off my other hand and race for the window. It's set high, but I can still reach the locks. After some prying and pushing, I manage to force the locks open. I try to push the window up, but it doesn't budge. I try again, harder. It still won't move. The old congealed paint around the edges acts like superglue. I spend the next few minutes fighting it from every angle with no success. A fluttering jolt seizes my chest, but I refuse to give in to it. I'll find a way out. I'll break the window. I look under the bed but only see the shoebox Eddie had in his hands last time I was here. That's not going to break a window. I turn and eye the metal dolls. Maybe. Then I hear footsteps clunking down the hallway.

I fly onto the bed, under the covers, placing my hands behind my back. The doorknob turns. I see the rope discarded on the floor. I want to reach for it, but it's too late. A lock turns, and the door swings open.

I shut my eyes. The air in the room shifts, changes, as a mass moves from the doorway to the room. Then something sharp pokes me. I flutter my eyes open. Eddie hovers over me, holding a long stick. He pokes me again. "Alive?"

"Of course she's alive."

Doyle moves from behind Eddie and studies me as if he may not be so sure. His cheeks are streaked with dried blood from where I scratched him.

I maneuver myself to a seated position. I focus on Doyle. I swallow the rage at what he's done. I have to stay calm, speak to him without putting him on the defense. "Doyle, I need to leave."

He shakes his head.

"No leave. Not safe," Eddie says. His face drops, and he starts to rock on his feet, heel to toe. He rubs his huge arms, and his breathing becomes labored.

"It's okay, Eddie." I glance at the rope on the floor. They haven't noticed it yet. "Everything's fine." He stops rocking.

I look at Doyle.

He shuffles on his feet. "I called the police."

A wave of relief washes over me. "Oh, thank God." Then I meet Doyle's gaze. "Which police did you call?"

"Raymond," he says.

I open my mouth to speak, and a loud knocking comes from the front room.

"Don't answer it," I say to Doyle.

"Hello? Anyone home?" a man yells from the front porch.

I recognize the voice. My heart stops a moment, then picks back up double time.

Another loud knock.

"Somebody answer the goddamn door!" Liv Arceneaux's voice erupts from a room nearby. I completely forgot about her. Does she know I'm trapped in here?

"Call Travis," I say to Doyle. "Get me out of here."

I hear the front door open. "Hello?"

Doyle studies me a minute, then runs from the room.

I shut the door and look at Eddie. "Eddie, I need you to do me a favor."

He stares at me but doesn't answer.

"I can get you more metal pieces, if you do."

He nods. I listen as Doyle and Raymond talk in the front room.

I look toward the window. "I need you to open that window for me."

The voices in the front room grow louder, heated.

"Now!" I whisper at Eddie.

Eddie lumbers to the window and lifts the pane with one motion, with one hand. The old paint pops and cracks as the pane slides upward. Hot night air and insects rush into the room.

The window is high enough that I'll have to hook my hands on the lower eave to pull myself up and through.

A gunshot erupts from the front of the house.

Eddie covers his ears and wails.

I hoist myself up and through the opening so fast that I fall out on the other side. My shoulder and side hit the ground hard. Mud splashes in my face. I ignore the pain in my arm, jumping up and running for the edge of the property before I can even think of where the road is. Mud from the recent rain sucks at my bare feet like quicksand, but I keep running, scanning the dark yard for the driveway. I feel disoriented and nauseated, and I'm having a hard time figuring out which direction I'm running. Then I see a car parked at an odd angle near the playground equipment. It's not an old junker like the others. It's new. It could have keys. I crouch as I run for it.

Clouds whisk overhead and cover the moon, plunging me into darkness, but my eyes have adjusted as I ease along the side of the car. I try the driver's door. It's locked. I try the remaining three doors, and they are locked as well. I peer through the window but don't see any keys.

Then I see a light, scanning the yard from the woods. A flashlight. I crouch low. I duck next to the back tire and watch the house. Frogs croak from every corner of the yard. I can see the driveway. It's so close. But how fast can I really run with bare feet and what feels like a slight concussion? The answer comes quickly: fast enough to save my life.

I push up from my crouched position and start for the road when large floodlights come to life on either side of the house. The front yard is illuminated like a runway. I duck back into the shadows, searching for another exit.

My gaze stops on the shed a few feet away. It looks like a work shed. Eddie's metal shop. Something catches my eye in the corner of the shed. A shape that looks familiar. But as I try to focus on it, the front door flies open. Eddie thunders out, yelling into the night, "She don't wanna be alone!"

Then I hear Travis yell. "Willa!"

A long, shuddering breath escapes me. "Over here," I yell back.

A flashlight beam whips in my direction. Travis runs for me, and when he reaches me, I collapse into his chest.

"It's okay," he says into my hair. "It's okay."

"Travis, Raymond . . ."

"I know." He lifts my head. "I followed him out here. I still have my police scanner. Willa, he's dead." He glances over my shoulder. "Where's Doyle?"

"What?"

"He ran when I came in."

Crickets sing their nightly sounds. My pulse pounds against my chest. Every noise feels amplified. Every shape becomes clearer. The shed. The car. I squint at it. The car. I know that car. Oh my God. It's Rita's. I turn to Travis, my mouth falling open but no words escaping.

"Where is he?" Travis says.

"I don't know."

"I don't like this." Travis grabs my hand and pulls me toward the back of the shed. His truck is parked on the back side, out of sight. He opens the passenger door. "Get in."

"I'm not staying out here alone."

"Lock the doors," he says, and he runs for the house.

My eyes dart to the car's console. I don't see the keys. I jump from the passenger seat and race around to the driver's side. When I'm behind the wheel, I press the brake and push the starter. A message appears on the dash: KEY NOT DETECTED. I try again. Same response. I scan the dash and its electronics. Nothing is illuminated. There's no way to call for help. Maybe a neighbor heard the gunshot and will call the police, but I can't bank on that. I have to assume we're out here alone. And I'm out here alone without a weapon.

A loud banging startles me, and I look up to see Eddie pounding on the back windshield. I slam the driver's door shut and punch the lock button. Eddie tromps to my side of the car. He presses his face to the window.

"Brother says to get you."

Brother. Doyle.

Eddie tries the door handle but can't get in. I back away. He bangs the window with a giant flat palm. I scramble over the middle console to the passenger side, keeping my eyes on him as he moves around the front and toward the passenger window.

He bangs the window again. Then he raises his other hand, and I scream. He's holding a hammer.

In one sharp movement, he smashes the passenger-side window. Shards of safety glass cover me. Eddie reaches through the window and unlocks the door. I try to scurry back across to the driver's side, but Eddie grabs my ankles and yanks me through the open car door. I hit the ground hard, my T-shirt now up around my head. I kick my legs as much as possible, but Eddie's grip is strong.

"No fight," he says. He releases my legs and grabs my arms instead, pulling me to standing. He smooths my T-shirt down, looking away from my bare chest as he does. "No hurt."

I stay very still. Eddie looks at me with sad eyes. "Mama's gone."

My breath catches in my throat. "Where is she?"

Eddie grips my arms tighter. "Dead."

"How'd she die, Eddie?"

He breaks my eye contact. "Brother." I feel his arms start to tremble.

I keep my voice as calm as I can. "Please don't let him hurt me."

Eddie's viselike grip doesn't let up. He wraps an arm around me and, with the other hand clamped over my mouth, drags me to the back of the house. I dig my bare feet into the ground, but little good it does. His strength is uncanny. At the back of the house, Doyle is waiting for us. The harder I struggle, the tighter Eddie holds me.

"Stop it," Doyle says in a sharp whisper.

I stop moving. Something about Doyle is bothering me. Confusing me. Then Doyle raises my gun. I flinch and struggle, but he doesn't point it at me. He points it over my shoulder.

Eddie lowers his hand from my mouth. Doyle finds my gaze. And that's when I see it. He's terrified. Slowly, I turn to look behind me.

Travis is standing there, his service weapon raised.

"Wait!" I scream, but it's too late.

A gunshot explodes in the thick night air, and the side of Doyle's skull explodes with it. He falls to the ground in a heap of blood. Eddie wails like an animal, his grip on my arms tightening as my legs weaken and my body sags.

"No! No, no, no, no, no." It's all I can say. Over and over and over.

My ears ring as Travis inches toward me. "I . . . I . . . don't think he was going to hurt me." I look at Travis. "He wanted to help me."

"I know that, Willa." Travis cocks his head to one side, runs the barrel of his gun down my cheek. "That was the problem."

Chapter
Twenty-Three

The truth flares in front of me like a match igniting. Hot adrenaline rushes through my veins, reigniting the strength in my legs. I kick and thrash at Eddie but make little impact on his thick body. My mind reels so quickly that I have a hard time holding on to one thought. Travis is the one I should have been focusing on. Not Doyle. Not poor Raymond. Not Liv Arceneaux. Travis. The man I compared myself to, felt empathy for. My stomach roils. The man I kissed. My brain refuses to connect the monster in front of me with the boy who once captured my heart. Everything, all of it, was a lie. His defensiveness about his brothers. His concern for his town. What happened to the boy who helped me that night all those years ago? I stare into his cold blue eyes, at the dimple as he smiles at me, and a sickening thought materializes in my mind. I was the one who helped *him* that summer, not the other way around.

"It's you." The words leave my mouth in a choked whisper.

Travis glares at Eddie. "Take her back to my truck."

"No, Travis! Listen to me."

"Shut up, Willa. This has gone too far." He looks down at Doyle, bleeding on the ground. "Now, it's messy."

"Brother?" Eddie says, staring at Doyle.

"That brother's gone now," Travis says. "He was a bad brother. I'm the only Brother now."

I stare at Travis in horror. "You killed those women. You put Emily in my mother's car."

Travis was the one who recommended the Delaroux farm. He was the one who disappeared to one of the shacks, coming back with garbage bags. But something had been off about one of them. The memory that crystallizes feels like a kick to my gut. I see it. So clearly. He was dragging the bags from the shack, one already looked full. In the panic of that night and after years of pushing that memory away, I distorted what I saw. But it's an avalanche now. I can't stop it. I see us frantically cleaning out the car, dumping garbage bags in the back of Travis's truck. What if, during the chaos, he slipped something back in? I heard him slam the trunk closed as I finished behind his truck. I heard myself telling him to leave: *I'll do the rest.*

"You put Emily in my mother's car." A sob escapes as I speak.

Travis tilts his head. "Emily had to be taught a lesson. She thought that asshole Raymond loved her. But I loved her more."

Eddie releases a long guttural cry. "She don't wanna be alone."

"She's not alone," Travis snaps at his brother. Then his face smooths over, and his voice becomes monotone. "Where I put Emily, she could have friends with her. Friends I brought to her. And no one would ever find her, question what happened to her in those woods. Poor thing thought Raymond was coming for her. My note worked."

My pulse throbs at an alarming pace. I force myself to breathe deeply. I will not pass out.

Travis leans closer to me. "Emily should have known better. She should've known she'd never get away from that house." I twist in Eddie's arms, but he holds me tight. "I made sure she'd never run away again."

His voice stays steady, no emotion. "People were talking about my mother. About Emily's death. I couldn't let them dig her up. Delaroux's shack was perfect. That is, until you called."

My legs give out from under me, but Eddie's grip keeps me from falling. Travis putting his dead sister in my mother's trunk. The women found in those barrels. How he must have hunted them. A nice-looking police officer in a fancy truck. Even wearing just a navy polo and khakis, he still looked official. Trustworthy. And he watched his mother medicate his sister daily. It wouldn't be a huge leap to learn how to over-medicate, how to incapacitate someone. A freezing claw clutches my throat. My breath catches, and I gulp for air. And Raymond. I warned Travis about him when it should have been the other way around. And now, Raymond is . . . I can't finish the thought because another image fills my head. The car by the shed. Rita's car. Rita who, the last time I saw her, was racing out to follow up on a lead. She knew.

I bend over and vomit. Travis is unfazed. He points at me.

"Because of her, I can't give our sister any more friends, Edward. Take her to my truck. We need to get out of here."

Eddie doesn't move. He's still got a tight grip on me, but he's not moving.

"Don't listen to him, Eddie," I say.

"Brother, take her back to the truck," Travis repeats in a calm tone.

I kick and flail as much as I can. Eddie feels none of it. He hefts me off the ground and over his shoulder like I weigh nothing. "Stop, Eddie. Stop." I writhe under his grip, but he holds firm, and adrenaline can only go so far. I give up fighting for now. I need to save my strength. Still balancing me on his shoulder, he squats down and retrieves something from the ground. Then he lumbers behind the shed and drops me next to the truck. That's when I see what he retrieved, my gun. It's in his waistband. I scramble to stand, but he presses me back down and holds my shoulders as Travis rummages in his back seat.

My whole life, I've trained to analyze people's behavior. To read them. Study them. And I'd missed all his signs. Smile for smile, frown for frown, he mimicked beautifully. He was charming and believable, and I'd been so busy analyzing everyone else, so blinded by my past with Travis, that I failed to analyze him.

I scan the ground around me for any kind of weapon. The shed is close, but there's no way I can get to it. Then I see the object I saw in the shadows earlier. The one that looked familiar, and a thudding terror shudders through my chest. There's not just one. There are several. And they're lined up in a neat line along the edge. Fifty-five-gallon steel drum barrels.

Travis finishes in his truck and returns to me, holding a clear plastic bag in his hand.

I push against Eddie, dig my feet into the ground, thrash, and yell, "Stop!" But nothing works. Eddie continues to hold me, and Travis slips the bag over my head. I suck in a wild breath, and the bag sticks to my face. I scream and kick, twist my head from side to side. I see Eddie looking down at me. I keep my eyes on his, pleading. Then I feel one of Eddie's hands let go of my shoulder, and in the next instant, something about the bag changes. I'm lightheaded, but I can taste it, fresh air. I gasp deeper. Darkness creeps in, and a second before I fall unconscious, I hear Travis say, "Help me in the shed, Eddie. Our little Emily is going to get one more friend after all."

It's dark. That's my first thought. My second thought is I'm moving. A loud truck engine roars around me. My knees are crammed into my chest, and my arms are folded in front of me. Screaming pain runs up my spine. I try to move my arms and can't. I try to move my legs. They're stuck as well. And then panic hits. I gasp and choke and feel the plastic bag on my face. Searing, claustrophobic heat surrounds me as I realize where I am. What I'm in. I scream, but the sound dies inside the barrel. I try to push off from the bottom, but my legs are wedged in front of me too closely to move them. Hot, blinding panic washes over me. I'm going to die in here. I have to get out. But the space is so small and cramped that I can't move my body. My breaths come fast and shallow. My throat constricts. I feel myself losing consciousness.

The next time I open my eyes, everything is still, quiet. I can't hear the truck anymore. I lean my head back, look up. A sliver of morning light greets me. There's a crack above my head, between the barrel lip and the lid. It's not secured. Then I hear voices. Travis and Eddie. Somewhere close by.

"Set her on the levee," I hear Travis say.

The barrel moves. I hear Eddie grunting as he works it side to side. His strength is uncanny, and I wonder if he had to help Travis with the other barrels as well. I also wonder what part of the bayou we are on. But the answer fills my head quickly: the deepest part.

Adrenaline burns in my veins. I work my right hand slowly, maneuvering my shoulder into a contorted position in order to make space as Eddie continues to move the barrel. My hand wiggles upward, and I reach for the plastic bag on my head, clawing it until I rip it free. I inhale a deep, scalding breath and will myself to stay conscious.

Something metal is perched on my chest. I lower my chin as much as I can to see it. One of Eddie's dolls and, next to it, a giant bolt. This doll is even less complete than the one in the bedroom. It's a metal skeleton made of screws and sharp pieces of metal. Sharp enough to cut the plastic bag over my head so I could breathe. Eddie wants to help me.

I raise my eyes to the lid again and an idea starts to form.

"Eddie," I whisper. My throat is dry, my voice scratchy.

The barrel stops moving. "Eddie," I say again. "I have something for you." I see a shadow near the lid. Morning air floods in. I smell my sweat and vomit on the front of my T-shirt, but there's another smell now. The warm stench of the bayou. "I know you want to help me. I want to help you too." The lid scrapes open a sliver more. "Good job, Eddie. Good—"

"That's far enough," Travis says, and I clamp my mouth shut. He's right over me. The shadows on the edge of the lid shift. "What the hell? Goddammit, Eddie. You put the lid on wrong." The lid pops back into place, and I'm plunged into complete darkness. I fight back my scream.

"Where's the bolt?" His voice is muted and sounds like it's coming to me through a tunnel. The bolt is in here with me.

"What the hell are you doing?" Travis yells.

Something bangs into the side of the barrel with a deafening sound. Then I feel it start to tip, and I can't hold back my scream. The barrel wobbles, then falls over and slams into the ground with a sickening thud. My shoulder cracks onto the metal side, and an excruciating pain travels down my arm. The breath is knocked out of me as the lid shoots off the top. Then the barrel starts to roll. My head knocks against the side. I bang against the inside as it rolls, and I try to brace myself for what's coming. When it does, my survival instincts don't disappoint me.

I hold my breath as I hear a giant splash and warm water floods into the open top. I wriggle my arms free and reach for the opening over my head. My fingers clamp onto the rim, and I pull myself through the opening. The barrel falls away from my body. Then I'm floating, my head above water. I gasp and kick until my bare feet find the mush and muck of the bank, and I stand, dripping wet, my left arm hanging at an odd angle. I wipe water from my face. Another body is on the bank, next to another barrel. Rita. And Eddie is running for me at full speed, toward the edge of the bayou. Behind him, Travis raises his gun.

"Eddie, stop!" I scream as he reaches the edge.

The gunshot cracks through the morning heat, and Eddie's lumbering body careens into mine and knocks me flat on my back. Winded and struggling to breathe, I push against Eddie's body. He's still breathing. I struggle to free myself using one arm. Travis is walking toward us. I'm not going to get out in time. Then I remember what Eddie had in his waistband. What he retrieved after Doyle was shot.

I wedge my hand into Eddie's waistband and move it across Eddie's clammy skin until I feel the familiar grip of my handgun. Travis looks down at Eddie's back with me pressed underneath him. Something flashes across his face, almost like sadness; then it's gone, and he turns his now glazed and empty eyes on me. The eyes of a sociopath.

"I could have saved you," he says. His eyes dart back to Eddie. "But they got involved. It's really too bad. You were a beautiful prop."

I keep my gaze on him, breathe, as I slowly pry my gun from Eddie's waistband.

"Travis."

He raises a single finger to his lips, like his sister in the picture Mabry drew. The sides of his mouth curl into a smile, and I don't wait for him to speak again. There's no more time.

I wrestle the gun free and fire. The shot misses. Travis opens his mouth, stunned. I fire off a second round. His shoulder whips back, and he screams. Travis regroups, raises his gun toward me, but I've already started to pull the trigger again, and I have no intention of stopping until this gun is empty. My third shot lands square in his chest. He drops his weapon. My fourth hits his stomach. He falls to his knees. I fire until there are no more rounds. My ears ring. Travis is on the ground, not moving.

I lower my shaking arm. Tears slide down my cheeks. I lie there in the bayou sludge, frozen underneath Eddie's weight, staring into Travis's dead eyes until I hear sirens approaching. Men are shouting. Someone yells at me to toss my weapon. I toss it. They hoist Eddie off me. Paramedics check my left arm, yell for a stretcher. I lie motionless as the chaos swirls above me, my cheek resting on the bank, my eyes fixated on the brown muddy water of Broken Bayou as it flows past me.

Chapter
Twenty-Four

Fort Worth, Texas
Six months later

I look through the windshield at the one-story, 1970s-style brick building in front of me. Two flags wave next to it: the American flag and the Texas flag, the Texas flag slightly bigger. Giant towers with satellite dishes affixed to them shoot up into the muddled sky on either side of the building. The KTFW studio is just as I remember. Only, today, I won't be interviewed by Harper Beaumont. She has graciously stepped aside in order for a guest host to do the honors.

I check my reflection in the rearview mirror one more time. It's not as bad as I thought. I actually slept last night. My body has healed since that night in Broken Bayou. My bones are strong again. But my mind still reels. Thankfully, I've found a trauma therapist. She's helping me navigate this new road I'm on. I still have nightmares. I wake up out of breath, pounding my pillow, trying to escape. And I accept this is part of it. Part of the healing.

I glance at the duffel bag and thermos in my back seat. Another part of the healing. As is the box of Legos also on the back seat.

Chief Wilson visited me while Eddie was hospitalized just down the hall. Told me Eddie's older brothers were unsure what to do with him, and he didn't have many answers for them. Wondered if I could help. Eddie was as much a victim of Travis's as I was. There's no way he understood what his brother was doing, and besides that, in the end, he helped save my life. I wanted to return the favor. Eddie deserved a second chance. Once I got back to Fort Worth, I did my research and started making calls. It gave me something positive to focus on, someone to advocate for. I spoke with a woman from the OCDD, the Office for Citizens with Developmental Disabilities, about getting Eddie assigned a caseworker. Someone who would monitor his social situation for life. I navigated through the mounds of paperwork and even paid his oldest brother to take Eddie to the dozens of appointments he needed to attend. Whatever worked. And it did work. Eddie got a caseworker and his own room at a group home in Baton Rouge. Then I called VR, vocational rehab, and set up skill testing for him. Not surprisingly, Eddie is good with his hands and was able to get a job mending and laundering linens for a local hospital.

I made one trip down to check his working and living conditions. Both exceeded my expectations. His work campus had beautiful green grounds with picnic tables and gardens. Eddie smiled when I surprised him there one day. The group home was clean and well appointed and run by a kind widow with a CPA degree, who I trusted to help monitor the money Eddie made at work. He had a safe place to live now, full of love and understanding. Something he'd never had. He also had his first chance to work. Like Freud believed, we all need a reason to get up in the morning. Eddie has one now. When I called last week to check in, he said more words than usual. He even laughed. But he also mentioned he missed his dolls. Sharp objects aren't allowed at the group home. That's when I decided that, on my next trip, I'd bring him a gift. I glance in the back seat at the Lego box. Something safe he can build a new family with.

Speaking of family. I check the clock, punch in my mother's cell phone number.

She answers by saying, "Your coffeepot's too fancy. How the hell do you turn it on?"

I smile. Miraculously enough, our relationship is healing as well as my bones. Not long after returning, I went to Texas Rose, spoke with her doctors. With her. We came up with a plan for her medication. A dose that helps even her out. Mama said she didn't like it, but I asked her to keep trying anyway. Told her we'd keep going until we got it right. And she, thankfully, agreed.

"Middle button," I say to my new roommate. "Your physical therapist will be there in ten minutes."

"I know that."

I shake my head. It won't be easy for either of us, but in our own ways, we need each other. We're the last of the Watters women. We're all we have left. We must work to embrace forgiveness. To maneuver those deep crevices between us and find the good memories among the carnage. Maybe it's time to make some new memories.

"Are you packed?" I say.

"I'm packed," Mama says.

"I'll pick you up after the show." I smell the sunscreen again, hear Mabry's laugh as we bob in the warm water. "It's time to set her free."

I hang up, open the car door, and step into the frigid February air. Gray clouds hover overhead. Sleet is expected later. We'll need to be on the road to Broken Bayou sooner rather than later. I rush across the lot in my sneakers and pull my coat closer. As hard as it's going to be to return to that town, it's the place for Mabry. It's where she was happiest. And besides, that bayou needs an angel watching over it.

Inside the studio, the air is warm, and Amy is waiting for me.

I don't remember much about that horrible day six months ago, but I remember Amy running into my hospital room out of breath. Ermine sitting beside me. The two of them comforting me as I was questioned by the police. I remember leaving the hospital, my arm in a cast, my heart full of hurt. Amy drove me to Shadow Bluff, and we retrieved my car. Then we drove all night to Fort Worth. She stayed at my high-rise for a week. Until I stopped screaming in my sleep.

She takes my hand. "Are you sure you're ready for this?"

I nod. "I'm ready."

Amy leads me down the hallway. We walk past the makeup room. No need to dress me up today. I need the world to see me as I am. Hurting, traumatized. Healing.

The lights in the studio are blinding. I sit in a chair I know all too well. A sound tech approaches me as if I'm a ticking bomb. He holds up the mic pack. I take it from him and slip it in the waistband of my jeans, then attach the mic to my sweater. He points to my hip and leans in. Then he twists a button on the mic, and it lights up green.

"Mikes are hot," he says over his shoulder.

A flutter of nervousness thumps in my chest. I inhale and exhale as slowly as I can. Then I hear her voice.

"Jesus, can't you people get your shit together? I told you to dim those damn lights. She doesn't need to feel like she's on an operating table. Hell, they're freaking me out, and I love being under lights."

Rita clicks around the corner in glossy black heels and a red skirt and jacket that hug her thin frame as if they were sewn onto her body. Our eyes meet, and I smile. She touches my arm as the mic tech secures her mic. She was transported to the same hospital as me. She'd been drugged but was otherwise unharmed. Apparently, Travis liked his victims to go into the water alive.

The mic tech finishes, and a makeup artist steps in. She blots Rita's perfect makeup.

"You've got this," she says to me.

"With your help," I say back.

We helped each other. In the days and months following that horrific night, Rita and I spoke with Chief Wilson and investigator Tom Bordelon several times. They kept us updated as the details unfolded. What a sick mess of details they were. The neighbors had indeed called the police that night after hearing gunshots.

The police found Raymond's body along with Doyle's. Both killed by the same gun. Travis's gun. The chief believed Raymond suspected Travis. Said Raymond lied to Travis about going to New Orleans so he could poke around and Travis wouldn't be suspicious. Raymond was following Travis that night he found me on the levee. He wanted to protect me. Like Doyle wanted to protect me.

I swallow, clear my throat, practice the breathing method I've preached to others, counting my breaths in a slow methodical rhythm.

Liv Arceneaux was also found that night, inside, strangled and hidden under a pile of old newspapers and magazines. They found cabinets full of medications, narcotics, syringes. Things, in his erratic state of mind, he hadn't thought to use on his mother or on me. Thank goodness.

They also found a shoebox. The one Eddie showed me. It was tucked under Emily's old bed. If only Eddie had opened it that day I visited. If only I'd seen the contents. Inside was a pile of Polaroid pictures. Women. The women from the barrels. The missing teacher. There was even one of Emily Arceneaux, who they now considered his first victim.

Her remains had finally been identified. The remains in my mother's trunk.

I bury my head in my hands.

Rita and I spent hours together, going over every detail. She had extensive notes and recordings. She'd researched everything, even the botched report filed years ago on the stolen barrels, which turned out to be just a clumsy mistake. Nothing at all to do with Raymond. She'd spoken with Travis's mother. Liv had confessed so much. Like she knew her time was limited. She painted a troubled picture of her son Travis. His obsession with her youngest child and only daughter, Emily. How she was scared for her daughter. Pulled her out of school to keep her close. Wanted to protect her not from the world but from her brother. Liv didn't mention Emily needed protection from her mother as well. She touched on Emily's illnesses, but mostly the conversation revolved around Travis and his dislike for her.

Liv confessed she knew about the barrels. She'd seen them in the outdoor shed. She told Rita she believed Travis was using them for something that was none of her business. She never said a word to the police. My guess is at some point, probably when Travis was physically larger than her, the dynamics in that house shifted. Instead of Travis being the scared one, Liv was. And she had good reason.

Rita hadn't spoken with only Travis's mother. She'd spoken to his other brothers as well. The ones who moved away. They seemed as oblivious to Travis's psychosis as the people who lived in Broken Bayou. As me. Or maybe, like me and everyone else, they chose to see what they wanted to see.

I look up from my hands, and Rita is staring at me. "We can do this," she says.

I nod.

The makeup artist finishes and walks off.

A man behind the camera yells, "Five minutes."

"We're covering it all," Rita says, keeping her gaze on me.

I nod again.

"Even Mabry."

"Even Mabry," I say, then add, "Especially Mabry."

"As harrowing as it is, your story is important. You've made the right decision to share it."

Making that decision wasn't easy. Hiding away in my high-rise felt much safer, but after long talks with Amy and my therapist, and even Rita, I saw how confronting what happened head on and telling it in my voice, on my terms, would be beneficial. Not only to me but to the people I want to eventually get back to helping. "Help people heal by showing them how to," Amy had said. And she was right. *Good Morning America* had been the first to call. I turned them down. I wanted to be at home for this.

Another man approaches Rita's side, and she turns her back to me as she talks with him.

As hard as I try to keep my mind clear and focused, it keeps reeling backward. Keeps going to the two words I know are not helpful but are so hard to avoid: what if.

What if Doyle just talked to me in the kitchen at Shadow Bluff instead of dragging me to that house? What if he told me then that he left the license plate to lead back to Travis, not as some cryptic message to scare me? He didn't realize by leaving that plate, he set himself up. So many mistakes made. And his ideas of helping me almost got me killed. I squeeze my eyes shut. What if Liv Arceneaux told the police she knew about the barrels?

A breath escapes me with a whimper. Rita, even with her back to me, still has my hand, and she squeezes it again.

Travis grew up in a home filled with abuse. I know enough about forensic psychology to know this is a dangerous setting for a son with sociopathic tendencies. And there's no doubt, Travis was a sociopath. He fit every mold: A mother who abused him. A father who was neglectful in his own right for not protecting his son from that abuse. His older brothers abandoning him, leaving him in that toxic home. All feeding into a person with an obvious mental illness and a dark, insatiable need for something that could never be satisfied. I read and studied every book on the subject I could get my hands on since coming home. I wanted to know how I missed it. How I could have cared for, given myself to, a boy who was so mentally disturbed? How could I have believed for all these years that he actually cared for me too? I'd laugh if it wasn't so fucked up.

His empathy, outrage, anger were all so well choreographed. Appropriate reactions at appropriate times. Even the worry I thought I saw in his eyes that day the convertible came out. The nervous energy. I read it wrong. He wasn't worried for me that day. He may not have even been worried for himself. Looking back, it seems more like he was excited. He wanted me with him on that bayou that day to see what he'd set in motion. Like the game was finally starting. A game he was confident he'd win.

His act fooled me and everyone else in that town. I'm horrified I wasn't able to identify the monster he really was. But I'd been leaning on my degrees, my years of training, not on the simplest answer staring me in the face.

The badge helped. Rita's notes described a man who entered the police academy with one goal: to help him kill.

The police surmised he hunted in crowds, starting with the woman at the casino. But her barrel had been found rather quickly. So Travis learned to sink them better. Then he figured out the sand.

Travis kept everything he needed at his mother's house. Syringes, a prescription pad, and injectable tranquilizers were all found in one of the kitchen cabinets. The best they could figure, he'd pick a victim, approach her, sedate her, and get her back to his truck, drive her to where he kept the barrels. The missing teacher was the only one who didn't fit his profile. He went rogue with her, broke his method. The police believed she was random. Maybe he came upon her car while scouting the bayou late at night. Maybe she drove upon him getting rid of a barrel. Whatever the case, he had his camera and saw an opportunity to kill. And he dumped her car just like I dumped my mother's. That's where things started to unravel for him. Her parents brought in the divers. Maybe that was his way of self-sabotaging, like he knew the game was almost over and he'd be caught soon, so he became reckless. Or even more likely, he was so overconfident that he felt he could get away with anything.

Rita showed up at the Arceneaux house to talk to Doyle about the sand. She believed Doyle was being set up. But Doyle was at Shadow Bluff that day, hiding and waiting for me, so she talked to Liv instead; then Travis showed up, also looking for Doyle, and found Rita. She only remembers coming to on the edge of the bayou, surrounded by paramedics.

I pull my hand away from Rita's. "I'll be right back," I say. I stand and ask one of the techs where the restroom is.

He points down the hall and says, "You've only got a couple of minutes."

In the bathroom, I run cold water and splash it on my face. Every time I think of Travis, my breathing falters just enough to make me panic.

There's still a running debate on if men like Travis are born or made. I'm starting to think both. People are abused and angry and resentful all the time. But when those traits surface in a person with an underlying psychosis, a person who watched his mother control his sister with poison, it changes everything.

I dry my face. It's unnerving to think how parallel my life was to Travis's. Toxic mothers. Losing our sisters. But even though our lives may have looked similar on paper, we couldn't be more different. I fought to overcome my traumas, learn from them. And I fought to not become one of Travis's victims. I will learn from that as well.

I return to the set as a man behind the camera yells, "One minute."

People scurry around the set. Rita rolls her neck. Amy runs to my side, bends down. "If at any point you need to stop, just say so. Even though it's live, you can take as many breaks as you need." She squeezes my arm and runs back behind the camera.

"Ten seconds," the man behind the camera yells.

So many lives lost; so many others affected by those losses.

"Nine."

Amy and I decided to take a hiatus from the podcast. I postponed my book tour as well. After this interview, I'm going to take the time I need to heal.

"Eight."

"Seven."

Rita beams at the camera.

"Six."

Her hand finds mine.

"Five."

Rita whispers, "Be brave."

"Four."

I'm not sure if she's talking to me or herself.

"Three."

I stare directly into the lens.

"Two."

"One."

The man behind the camera points to us. Rita gives my hand one final squeeze. I take a breath.

Time to tell my story.

Acknowledgments

Writing is not a solo endeavor. It takes a team. And I love a team; just ask my tennis squad. I'm so fortunate to be surrounded by people who lift me up and help me shine.

Thank you to Renaissance Literary & Talent and to Jacklyn Saferstein-Hansen for plucking me from a slush pile and giving me my yes. Your enthusiasm for this book gave me a renewed sense of energy and gratitude. Thank you for supporting my vision and championing me at every turn.

Thank you to my team at Amazon Publishing and Thomas & Mercer. Alexandra Torrealba, you shared my love for this story and used your keen eye to hone it into something sharp and exciting. Michelle Flythe, you are a goddess. Your edits were sublime and spot on. Lindsey Bragg, Harriet Hammersmith, Jenna Justice, and Heather Buzila, thank you for your finishing touches, icing on the cake.

Kristen Weber, thank you for your compassion and expert skills. You not only helped shape this book into something magical but also helped me navigate a process that at times felt impossible. I would not be here without you. You are an amazing editor and advocate for writers!

Thank you to Elizabeth Kracht for kicking off my editing journey years ago and for providing much-needed guidance. You were one of the first advocates for this book.

I'm in awe of the following experts. Any mistakes made in these fields are mine and mine alone.

Thank you, Dr. Michelle Yetman, for providing me with research on top of research about child psychology, especially when it relates to children on the autism spectrum. And for inviting me to do fun things like tour the North Louisiana Crime Lab! I'm grateful for both your expertise and your friendship. Our Friday lunches are the highlight of my week.

Thank you to forensic pathologist Dr. James Traylor for taking time out of your busy days to answer my questions on all things bodies, barrels, and forensic science. Also, many thanks to Assistant District Attorney Lea Hall for the endless phone calls about law enforcement, serial killers, and crime in southern Louisiana. Your stories gave me chills, in the best way!

Thank you to my plod-and-plot partners, Liz Talley and Phylis Caskey. Our weekly walks kept this book on track (literally) and provided much-needed comic relief!

Thank you, Ashley Elston, for talking me off the writing ledge more times than I can count and for all the times you said, "What if . . ." Bless you for still answering the phone when I call.

A special thank you to all my early beta readers. We did it! And to Dr. Gerald Baker, thank you for showing me I was wearing the ruby slippers all along.

Rachel Thomas, thank you for being you. You've celebrated with me every step of the way (and lifted me up when I tripped on a few of those steps). You are the foxiest Gemini on the planet.

Thank you to my families-in-law, the Boulder-Mos and the Crosby crew. You have been my number one fans since the beginning, and I love you dearly.

To my parents, Margo and David Myatt, thank you for your endless support, emphatic love, and countless hours of laughter. I'm so lucky I get to call you Mom and Dad. Tonight, we ride!

To my sister, Maggie, where do I begin? Your sidesplitting humor and fierce loyalty are second to none. You fill my world with joy. Thank you for being the best sister, friend, and cheerleader I could ever ask for.

And to my own family, words are not enough. To my husband, Mike, and my daughters, Mackenzie and Mia, I love you to the moon and back. You are gifts that keep on giving. And what you give to me is priceless. My heart is full. Mike, I promise I'll go to the grocery store now, right after I finish this next scene.

ABOUT THE AUTHOR

Photo © 2023 Ashley Elston

Jennifer Moorhead graduated from Louisiana State University in Baton Rouge. Geaux Tigers! She has written and produced three indie short films, which made Top 20 at Louisiana Film Prize and were presented with awards at festivals around the world. She lives in Louisiana with her husband, two daughters, two dogs, and one cat—plus plenty of horses, mini ponies, and donkeys—in a place where swamps and winding trails are the norm. When she's not writing or spoiling her pets, she's on a tennis court laughing and providing job security for her coach. *Broken Bayou* is her debut novel.